Teacher:
The Final Act

By

R.L. Merrill

Teacher: The Final Act
Copyright © 2015, Celie Bay Publications, LLC
All rights reserved.

Published By: Celie Bay Publications, LLC

ISBN: 978-0-9962803-4-1

Cover design by: Yosbe Design
Edited by: LTE Editing
Interior book design by: Bob Houston eBook Formatting

Dedication

To Jennifer
How you continue to soldier on, despite your debilitating condition, by educating our children, I'll never comprehend. Thank you for inspiring my Teacher, Jesse, and for always supporting me in my endeavors. You are my hero!

Teacher:
The Final Act

A Hollywood Rock 'n' Romance Trilogy

Book Three

By

R.L. Merrill

Teacher: The Final Act

Prologue

November 2013

"This shit is itchy as fuck! God damn! How much longer, Nikki?"

Danny was trying desperately not to scratch, but the black body paint was getting to both of us. I was just not about to complain. Not in front of Nikki Sixx. I was having a hard enough time focusing on what he was telling us to do. The music playing, "A Touch of Evil" by Judas Priest, was blaring, making it hard to hear anything. Except when Danny sang along in my ear. I could listen to his voice all the time and it would never stop giving me chills.

"I think I'm getting a fucking rash," he grumbled.

Nikki laughed and said, "Nah, dude, it's probably just your hair growing back already. You sure are a hairy bastard for a red head."

Danny told him off in such a creative diatribe, he had us all in stitches.

I moved just a little to ease his weight off my thigh. We were lying on a padded platform draped with white, gauzy fabric, and surrounded by crows. Trained crows, apparently. They had a handler and everything.

Nikki directed Danny to move around behind me as I rested on my side. Danny pulled my top leg back over his hip, once again delighting in my flexibility. I pressed my hips back against Danny's and he made a strangled sound.

"God, you feel so fucking good," he whispered, his breath giving me goosebumps.

"Jesse you are amazing! Now can you reach back over your head and grab his head? Yeah, like that, and arch your back as much as you can. Danny, I want your cheek against her shoulder, and close your eyes. Fuck, that's hot!"

Now before you assume our relationship has progressed to pornographic filmmaking, let me explain. Way back when, the night Danny and I went to the Roxy, Nikki told him he wanted to use Danny in a photo shoot at his studio sometime. He had some ideas he wanted to play with and thought Danny would be a good subject. Nikki had spent the last few years really exploring photography and loved to play with the borderline between beautiful and profane. After that night, Danny and Nikki talked a few times about Nikki shooting the cover for the next Blackened album, which Danny and 'the guys' wrapped up recording just a week ago. Nikki agreed, but after Danny called him about something totally unrelated, he asked a favor in return. Danny and I were now covered in splashes of black body paint and black feathers, returning the favor.

Nikki asked us to pose nude for him, a request that had me cringing, but he promised our intimate bits would be covered. I agreed after some lengthy discussions with Danny as well as my mother and my boss. I didn't want anything to jeopardize my career and certainly didn't want to disappoint my folks. I'd seen Nikki's photography and found it very tasteful, dramatic, and sometimes, quite disturbing. My mom thought it sounded exciting. My boss, Gloria, made me promise to show her the results.

Danny's major concern, other than my bits being on display to anyone other than him, was the fact that he'd have to have a full body wax. Nikki explained that his red and blonde curls would interfere with the body paint that would cover large swaths of our bodies. He'd had it done the day before, and he assured me it was far worse than the scene from "40-year-old Virgin." I promised to kiss it and make it better, which made it worthwhile to him. I promised to be very thorough.

"Now let's get some standing shots." Danny helped me up from the draped platform we'd been on. I think the only thing keeping him from an aroused state was the itchiness he was experiencing, and the small, but very present, audience of Nikki, his girlfriend, the crow handler, and two assistants.

Danny looked demonic and angelic all at once. He had black paint across his eyes, his chest, and patches on his ass and legs. He had large wings made of black feathers attached to his shoulders, and more feathers covering his groin. My breasts and parts further south were covered in black feathers, and I, too, had the black paint across parts of my body. Nikki's makeup artist had done elaborate eye makeup, including thick, black, sparkly lashes that extended about an inch on top and bottom. My hair had black feathers woven into it. Danny recently shaved his hair off again, but his goatee was the longest I'd ever seen it at around three inches. He'd started back at the gym about a month or so ago to get ready for being on tour. He was already looking much more toned, even though he was perfectly fit before. Now, his muscles were well defined and his stamina, well, I never thought that could get any better, but then I should really cease to be amazed by him.

I'd followed the doctor's orders and gained fifteen pounds since my flare up of Rheumatoid Arthritis this summer. I was definitely at my curviest. I'd even gone up a bra cup size from a barely B to a sure thing C. A change Danny could not stop admiring. My bruises and cuts were all healed as well, thankfully.

I had to pull myself away from admiring Danny's mouthwatering physique to follow Nikki's directions. He tried a few poses, but wasn't getting what he wanted. Danny got an evil grin and I knew I was in for it.

"Hey honey, how about you do that thing where..."

He whispered the rest to me and I blushed.

"Okay, hold me tight," I said, a little embarrassed to do this trick in front of our audience. Nikki took pictures the whole time. I was facing Danny, and he must have sensed my nerves. He leaned in to kiss me so deeply, my knees got weak.

"Relax, babe. Pretend like it's just the two of us and we're not in some demented Mapplethorpe photo session."

That got a chuckle from Nikki. He winked at me and I took a deep breath. I held on to Danny's shoulders and brought my right leg out to the side and into a full extension. I rolled my hip and placed my heel on his shoulder.

"You ready?" I whispered with a giggle, and his eyes rolled back in his head.

"I don't know. I'm not sure I can stay in control with you like this," he said in a gravelly voice.

Nikki stepped in close and said quietly, "You two are fucking beautiful. Just a few more, then we'll leave you alone. Show me what you've got, Jesse."

I nodded at Danny and then I raised my hands over my head and continued leaning back, arching, until I was in a full extension and my fingertips brushed the floor. I heard Danny groan, heard the two assistants gasp, and Nikki cursed.

"Jesus, woman! This is fucking perfect! Babe," he called over his shoulder, "I hope you don't have plans this afternoon." His girlfriend giggled and gave a sigh.

"You two are incredibly sensual. Danny, lean back a little and roll your hips forward. Close your eyes. That's it. That's so fucking it!" He made appreciative sounds as he took a few more shots, making sure to get additional angles.

"I'm going to bring you back up now," Danny whispered and he pulled me back to standing. My hair spilled across both of us and he took advantage of our position to kiss me again. I slid my leg down to around his waist, pulling him close, but then he lifted me and I brought the other leg around him. I held on to his shoulders and squeezed with my thighs as he kissed my neck, missing the body paint. My head fell back and I closed my eyes, completely forgetting we weren't alone. I felt Danny start walking and next thing I knew, my back was against a wall. I vaguely heard Nikki snap a few more pictures and then put down his camera. He called to Danny to take his time, and I felt Danny growl.

He frantically pulled at the feathers that had been attached to bra cups and stuck to my skin with adhesive. I smiled down at him and helped him peel the cups off. His hands and mouth replaced the feathers and I started to squirm in his arms. He tried to pull off the rest of our feather coverings and still hold me up.

"Put me down, baby, and I'll help you," I murmured.

He just growled and kept at it. He kissed my breasts hard, which would probably leave marks, and finally got his covering off, shortly followed by mine. Once it was off, his fingers found my center. He pushed in and out, my cries getting louder and more insistent.

"Danny, please, I need you," I groaned against him. He grabbed my hips hard, hoisted me up, and carried me over to the platform. I slid down his body and laughed when I looked down.

"Look at the mess we've made."

He looked down at our bodies and chuckled. The black body paint was smeared everywhere and there were fingerprints all over where we'd touched each other. My eyelashes were even stuck to his head and his chest! We playfully made an even bigger mess, and soon we were covered from head to toe with smudges.

"Nikki would probably like us like this," Danny said, pulling on his goatee. He grabbed the camera and took a few shots of me, during which I covered myself. Then I took the camera from him and took several shots from different angles, making sure to keep my favorite part out of view!

He was so beautiful, even covered in black smudges. I couldn't wait to see the prints. I did some close-ups of his face with different expressions, and one of his back and his profile.

Danny set the camera on the tripod and started a timer. He trotted over to me and wrapped me in his arms. The camera flashed several times over the next few minutes while Danny kissed me, and then we just looked into the camera together, Danny blocking my body with his shoulder.

"I'm going to want copies of these," he said, kissing my neck. Then he started itching again.

"You poor thing! Why don't we finish this at home, after we've had a shower? Then I can rub you down with some lotion to help with the itching," I suggested.

He smirked down at me. "A rub down sounds like a great idea, honey."

Chapter - One

Two months prior...

End of August 2013

"I don't know what the hell is wrong with me! Where's the strong, confident Jesse, who stood up to Her Hungarian Highness that day on Melrose? Where's the assertive Jesse, who told off Danny's ex-wife when she insulted him about not having a diploma?"

This Jesse was currently cowering in the bathroom in Danny's room, feeling unworthy and considering giving up on a nearly perfect love with a complicated man.

After a tumultuous week where we travelled back to our homes to meet each other's parents, things were fantastic between Danny and me. He made it clear to both sets of parents that he planned on marrying me and had even shared the news with his amazing daughter Jane. We'd gone to a wedding today for the daughter of Danny's producer and it should have been another of our best days. Instead, I'd stupidly gone without food all day and only picked at my dinner because I was hot and feeling a little off.

Unfortunately, Danny's ex, former A-list actress Brooke Jones, took this moment to make a grand entrance. The stress of her reaction to seeing Danny and me together and not just as a student-teacher, and the reaction of the Mannings' mother, Grace, to seeing Brooke brought my happiness crashing down. I'd begged Alex's sister to drive me home and then arrived to find myself locked out of the house and physically a disaster. Danny had come home to find me passed out on the porch.

Now, after purging what little had actually made it into my stomach, I was shaking and angry at my behavior.

"Snap the fuck out of it," I shouted at the sniveling woman in the mirror. "Who the hell is Brooke Jones or Grace Manning to tell you whether you are worthy of Danny?! One thing's for sure, if you run away, you're going to lose the best thing that ever happened to you."

I turned and threw up in the toilet one more time. I was washing my face when I heard Danny clear his throat.

Embarrassed, I turned to him, wiping the last of my tears away. I threw back my shoulders and faced him. "How much of that, did you hear?"

He uncrossed his arms and stepped over to the counter, leaning his hips against it and looking at me, curiously. "All of it." I dropped my head and he took a deep breath. "Were you really going to run away? Are you leaving me?" he asked in a cracked voice.

I touched his hand that rested on the counter and then pulled back. "No. Not really. I just panicked, Danny! When I got back here and I couldn't get in, I felt lost. It was one more reminder that I'm an outsider in your life, and as much as we love each other, there's always going to be someone or something trying to keep us apart. I didn't feel strong enough to fight anymore. I never told you this, but there's this cop that patrols around here that's stopped me a couple of times and given me a hard time for being here. It always seems to happen when I'm feeling a little nervous about moving things forward with you. And every time I have let him know I belonged here, with you, and he let me go. I don't know what happened today, but the more upset I got, the more physically sick I became. I felt like me being there was making it worse for you, like if Brooke hadn't seen me, you wouldn't have had a fight with her."

I took a deep breath and slid down the wall to sit on the floor, no longer able to stand. Danny watched me, then slid down next to me. He still didn't speak, just stared at me. I took another deep breath and continued.

"A major difference between you and me is that I've never had to deal with anyone's obstacles other than my own. I've always fought for everything I had. I don't know why I thought our relationship was going to be any different from the challenges I've faced before. So as soon as I can quit throwing up, I intend to fight for you. For Jane. For us. That is, if you still want me to."

And with that, the digestive pyrotechnics continued. I heaved so hard I was afraid to open my eyes because I just knew some internal organs had to be sitting in the bottom of the toilet. So not a dignified way to end such a statement.

I felt his strong arms come around me, supporting me and holding my hair. When I finally stopped, he started the tub. He waited until the water was warm enough before he pulled my dress off over my head, took off my undergarments, and helped me up.

"Brush teeth first," I whispered.

He handed me my toothbrush and pasted it for me. I brushed until I thought my gums had probably been scraped off. I just wanted to scrub this whole horrid experience away. I rinsed and let Danny help me into the tub.

"I'll be right back," he said quietly, and stood to leave.

I heaved a big sigh, too tired to cry anymore. I felt like every nerve in my body was exposed, completely raw. I started to reach for the soap and Danny beat me to it. He'd gone to change out of his suit and was now just in his black boxer briefs. He took the bottle of body wash and squirted some on his hands, urging me to kneel just for a moment so he could wash all of me. He worked his way down to my toes, massaging my legs and feet. When he was finished, he grabbed the shampoo from the shower, used the hand held nozzle, and washed and conditioned my hair. When it was done, he towel dried the mass and wrapped it up. I rested my head back and closed my eyes. I sensed him moving and opened one eye to find him sitting on the edge of the tub, gazing down at me.

"I would have understood if you left. I kept getting angry and frustrated with you when it felt like you weren't moving at the pace I thought we should. I felt like you were holding back, like you didn't care enough. And the whole time you kept worrying you were going to be a problem for me, I would get mad and tell you to stop worrying. What I didn't see was what all you were taking on by getting involved with me. I have a fucked up ex-wife. I have a beautiful, but troubled daughter. I'm surrounded by people who expect a lot of shit from me. You are the first person in so long that didn't expect something from me, and I took it for granted. I thought if I just didn't worry about the other shit, and if you didn't worry about it, it would just go away. But it's not going to go away." His shoulders bunched up and he pulled at his lip.

"Brooke was there tonight to stir up shit. She's definitely using, and when I confronted her about it, she got really fucking nasty. She started screaming at me. Her fiancé, Oliver, or whatever the fuck his name is, had to carry her out. She made a huge scene. Grace came running up, apologizing, said she didn't know Brooke was in such bad shape, blah blah blah. I feel awful for Trina and Elliot, but Ron assured me they were fine. They wanted to leave early for their honeymoon anyway, but I still feel terrible. Then I got to thinking about how much shit you've had to deal with because of me, and I just wanted to fucking hit something. I looked all over for you until Alex told me Rebecca had taken you home. I was relieved momentarily, thinking at least you hadn't seen all that. Then I saw your purse with your wrap and I..."

He put his head in his hands and took a couple of shaky breaths. He sat like that for a long time. When he finally spoke, he said, "I was so afraid you wouldn't be here when I got back, and I wouldn't have blamed you if you weren't."

I unplugged the drain and got to my feet, not without some effort. I stood before Danny. "Will you get me a towel?"

He looked up at me with tears in his eyes and nodded. He dried me off, wrapped the towel around me, and led me to his bed, where he hesitated.

"Will you sleep with me, Jesse? You don't have to tell me if we're ok—"

I grabbed his face and kissed him firmly. "I'm going to operate under the assumption that what you said to me when I moved in here, that you were 'never fucking letting me go,' is still in effect. You'll need to correct me if I'm mistaken."

He blinked once and fell to his knees, his arms around my waist. "I don't want to lose you, Jesse. Please tell me you'll stay."

I gently pulled his arms away from me and let the towel fall to the floor. I grabbed his t-shirt he'd worn earlier, slipping it over my head. I lifted the covers and crawled into bed, holding my arms out for him to join me. Which he did. And he held me all night.

We spent the next week, starting Sunday, with him in the studio all day. He'd have breakfast with Jane, leave until ten or eleven at night, and then we'd talk and hold each other. We both needed this time to work out some things alone and together. Some nights our discussions got heated, and we never really resolved anything, but we still held each other every night.

The Friday after the wedding, Danny and Brooke had a court date to finalize custody and some other issues. I met his attorney, Jordan Simmons, Thursday morning when she came to the house for a breakfast meeting. She was smartly dressed in a plum colored suit that contrasted nicely with her dark chocolate skin. She wore her hair smoothed back into a bun and wore her makeup to highlight her features. She had a tough-as-nails attitude. She had a similar way of dealing with Danny as Nora did.

Danny had Jane sit with us to hear what he was going to say to Brooke. He hadn't told her about the blow up over the weekend and he didn't mention his concerns about her drug use, although I knew he'd told Jordan everything. After breakfast, I took Jane out for some school supply shopping so he and Jordan could work out the uglier stuff. I liked her. She was confident in Danny's ability to get everything he wanted and she'd heard from Brooke's attorney that she wasn't going to contest anything.

Thursday night he was unsettled about meeting with her, but glad that everything was finally going to be decided. We sat outside by the fire until two in the morning talking. He was just so relieved that Brooke was moving away and wasn't going to be able to cause him and Jane so much grief. Again, we held each other all night, but we hadn't made love since before the disastrous wedding. I told myself it was only because Danny had so much on his mind. It made me a little nervous.

Friday I got Jane up just after Danny left so that I could take her to meet Ivana and Sasha at Universal Studios. We both needed a break from the stress in the house. Danny texted me when the meeting was over:

Leaving court now. Very weird. Full custody granted with supervised visitation. Will tell all later. My love to my girls. Going to the studio, probably be home late. Going to get Jane's shit tomorrow and spend time with my family. IFLY

"I fucking love you, too," I whispered with a relieved sigh.

"What was that?" Ivana asked me and I blushed, not realizing she'd heard me.

"Sorry. Danny was just texting me to say that court was finished. He met with Brooke this morning." She nodded seriously.

While the girls were on the Jurassic Park ride for the fourth time, I told her a very sanitized version of the previous weekend's blow up.

"I hope she doesn't involve Jane in her drama. I hate that you and Danny are having to deal with it, but I sure hate to see Jane getting dragged into it."

I assured her that while Danny was keeping Jane informed, he wanted to protect her as well.

Danny came home after two in the morning and it was obvious he'd had several beers. He kissed me good night and crashed hard. Alex had driven him home, so I knew he was safe. I gave him his space, although I had hoped we would talk. Saturday he was up before me and in the pool. He didn't say much, so I did my own workout and dressed in sweats and sneakers so I could help at Brooke's. She told him she would be gone until Tuesday, when she was overseeing the moving company that was going to pack and store her things for the time being. She'd already found a buyer, and since Danny bought the place for her, he would be receiving half of the proceeds, a quarter would go into Jane's trust, and Danny generously let Brooke keep a quarter. The townhouse sold for over 1.75 million dollars so this was pretty big money.

It took us several hours to pack up her room. I had asked Jinx to bring the van over in case the Range Rover wasn't big enough. He and Cosmo came and helped Danny carry out all of the boxes so Jane and I could pack and sort. Jane said she preferred her furniture at Danny's, so we left it behind for Brooke to deal with. Jane donated several garment bags and boxes full of clothes and shoes she never wore or that were too small. It made her feel good and made Danny and I proud of her.

When it was over and everything was moved out, we drove back to the house in silence. Jane seemed overwhelmed, Danny was pensive, and I was exhausted. Nora had dinner waiting for us and we wolfed down our food. Danny explained that we forgot to eat lunch when Nora looked worried. My appetite had been off for most of the week, I'd even had a few more meetings with the porcelain boss, but tonight I ate like I hadn't had a meal in weeks. I hadn't told Danny, but I was losing weight again. I decided I'd go see the doctor this week if it continued.

After dinner, Danny and Jane went to watch a movie in the theater and I went to the library to read. I just needed to stop thinking for a little while.

"Hey, sugar. You okay?" Nora must have been tidying up the various rooms when she found me a couple hours later.

"Yeah," I answered. "It's just been a weird week and I'm a little tired."

She put a hand to my forehead. "No fever, but you don't look well."

I confessed about the nausea and she thought it might be some combination of the medicines.

"You're not pregnant, are you?" she asked and I shook my head.

"I took a test, so no. I haven't missed any pills or anything either. I might talk to the doctor about another form of birth control, though. Maybe even something permanent."

Nora brushed my hair back and smiled sadly. "I know you said you're okay with that, but you're so young to do something so permanent. Maybe there's another way."

I shrugged. "I don't think it matters. I want to live the life I have. If I were to get pregnant, I'm worried it would cripple me and as underweight as I am, the baby might not make it."

She sat next to me and took my hand. "And as crazy as life can be around here, it's going to take a lot out of you to keep up."

I smiled weakly at her, figuring she just might know what's been going on. Even though we were close, there was a chasm between Danny and I, and I had no idea how to get across it. She pulled me into one of her awesome hugs, and I let myself relax there for a moment.

"Jesse, I wanted to say goodnight." Jane came in and stopped in the doorway with a worried look on her face.

"Baby, did you find... There you..." He stopped with the same pose and worried look as Jane. Nora and I looked up and laughed.

"You two look more alike all the time," Nora said, motioning for Jane to come join our hug. She squeezed us both really tight.

"Jesse, will you tuck me in?" Janey asked, turning her big blues on me.

I kissed her forehead and followed her out of the room, saying goodnight to Nora.

"I'll wait for you," Danny whispered as I passed him, and I smiled at him, relieved. In Jane's room, I braided her hair for her and gently scratched her back until she was asleep. Poor thing just went through a huge upheaval. It was no wonder she was upset.

I stepped out into the hall maybe a half hour later and heard Danny playing the piano. He smiled slightly as I walked up, glancing down at the bench next to him so I sat down. He played a tune I recognized from the night before they went into the studio. His music was really soulful. I wondered how it would transfer to the Blackened hard rock sound.

He stopped about ten minutes later and stretched his back.

"I've missed you," he said quietly. "I know we've been talking a lot this week, but I feel..."

I nodded, running my fingers along the top of his thigh. "You've had a lot going on, baby."

He covered my hand with his. "So have you," he said in a gravelly voice. "Are you feeling okay?" While I wanted to be honest with him, I didn't want to upset him.

"Can we talk about that tomorrow? I just want to be with you tonight," I said, feeling a little shy. I wasn't sure where his head was at, and with him being a little distant, I was worried.

He frowned, looked down at my hand in his, and stood, leading me to the bedroom.

"Do I need to be worried?" he asked as he led me down the hall.

I shook my head. "No, just having some side effects. I'm calling the doctor Monday morning." I really didn't want to worry him and I didn't want my health to get in the way of us being intimate. I needed to be close to him.

When we got to his room, well, our room, there was a lot of tension in the air. We looked at each other nervously. Thankfully, he spoke first.

"I've wanted to touch you every night this week," he said quietly, while keeping his hands in his pockets.

I was so afraid a bomb was about to drop. He was acting so hesitant. "And you didn't because?" I desperately tried to figure him out.

He cleared his throat and said, "I wasn't sure if it was okay. I still don't." He looked deep into my eyes and spoke so honestly, it was probably the most difficult thing he'd ever had to say to me. "I'm afraid."

I wanted to cross the space between us and take him into my arms, but I felt exactly as he did. "What are you afraid of?"

He took in a shaky breath and ran his hands through his hair. "I'm afraid of how out of control I feel. I'm afraid of you leaving. I'm afraid of losing the best friend I've ever had. You. Before the wedding I thought I could read you, thought I had a handle on my feelings for you. Now..."

Oh, God. This was scaring the crap out of me. I wanted him to stop talking. I was petrified of what else he might say. I felt like we were standing on the edge of a cliff, and the rocks were slipping away.

"Now?" *Please don't let him say it's over*, was all I could think. "What's changed for you, Danny?" I was shaking. I was so scared. Obviously all the talking we'd done this week had unsettled him more than anything.

His expression was all over the place. "Everything just feels so much more real. And fragile. My feelings have changed only in that I love you even more, and I need you even more, and I got a taste of what it would feel like to lose it all. I don't think I would survive that. So part of me wonders if I shouldn't just let you go so I never have to worry."

My heart stopped. This was it. I'd heard people describe the feeling of a broken heart before. I thought I knew how it would feel from the previous times he'd pushed me away. But there was no describing this fear, this pain. If he said it was over, I thought it would end me.

Scrounging up the last ounce of courage I had, I asked, "So what are you going to do about that part?"

He cocked his head and narrowed his eyes. "I'm going to tell it to shut the fuck up because there's no way I ever want to live without you. No safe route will ever compare to how whole I feel with you. But I'm so scared you're going to tell me to fuck off. I can't take not knowing anymore, Jesse. Can we fix this? Please? I love you so fucking much! I can't take it anymore, not knowing."

When I could convince my lungs to function again and when I could force myself to take in a breath, I slowly stepped across the space between us. I lifted Danny's left wrist, the one still thankfully wearing the cuff I'd given him. I lifted it up so the heart was facing him and I held it up in front of him.

"The only thing that has changed for me is the determination to love you even more, to fight for us even more, and to do whatever it takes for us to get past this. I can't stand this space between us either, Danny. You're my lover, my best friend, and you hold my soul in your hands. Please, don't be afraid. Come back to me." The last words were barely above a whisper.

"I want to," he said, shaking his head. "But I know there's going to be more drama. I wish I could say there won't be, but Brooke's shit isn't going to go away just because she's in New York and marrying this dude. And neither is Grace Manning, although I think she'll be singing a different tune now that she's seen Brooke at her worst. I guess what I'm trying to say is I wish I could shield you from the ugly parts of my life, but I won't always be able to." He swallowed hard and took my hands in his. "Knowing all that, do you still want to be with me, Jesse?"

I answered him without hesitation.

"For as long as you'll have me, Danny, and I sure as hell hope that's for good."

He squeezed my hands in his and pressed his forehead against mine. "God, I want that. I want you! I've been so afraid to ask you because I thought you'd say no." His hands came up to cradle my face. "So you promise me that we'll deal with this? Together? No running away?"

I nodded and lifted my chin. "No running away. We're in this, for better or worse."

His lips curled up on the sides. "That sounds a little like a vow," he said, playfully, while dropping kisses on my bottom lip and jaw.

I smiled up at him, raising an eyebrow. "It does, doesn't it?"

He leaned back so he could look deeply into my eyes. "I'm going to fucking marry you, Jesse. I swear it. I hope you're ready for it when the time comes."

I giggled. I couldn't help it when he was so serious. "Name a time and place, Danny. I'll be the one in the dress."

His eyes bugged out and he clutched at his chest. "You mean it?! You will? Even after what I just said?"

I rolled my eyes. "The only way I would say no at this point is if you decided you were done with me. Or, I guess, if you decide to rekindle your relationship with Alex. I'm not sure I could compete with him."

He laughed and picked me up, spun me around, and fell on the bed with me on top of him. He brushed my hair back out of my face and laughed. "I told you he's a sloppy kisser, and you're an amazing kisser, so I think we're safe from that fucking scenario."

I gave him a non-serious look of scorn. "You keep bringing up his kissing skills, or lack of them. I think I'm going to have to make you give me the gory details." I tickled him a little and he squirmed wildly.

He tossed me off him and pinned me down with my arms over my head. "You want me to talk?"

I nodded. "I think if we're going to be married eventually, I should know about your sexual escapades. Especially with Alex! For all intents and purposes, he'll be my brother-in-law, so it's kind of weird that he kissed my future husband."

He groaned and bit my neck, eliciting a gasp from me. "I fucking love it when the words 'married' and 'husband' cross your lips. Fine. I'll give you the fucking gory details."

I stopped struggling against his hold and looked up at him in anticipation. "We, uh, experimented a little. When we were younger. Like when we first left home."

He blushed and I could tell that he was really worried about what I would think. He let go of my hands and I wrapped them around his waist, slipping my fingers under his waistband.

"Experimented, huh? I think I need more details." Nothing disturbed me about this information. In fact, I thought it was exciting.

He cleared his throat nervously. "You sure about that?"

I nodded, licking my lips. "Danny, you are the sexiest man I have ever met. It would in no way surprise me to hear that straight men aren't immune to your sensuality."

He shook his head. "You are unbelievable," he murmured, kissing me deeply. My hands slid further down, squeezing his perfect ass. He moaned softly and I could feel his arousal thickening.

"Did you have sex with him?"

He dropped his head on my shoulder and laughed. "No. Well, not totally. We couldn't decide who should bottom, and I think we just kind of reached a point where we both said, 'Nope, not interested,' so we stopped. Then we went out, grabbed a couple of chicks, and looked at each other like, 'Yep. Way better.'"

I could totally see that happening. "So you kissed, though. Anything else?"

He smiled, moving ever so slightly against me. "Aren't you the curious kitten?"

I nibbled on his jaw and he ground a little harder. "I am curious. Did you touch each other?"

He nodded, slipping a hand under my shirt to caress my breast. "We did."

I opened my legs a little further and he pressed hard against my core, like he really wanted inside. "Did you use that talented mouth on him?" I asked, feeling myself getting wet.

His eyes searched mine, perhaps unsure of what I'd think. "Yeah," he said and I sighed.

"I bet he enjoyed that. You are so good with your tongue."

His eyes rolled back in his head. "Jesus, Jesse. I never thought talking to you about being intimate with Alex would have this effect."

I reached under him and unfastened his jeans. "Did he return the favor?" I murmured against his throat. When I touched him, he shivered.

"God, yes, he did. Fuck, Jesse! I love it when you touch me." He moved against my hand and kissed me hard. Then he stilled, holding my face in his hands.

"Jesse, you need to know that I mean it when I say that no one, and I mean no one, has ever made me feel as good as you do. I don't mind telling you this stuff. It's surprisingly kinda hot. But I can honestly say that you're the best I've ever had. Hands down, no competition."

I smiled up at him. "I'm glad to hear you say that, but I wasn't worried. If Alex was better than me, I don't think we'd be here right now. Now roll over."

He grinned and complied. He rolled onto his back with his hands behind his head, and watched me stand before him intently.

"I think we both have too much clothing on for this conversation, and I don't know about you, but I've really missed being naked with you."

His smile fell and he sat up. His hands came around my waist, pulling me close. "I've missed you, too. I was afraid you wouldn't want me to touch you..."

"How about we show each other how much we missed each other," I said hoarsely. "No more being afraid."

He smiled up at me and proceeded to undress us both. We spent the rest of the night getting reacquainted with each other's bodies and all the things we loved to do together. When the first rays of the sun filtered in, we were still making love, covered in sweat and each other.

"I kept you up all night," he panted.

I laughed. "You mean, I kept you up all night."

He laughed, nuzzling my neck. "And I loved every minute of it. You can keep me up whenever you like, honey."

We kissed lovingly and then Danny began to thrust into me like he meant business. It was difficult not to scream when I came. It gave me a rush, like riding the downward path on a roller coaster. Danny watched me the whole time and when I smiled at him he pulled me over on top of him and I moved against him until his whole body was quaking, his head thrashing from side to side.

"Let go, baby," I whispered, but his movements grew more desperate.

He gripped my hips hard enough that it caused me pain, but it felt so good to watch him experience such ecstasy. His head kicked back and he moaned.

"I love you, Jesse. I love you," he cried over and over. Suddenly his eyes opened, he reached up to touch my face, and then his whole body bowed up off the bed. "Ahhh, God! GOD! Jesse, Jesse." His breath was labored, his body slack.

I climbed off of him and he gasped. "I can't even pull you over here, I'm so fucking spent. Hold me? Please?"

I pulled him over to me, using the last of my strength, so his head was resting on my chest. I stroked his back and laughed at the cries coming from him.

"I've died and gone to heaven," was the last thing he mumbled before he finally fell asleep.

I rolled him off of me so I could use the bathroom. When I came out, I put on the t-shirt he took off last night and walked over to the window.

The sunrise was so beautiful. It left me feeling even more optimistic.

Chapter - Two

For once, Jane woke before Danny. She knocked quietly and I looked up from the book I was reading. She giggled when she saw him sprawled out on his stomach, his face turned to the side with his mouth open, snoring. I motioned her over and gave her a hug.

"I so want to mess with him right now," she whispered.

I nodded and whispered some suggestions in her ear. She crept quietly into the bathroom and came back with my makeup bag. I handed her a bottle of nail polish and she painted his toenails and fingernails on his right side bright pink. He barely stirred. Next she lined his lips with my purple eyeliner, his eyebrows in dark pink lip liner, and finished off by writing "ROCK STAR" across his forehead. She grabbed his phone off the nightstand and took pictures before he woke up and all was lost. Her giggling must have disturbed him, because he rolled over on his back and rubbed at his mouth, smearing the lip color everywhere. I snorted and we both cracked up.

"What the hell?" he groaned, scowling.

Jane smiled sweetly and tried to hide the evidence. "Good morning, Daddy! Did you sleep well?" She was overdoing it with the cheese and he picked up on it.

"I slept fine, thank you. What are you doing up so early, acting so damn chipper?" He winked at me and pushed himself up to sit against the headboard. I tried not to gawk at the sight of him like that.

Jane sat on the end of the bed towards my side, still giggling. "It's eleven o'clock! I've already had breakfast. Nora was going to take me and Legs to the ranch, but I wanted to give you a kiss first." She skittered around to his side, kissed him quickly, and then hurried around to my side for protection.

Danny laughed at her behavior, only a little confused. Then he noticed the polish she'd left on the bedside table. He looked at his hands and feet and frowned. "Baby, this totally isn't my color. It pales next to my skin. Didn't you have anything brighter?"

She laughed hysterically, falling back on the bed and I knew she was only saved from a mauling by his lack of clothing.

"Oh, my sweet daughter...Beware what you start with your old man."

She giggled, a little more nervous. "Gotta go! Love you! Oh! Can we go do something this afternoon? I wanna hang out with you. And Jesse. Bye!" She shut the door behind her and I felt Danny's eyes on me.

"How bad is it?" he asked, stretching out and rolling over towards me.

I covered my mouth with a hand to hide my smile. "I believe there's some damning evidence on your phone."

He rolled his eyes and leaned over to grab his phone, exposing his delicious skin and delectable ass. I noticed I'd left teeth marks the night before. Oops. I put my book aside so I could fully appreciate the view.

"Nice touch with the forehead tattoo," he chuckled, setting the phone aside. He reached for me and pulled me up against him, essentially trapping me so he could interrogate me. I reached for a tissue to try to get some of the makeup off. It was hard to take him seriously with writing on his forehead.

"So what was your role in this? Co-conspirator? Accessory? Or were you an innocent bysleeper?"

I wiggled, trying to get loose, but he had a good hold on me and used his bulk to keep me pinned beneath him. He yanked his shirt off me with one hand while using the other to keep me from escaping. He kissed my neck, shoulders and breasts enthusiastically, his version of coercion.

"I swear, I had nothing to...Ok, maybe she used my makeup, but it was all her...I might have told her where it was, but she intimidated me.

Hey, I didn't think cops were allowed to use excessive force," I said the last part with a groan as he entered me deeply. Even after our marathon session the night before, I welcomed him with a happy sigh. "What happens if I plead the fifth, officer?"

He kissed me hard on the lips and then pulled back. "Vell, ve have vays of makink you talk," he said as he moved down my body, nibbling, sucking, and kissing. Until he got to my hips.

"Did I do this? Shit, Jesse!" He noticed the bruises from his fingers.

I laughed and said, "Police brutality! Police brutality!" He frowned, looking really upset so I grabbed his jaw and made him look at me. "Baby, I loved it. I'm fine. I just bruise easy. And you were going to make me talk, remember?"

Once he could tell I really was fine, he grinned wickedly. He got to work, and with his skills, he had me singing like a canary in no time. It didn't take much more effort on his part for me to give him a full confession. He worked me over until he was completely satisfied there was nothing left to add to the story. He said I could go free, since I was a good little prisoner, and I was rewarded with a shower. After we dressed, I was fed a delicious breakfast. By hand. I made sure to savor every bite and nibble every one of his fingers.

"I fucking love you, honey. I feel so good after last night. In so many ways," he said with a mischievous smile.

"Me, too, baby," I answered, leaning forward to link my fingers around his neck. "So let's talk schedule."

He stepped closer to my barstool and leaned in close. "Absolutely, although mine is pretty set. Breakfast with my ladies, studio with my boys, home to make love to my woman." His hands started to get busy, so I slapped at them.

"Serious talk time, mister! Now, I know what your schedule is, and I know Jane's going to horse camp until Friday, but I also go back to work on Tuesday."

His smile was gone and he was all serious. "Work. Right. I forgot." He pulled back a little and leaned his elbows on the counter. "Do you know what your schedule is going to be like?"

"I think Gloria has me scheduled to work Monday, Tuesday, and Wednesday. I'll work from eight to three, and then I was thinking of talking to the dance studio to see if I could have flexibility with my nights. Nora said her cooking will be on Wednesdays and Thursdays. I was going to see if I could teach Mondays and Tuesdays so I can be here with Jane."

Danny smiled at me and then shook his head. "You are so fucking good to me." He leaned over to kiss me lightly on the lips and I almost lost my focus.

"I just want to help. Anyway, this week, I'm going to go to acupuncture and the doctor tomorrow, training Tuesday through Thursday, and Friday I was going to go clean up the rest of my apartment. Nora said she'd come help me."

Danny took my hands in his. "I'll come help. I can tell the guys—"

"There's really not much more to do. It's fine."

He exhaled, frustrated, and then nodded. "Okay." He walked around behind me and rubbed my shoulders. "You know what I like about your schedule?" He spoke close to my ear, giving me shivers.

"What do you like about it?" I asked, enjoying his touch.

"You will have four days off each week. It'll make it easy for you to fly out and spend weekends with me when I'm on tour."

I turned to face him, a surprised smile on my face. "Really? You'd want me to?" I attempted to hide my excitement.

"Of course, honey! I'd love for you to be with me all the time, but I know you have to work. It might not be possible when we're in Europe, but when we're here in the states, hell yeah I'm going to want you with me! We've already decided to only be out two or three weeks and then a week home. I want you to send your school calendar to Patricia when you have it so she can work her magic. Oh, and if you don't already have a passport, I'll want you to go with Patricia to get one."

I snorted. "Oh yeah, because I've had so much need for a passport. I'll talk to her about it. But why?"

He grinned like he had been busy making plans. "I have my reasons," was all he would say.

We spent some time doing business type stuff. I pulled up my calendar and sent it to Patricia using Danny's computer in the office. I sat on his lap, at his insistence, and he told me a little bit about the business of being Danny Black. He slid on his reading glasses. Very hot.

"So Patricia handles the band stuff, but she also handles a lot of my personal business." He ran his hand up and down my back while scanning his email. He flipped through the snail mail and sorted it. Bills, music catalogs, requests for donations, invitations to appearances. The stack was pretty hefty.

"I know she handles your schedule, but what other kind of business?"

He laughed, shaking his head. "Taking my girlfriend shopping, finding rehearsal space and booking it for a bunch of ruffians that live next door to my girlfriend. Well, used to. Let's see, helping me order jewelry for my girlfriend." I pinched his side and he jumped, almost knocking us out of the chair.

"I get it that she takes care of stuff for your girlfriend," I said with an exaggerated eye roll. "I'm just curious what else?"

"Ah, she helps me with my finances, she oversees my accountant, insurance, stuff like that. She helps me hire people I might need, like my attorney. Pretty much she's my go-to girl. Nora, on the other hand, is my business partner and personal assistant. We make decisions about the house together. She pays the bills, handles household maintenance, oversees the cleaners when they come...We do have a cleaning crew that comes through once a month, taking care of the heavy-duty stuff that Nora hates to do. She schedules the gardeners. She handles the dry-cleaning. She'll be Janey's chauffeur for all of her stuff. You've already seen that. Pretty much she's the boss. I just live here."

I giggled and kissed his temple. "So what's my job, then? Seems like other competent women already take all of the jobs in your life. Speaking of which, do you consciously surround yourself with women? I think it's really cool. I was just wondering if you did it on purpose."

He made a face and then laughed. "Wow, I guess I hadn't thought of it that way. Does that make me a mama's boy?" More pinching from me. "Ow! I guess it started with Patricia. Nora came with the house. Jordan and Connie came with the territory. My accountant is a dude. My band members are dudes. I'm an equal opportunist." He wrapped his arms around me and rested his head on my shoulder.

"You have the most important job," he murmured, the rumble of his voice giving me shivers. There was a time when he couldn't speak, when I didn't know what his voice even sounded like. Now I got to hear it and feel it. No wonder I was so in love with him. He assaulted all of my senses.

"And what does my job description say?" I asked in a low voice.

His lips spread into a most sexy smile and he said, "To love, honor and cherish me. To hold me in sickness and in health..."

"Hey, those are vows, buddy!"

"Hmmmm," he murmured. "How about sleep aide, muse, swim partner, masseuse, hair washer, well, total body bather..." He kept on with his list, getting quite graphic, but then he stopped and smiled again. "And most importantly, my best friend, my sounding board, and, of course, my teacher. That's how you started, that's who you'll always be, because you've taught me so much, honey." He was so sweet. I had been determined not to cry anymore, but my eyes welled up with tears. "I didn't mean to make you cry. It's just the truth, honey." I sniffled and he kissed me. And kissed me again. And some more. He lifted me onto his desk and started assaulting my neck when we heard the front door open.

"You guys home?" Nora yelled, probably meaning "are you guys decent?"

Danny smirked and said, "We'll have to save this for another time. Mmmm, don't think I'll be able to work in here without thinking of you on top of..."

"Hi Daddy!" Jane came running in and I turned to hide my blush.

"Baby girl! How was the ranch?" He gave her a big hug and she beamed up at him.

"Great as usual! But I think I need new riding pants." She pointed down at her legs and the bottoms barely reached the top of her boots.

Danny barked out a laugh. "Yeah, I would say so! The flood waters are coming in!" She slugged him in the arm. "Ow! How about we go this afternoon? Do you need anything else?"

She shook her head. "Well, yeah. Maybe some boots? Tall boots? Mine are getting tight."

I reached down and felt to see where her big toe was and all her toes were pushing against the front. "These are way too tight."

Danny nodded at both of us. "Well, that settles it. Let's go to the country and western store. I better get mah Ropers and mah Wranglers on, little darlins."

Jane groaned and I cracked up at Danny's bowlegged cowboy walk down the hallway. He even turned and tipped a pretend Stetson at us, and then he fake spat.

"My dad is such a weirdo," Jane groaned.

I hugged her close and said, "Yes, but he's our weirdo."

She looked up at me quizzically. "Everything ok with you two?" she whispered.

I frowned down at her, smoothing her hair back. "Why do you ask? Yes, we're fine, but what made you think something was wrong?"

She shrugged and rested her head on my chest. "My dad seemed kinda depressed. You did too, I guess. Is it always like this when you're in love? The ups and downs?"

I kissed her hair and rested my chin. "I think so. At least that's what I'm learning. I hope he and I won't have too many of the downs. It's just been a tough adjustment for us both, but I think we've worked things out. Don't worry. I'm not going anywhere. Certainly not without a fight."

She smiled at me and squeezed. "Good! Because I love you, Jesse. I don't want you to go."

I smiled at her and said, "I love you, too. And the only place we're going is to get your new supplies! Let's git along little dowggie!" I smacked her butt and she scooted out of the room, laughing.

Danny in the Western Supply Depot was almost as bad as Danny in the drug store.

"Hey darlin'," he called out to Janey, continuing with his horrible attempt at a Texas drawl. "You think I need a ten gallon or a twenty gallon hat? Maybe they make a keg sized one." Then he held up the gaudiest Western shirts and asked, "Honey pie, think I should git me some of these to wear on tour?"

I grabbed my forehead and shook my head. Jane leaned into me and tried to hide.

"I think this hot pink one with all the sparklies is totally me! Oh shit, this one's a chick shirt. Dayam! Can't tell the difference."

I pulled his arm to get him out of the clothing aisle as he was starting to get frowns from some of the real cowfolk.

"Danny, don't be offensive. Those cowboys over there don't much like your kind in here, and you promised Jane no fighting."

Danny looked down at himself in his black jeans, black Chucks, Motorhead t-shirt, tattoos everywhere, and his hair styled like the rock star he was. He looked thoroughly admonished and he whispered an apology to Jane, who was still giggling.

We got her two pairs of riding pants and some new boots, socks, riding gloves, a new helmet because, well yeah, the one she'd been wearing was from three years ago and kinda small. An hour and a half, and close to a thousand dollars later, we loaded the purchases into the Challenger's trunk and pulled out into traffic.

"Phew," I said. "That was a close one! I think the shurriff was coming after ya." Both of them burst out laughing.

"Yeah, I don't think I have to worry about getting recognized in that place. They'd probably think Blackened is just how we cook our food." He gave a comic drum roll and Jane laughed so hard she got the hiccups.

Danny shook himself. "I think we need to go to a rockin' place to wash all that country out of our mouths. Hey Janey baby, how about we go get you your own guitar?"

She stopped laughing and her eyes lit up. "For real? Are you serious?"

He laughed and shrugged. "Why not? You're doing really good with the stuff I taught you, and you've been practicing, right?" She nodded enthusiastically. "You want to keep learning?"

"I do, Daddy, I do! It's so cool!"

His face broke out into a large, proud papa grin. "Well, alrighty then! Let's go get you a good starter."

She clapped her hands together and he reached over to take my hand, raised it to his lips and kissed my swollen joints, just like he used to. All was really right with my world tonight.

The Guitar Center on Sunset was like a museum. Jane and I stopped and looked at all the names carved into the sidewalk and the busts on the wall. Jane asked Danny who his favorites were. He pointed out Stevie Ray Vaughn, Eddie Van Halen, Jimi Hendrix, Tony Iommi, and several others. Jane listened to him, hanging on every word.

"Ok, but you're going to have to make me a playlist with all those guys because I've never heard—"

"Shhhh!" Danny held a hand to her mouth. "Baby! That's blasphemous talk in here. We'll remedy this situation after we leave. Just don't tell any of these guys you've never heard of those guitar players, all right? I got a rep to protect."

We cracked up as we entered the store. Several anxious sales kids immediately surrounded Danny. Kids. None of them were over twenty-two years old.

"I'm here to pick up a good starter for my daughter."

Their eyes glazed over and they practically drooled at the potential commission they could earn. Danny tried out all the guitars they suggested and then gave them to Jane to try. She decided on a vintage sunburst Les Paul Jr., but made sure she got the furry pink zebra print strap, a velvet lined case and some rainbow picks to go with it.

Danny perused the high-end guitars and let one of the young salesmen follow him around, talking excitedly to him the whole time. He was very patient with the kid.

"And over here, we just came into possession of this nineteen fifty-nine Les Paul Custom. Its owner hocked it at a pawn shop in Las Vegas. Our manager knows the shop owner. It arrived about two weeks ago."

Danny gazed longingly at the beautiful guitar hanging on the wall. He started pulling on his lip so I nudged his shoulder.

"Why don't you try it out, babe?"

He looked at me, startled. He'd obviously been in his own world. For a moment I worried that I'd interrupted some sacred musician experience, but then his lips split into a kid-in-a-candy-store grin and I could breathe again.

"Mind if I play it?" he asked and the kid broke out into a sweat.

"Ummm, yes, of course, Mr. Black. I, uh, need to just, uh, have my manager unlock it. Excuse me for a moment?'

The poor kid almost took out a whole display of amps, tripping over his feet to get Danny what he wanted. Danny didn't notice, however. His eyes were appraising this guitar.

"So what makes this one special?" I asked.

He turned to me, again looking surprised. "Well, these customs are pretty rare and were the first to have these Humbucker pickups. Humbuckers give them a soft tone, a really nice sound. They're hard to find." He was so taken with the guitar. I wanted to know more about what made this guitar so attractive, but before I could ask any more questions, the kid, Randy, was back, and he had the keys to unlock the guitar.

"Here you are, M-Mr. Black. You can plug into this Marshall over here." Danny thanked him while cradling the guitar lovingly in his hands.

I figured I would distract the poor kid before he had an accident. I walked over to him and asked him a few questions about the guitar. He smiled brightly at me, stopped chewing on his fingernail, and launched into a history of Les Paul, telling me about the guitar legend, and about his collaboration with Gibson to make these amazing guitars. He talked about this particular model, called the "Black Beauty," and how it incorporated the PAF, or "patent applied for" Humbucker pickups and repeated what Danny said about them being rare and hard to find.

By now Danny was seated and had finished looking over the guitar for wear and tear. Surprisingly, there was little damage to find on this old guitar. When he plugged in and started to play, I noticed that the majority of people in the store stopped what they were doing and were peering over displays and around corners, trying to get a look at Danny. He had his eyes closed as he played a blues riff I recognized from a song Eric Clapton recorded with the John Mayall Blues Breakers. He played a part of a Guns N' Roses song, and then he played some pieces I didn't recognize. All of the sales people were hovering and shaking their heads. I bet they loved when a true genius like Danny came in. He stopped playing and looked around, blushing a little.

Randy cleared his throat and said, "What do you think, Mr. Black?"

Danny smiled and looked down at the guitar. "It's beautiful. I have a couple of signatures, but I've wanted the right custom." He looked up at me and asked, "What do you think?"

I laughed and leaned down to talk to him in a low voice. "You're asking me? I have the least bit of knowledge of anyone in this store about this guitar. I think it sounds amazing. I think you look sexy as hell playing it. But that's really all I can comment on."

He grinned at me and grabbed my hand, leaning his head back to kiss me. I heard Jane giggle and he whispered loudly, "I fucking love you, honey."

The crowd started to dissipate, and Danny played a few more chords.

"Well, Randy, I think this Beauty needs to come home with me. Can you ring this up, along with my daughter's purchases?"

Randy turned awfully pale and it took him a minute to collect himself. "S-s-sure, Mr. Black. I'll, uh, get you the case."

Danny stopped him. "Hey, how long have you been working here?"

"About four months, sir. I, uh, moved out here from Iowa to go to school and found a job here."

Danny smiled at him and said, "You've got a lot of knowledge. What are you going to school for?"

Randy rubbed the back of his neck. "Um, I want to be a music teacher," he said in a shaky voice.

I smiled at him, glad to hear he had such a great goal.

Danny noticed my smile and said, "That's great. We need more teachers." He winked at me and asked, "You in a band?"

Randy shook his head. This time he spoke with a much more confident voice. "No. I get too nervous. I've played with a few, but it never works out because I hate being on stage. I want to do some studio work. I've been playing guitar since I was five and I love it. It's everything to me."

Danny grinned. "I totally get it. I wish you luck, man." He reached for his wallet and took out a card. "Here. Call Jerry. He's the owner of the studio where we record. I think he's looking for some good sessions guys. Tell him I told you to call."

Randy looked like he'd just won the lotto. "Th-thank you, so much, Mr. Black. This is huge. Thank you, I'll call." He took the card from Danny and put it in his pocket. He carefully lifted the Les Paul from Danny's outstretched hand and carried it into the back.

Danny stood and hugged Jane. "You like your guitar, baby?"

She nodded. "Do I get to play that one, too?"

Danny laughed. "Maybe when you get a little further along. That guitar is worth about two years of your future college education, so we're going to take really good care of it."

My stomach plunged. He was about to drop over $40,000 on a guitar! Sometimes I forgot just what different worlds he and I lived in. Although, now I was living in his...And it was weird. He wanted to marry me! How the hell was this going to work, because in no way was I ready to be making $40,000 purchases on a random Sunday afternoon.

Danny must have noticed my shock. He kissed Jane on the head and she walked over to look at the books. He turned and wrapped me in his arms, kissing me. "You probably think this is pretty crazy," he said in a low voice.

I swallowed hard. "For me, yes. But I guess it's not for you?"

He shrugged. "It's probably the most I've spent on one guitar. I felt like celebrating today." He kissed me again and I could have easily forgotten we were in public, until I heard giggles from across the store. Jane. Danny pulled back and studied me. "I don't blow money like this on a regular basis, though. I want you to know that."

"You can do what you want, Danny. It's your hard earned cash, right?"

He shook his head. "Yeah, but I don't want you to think that...I don't know. I know how you feel about—"

"Danny, it's fine. I can see how much you love it. You deserve to treat yourself, and it's not like you're not going to use it. Besides, I'm sure down the road if you wanted to sell it, it would fetch a pretty penny after being in your capable hands." I smiled up at him, biting my lower lip a little and I felt him growl.

"God, you are so fucking hot, Jesse. You can't do that in public." His face turned a little red and I laughed.

"I'm sorry. Let's change the subject. You were very sweet to the salesman."

He took my hands in his and stepped back, taking a deep breath. "He's a good kid. And I wasn't kidding about Jerry needing a sessions musician. He fired Stacey for being drunk at work. That guy is a disaster."

Sadly, I could believe it. "He's got a real problem. After the day at your house, and the fight, you'd think he'd realize..." I shook my head. People who are in the throes of addiction don't see what's going on, usually until it's too late.

"I hope he figures it out soon. He's got a lot of talent. It's a shame he's throwing it all away on the bottle and drugs." Danny seemed genuinely concerned about the guy, even though I knew how angry he was with him. Chalk that up as one more reason I loved this man.

Randy came out and rang up Danny's purchases. He and Jane both walked out with huge grins on their faces, and guitar cases in hand. We locked their purchases in the trunk of the Challenger and climbed in.

"Who's hungry?" Danny called.

"Me!" Jane was actually never *not* hungry.

I wasn't feeling much like food, but I was enjoying our afternoon.

"How 'bout a stop down memory lane?" Danny pulled out onto Sunset, made a right onto LaBrea, and then a right onto Santa Monica, pulling up to the Formosa Cafe. Danny looked at me, a loving expression on his face, and I melted.

"What's this place?" Jane asked as Danny opened my door for me.

He helped me out, grinning, and then helped Jane. He had the valet park the car and gave him extra to keep a close eye on it. We watched the guy park it in a corner, closest to his stand.

"This, my dearest Jane, is where I met Jesse. We had our dinner interview here with Patricia."

We walked in together and were seated immediately, the hostess gawking at us. She walked us back to the streetcar section and Danny asked if we could be seated at 'our booth.'

"Can I get you something to drink, Mr. Black?" she asked, batting her eyelashes.

"Ladies? What would you like?" I was tickled by the way he ignored the hostess.

Jane asked for a root beer and I ordered a Diet Coke. Danny asked for ice water and the hostess, lingering a tad too long, told us our server would be over shortly.

Jane gave her a funny look and I leaned in to whisper, "He gets that a lot, doesn't he?"

She rolled her eyes and nodded.

Danny continued with his version of our first meeting. "So yeah, I looked like shit, my hair was a wreck, and I was in my ratty sweats. In walks this long-legged, fucking gorgeous woman dressed in a suit with her blonde hair piled on top. She took my fucking breath away. I couldn't believe it when Patricia introduced her. I thought she was a damn supermodel. She was so perfect. But no, she was to be my teacher, and a cranky one at that." I kicked him under the table. I was sitting next to Jane across from him, and he laughed. "You were kinda cranky, honey."

"Me? You were the one who looked pissed off at the world!"

He blushed a little and nodded. "Yeah, you're right. I was in a bad place. I'd gotten sick from the anesthesia after my surgery and had been throwing up for a couple of days."

I frowned. "I didn't know it was so close to your surgery," I said, quietly.

His smile slipped a little. "The doc thinks that's why it took me so long to heal, because of the, you know, being sick part."

Poor Danny. "If I would have known that, I would've gone easier on you," I said seriously and he laughed, shaking his head.

"Thank God you didn't. Janey, this lady here didn't take any of my crap. She even tried to take care of me, and she didn't even know me. When my food came and I couldn't eat it, she ordered me ice cream." His face morphed into that of a lovesick puppy.

"You are too much," I said, laughing. "I was just afraid I would be fired before I was even hired. I'm glad I wasn't."

Jane looked back and forth between us and made retching sounds. "Okay, okay, I get it. You met, you fell in love, and now you're going to get married. By the way, when is that happening and do I get to be a bridesmaid?" She looked up at me expectantly.

"I don't know, sweetie, but I would be honored, if and when it happens, if you would be my Maid of Honor. Not just some measly bridesmaid."

Her eyes got big and she smiled up at me. "Really? Don't you have like a friend, or something, you'd want?"

"Besides your dad, my best friend is Cosmo, and he'd be a little hairy for a bridesmaid dress. Not to mention I think he wears like size fifteen shoes. He definitely wouldn't be able to wear the heels."

She burst out laughing and Danny nudged my foot under the table.

"There's no *if*, Jane. I am going to marry Jesse. I'm just waiting for the right moment to ask her officially," he said, with a wink. "And you'll be the first to know when that is going to happen, okay baby?"

She nodded.

I thought that was a good idea.

The server came, a bored looking guy with a rockabilly 'do going on and full tattoo sleeves on each arm. He took our orders and huffed off to put them in.

Danny asked Jane what she was going to be learning at horse camp, and we fell into easy conversation. Jane was bummed I was going back to work. Her school didn't start for two more weeks. She and Nora were going to take Legs to the beach one day and she was going to hang out at Sasha's for a couple of days.

Summer was over and we all had to get our game faces on. Well, except Danny. He'd already been back at work. He shared with us the band's progress in the studio. Jane asked if we could come visit and he thought maybe in a week or so.

"And we're going to start dance class, too, Jane. You're going to be a busy girl," I said to her, hugging her close to me.

She smiled happily. Danny seemed pleased that we were happy and getting along so well together. Everything felt great today.

We drove home after dinner and Danny and Jane carried their guitars straight to Danny's room and got to work practicing. I went to talk to Nora, who was putting away groceries. We talked over the schedule for the week and then we went to the bedroom to listen to the Blacks play together. She drooled over his guitar and admired Jane's as well. I lay down on the bed, stretched out and watched them.

The next thing I knew, Danny was crawling into bed with me. "Did I fall asleep?" He chuckled close to my ear.

"You did. Don't worry. We didn't do too much damage."

I shot up and touched my face, feeling something sticky. "Oh no," I groaned and stood up shakily to go to the bathroom. The room was spinning a little so I stopped in the doorway to take a break.

"You okay, babe?" Danny called, nervously.

"Just need the room to stop spinning a bit. No problem."

He stood up to help me into the bathroom and when I got a look at the mirror, I cracked up.

"Nice moustache," I said sarcastically.

Danny was giggling behind me. "The goatee was my idea," he said, backing away from me.

I rolled my eyes. "Of course it was." I grabbed some makeup remover and got to work.

Danny cautiously approached, staying at least an arm's length away. "Am I in trouble?" he whispered.

"How could you be in trouble?" I asked him so sweetly, he flinched with anxiety. "Just remember what I said to you when we first started working together. When students mess with me, I'm pretty sneaky about getting them back."

He laughed and buried his face in my neck. I got the rest of the black eye pencil off my face, and turned to kiss him. We undressed and got into bed, loving each other until early the next morning.

Chapter - Three

September 2013

Life fell into a busy, blissful pattern for the next month. School started and I was glad I had a shorter schedule. It gave me more energy to give to Danny and Jane. I was able to get my classes moved at the studio so I worked at the school Monday through Wednesday, taught dance on Monday and Tuesday evenings, and had Thursday and Friday to go to acupuncture, see Connie for massage, run errands, and just be at home. Danny drove Jane to school each day. He'd come back and we'd spend some quality time together. He'd go to the studio at noon and I'd pick up Jane from school. Nora was at class Wednesday and Thursday nights, but she left dinner for us. Jane totally loved jazz class and thought, soon, she might want to try tap, too.

The doctor adjusted my meds, so I was feeling great and putting on weight. One morning, the last week of September, Danny noticed me fighting with my wardrobe before work and decided to intervene. He was lying back against the headboard, naked, and groaning about how he loved to watch me dress almost as much as he liked me to undress. This particular morning, however, none of my zippers would zip and my buttons wouldn't even reach.

"I know I'm supposed to be gaining weight, but I feel like a fucking cow right now." I fought back tears of frustration. Danny approached and wrapped his arms around me from behind.

"Honey, it's what's healthy for you. I know you hate it, but you look so fucking good, I can't say I'm sorry."

I knew he was right, but I dreaded getting dressed in the mornings.

That Thursday, I was playing with Legs in the backyard, dressed in Danny's boxer briefs and a t-shirt, about all that was comfortable, when I had an unexpected visitor.

"Surprise!" It was Patricia, on another mission from Danny. "I'm under orders," she said with a wicked grin. She hurried me into my room to get dressed and informed me we would be dropping Legs at the pet sitter on the way.

She took me shopping to her favorite boutiques as well as some discount stores (at my insistence) and she showered me with clothes to try on. Most of them were a little edgier than I was used to, but all were absolutely gorgeous. It was no wonder my clothes weren't fitting. I'd gone up two sizes!

Lingerie shopping was the most fun.

"Patricia! I have boobs!"

She laughed hysterically at me trying on bras and delighting that I actually had cleavage.

"Congratulations, my dear! I think we should go celebrate!"

After we'd spent several hours shopping, we had lunch, and then she took me to a spa.

"Also part of my orders," she said when I started to protest. "And Jane is going home after school with Sasha. They have the day off tomorrow, so she's spending the night." She wiggled her eyebrows at me. "Danny wanted you 'perfectly outfitted, relaxed, and ready for me when I get home.' Direct quote, I promise!"

My phone rang at that minute. It was Gloria.

"Oh Future Mrs. Black," she said in a singsong voice. "The exit exam results are in. You can officially say you are living with a high school graduate."

I squealed so loud Patricia swerved the Corvette.

"Thank you so much for calling! I can't wait to tell him!" I hung up and hooped and hollered some more.

"What in the world?"

"He passed! He passed! Oh! I gotta call him. I gotta—"

"Wait until he gets home. What a nice surprise you'll have for him." I looked at Patricia and grinned like a crazy person.

"The best surprise. All right. You convinced me." She laughed at me and gave me a fist bump.

I had known that he would pass the exams, but hearing the news officially just warmed my heart. All of our hard work had paid off. I'd accomplished something really important by being his teacher. Handing him his diploma would be incredibly fulfilling for us both.

The spa was phenomenal. I had my first facial, a manicure and pedicure, and even a massage, although it wasn't as good as what I got from Connie. I needed to remember to tell her the next time I saw her. Patricia dropped me off at the house and I let myself in, loaded down with bags. So many thoughts were running through my head. How was I going to tell him? How would he react? I had to let his mother know...

As I was struggling to get in the door, I felt someone push me from behind.

"Where is he," I heard a male voice growl. I pulled away as he shut the door. "Where the fuck is Danny?"

I vaguely recognized the intruder as Stacey. He had lost a lot of weight, his hair was all stringy and gross, and he smelled terrible. I dropped my bags and backed up to the wall where the alarm pad was located.

"He's not here, Stacey. They're in the studio. Do you want me to call him for you?" I asked, pulling out my phone with shaking hands.

He knocked it out of my hand and stepped closer to me. "He got me fucking fired," he shouted. "Because of him, no fucking musicians will work with me. I can't get work. I even lost my fucking apartment and had to hock my guitar, that sonofabitch."

I was able to reach behind me and hit the silent alarm, thankful Danny had a good security system and that I had finally learned how to use it.

But then Stacey turned his hatred on me. He grabbed my arm hard and jerked me away from the wall. He yanked me into the living room and threw me down on the sofa.

"Stacey, maybe if you just sit down, we can talk about this."

He started pacing and I saw he had a knife clipped to his pocket. Please, God, don't let him take that out! I wasn't sure how long it would take the police to get here, but it wouldn't take long for him to really hurt me if he used a blade.

He stepped over to me and grabbed me by the hair. "If only I'd never laid eyes on you at that party. If only I hadn't touched you." He ran a hand down his face and his cracked lips split into a disgusting grin. "Or, maybe I should have just made it more worth my while."

I started to panic. This wasn't a man afraid of the consequences of his actions. He yanked me back, pinning me to the couch, and pulled at the front of my dress, popping the buttons off. I screamed and clawed at him, but even at his smaller size, he was way too strong for me. I vowed that if I made it through this, I was going to learn how to defend myself. I'd take Janey with me to training, too. I was so grateful she wasn't here. I prayed that if this turned ugly, that Danny wouldn't be the one to find me.

I tried to kick at him and he backhanded me with his other hand, splitting my lip. He held me down by my throat until I started to suffocate. With my vision going spotty, I could barely think, but I knew I needed to get away from him. I let myself relax, going completely slack, and he took that as a surrender. He let go of my neck, unfastened his pants, and climbed on top of me.

"That's right, Teacher. I'll show you who's the better man." He got right in my face with his rank breath and let go of my hair so he could rip the bottom off of my dress. He got a grasp on my panties and tore the side off.

I smiled at him invitingly and then hauled back and head-butted him as hard as I could. I heard the sickening crack of his nose as my forehead connected with his. I felt his blood splash on my face.

He clutched at his nose and screamed, "YOU FUCKING BITCH!" He sat back enough for me to get out from under him, but then he caught what was left of the bottom of my dress, ripping it the rest of the way. My sandal strap broke and I fell down, catching myself before I face planted on the marble floor. Stacey was right behind me on the floor, reaching for my ankle.

"Come here! I'll make sure you bleed even more, bitch."

I heard the flick of his knife as he opened it and I screamed.

The door flew open in front of me. "FREEZE!"

Two officers came running in, guns drawn. Stacey cursed and dropped the knife. I scrambled over to the wall, breathing hard. The first officer stepped forward to subdue him, but Stacey turned over and reached in his pocket. The second officer fired three rounds into his chest. It was over.

The other officer came to check on me, and at that moment, I recognized the shooter as the cop who'd stopped me.

"Jesus! You're the teacher," he yelled. "Are you hurt? Did he hurt you?"

I shook my head, but I was too dazed to speak. The other officer called for the paramedics.

"Can you stand up, Miss—"

"Martin. Jesse Martin. I think so."

He tried to help me into the kitchen so I wouldn't have to look at Stacey anymore, but instead I dashed into the bathroom, barely making it to the toilet before I threw up violently. He stood in the doorway, offering me a towel when I was finished, and then helped me to stand. I wrapped the large bath sheet around me since my dress and panties were practically gone. "Is there anyone else home, ma'am?"

I shook my head. "No. Danny is at the studio. Jane is staying at a friend's house, and Nora is probably at class." I looked at the clock and saw that it was seven o'clock. Legs was at the pet sitter. No one would have been home for at least another three hours. Thank God I was able to hit the alarm.

"Danny? You mean Danny Black?"

I nodded, my head screaming at me with the movement. My neck was sore and it hurt to talk. "Yes. He's my boyfriend."

The cop nodded and stepped away, speaking into his radio. He and his partner conferred in the entryway for a few minutes, and then I heard more voices. Two paramedics came in and started to look me over. They cleaned the wounds on my face and said they thought I needed stitches on both my lip and my forehead where I'd split my skin hitting Stacey.

"We're going to need to take you to the hospital," the female said.

I nodded, wanting Stacey's blood and whatever else off of me. I wished I could just shower and scrub it all off.

"Just let me grab my purse."

The other paramedic said, "Ma'am, I think it's in the hallway with the other bags and we'll need to use another exit. The crime scene techs need to have that area sealed off."

"We can go through the garage," I said quietly.

The officer leaned in the doorway and said, "Is there someone we should call for you?"

Just then I heard tires squealing outside and a door slam.

"JESSE! JESSE! Fucking HELL! JESSE!" I heard the officer try to calm him down and he screamed, "Where's my fucking girlfriend? Jesse!"

I hurried over to the garage, opening the outer door. "Danny, in here."

He flew around the corner and stopped running when he saw me. He looked like he'd just been sucker punched. He stalked over to me, grabbing my arms. "Oh, honey. Oh my God, Jesse?" He crushed me to him. I was so grateful to see him. We were both shaking. He pulled back to look at my face.

"Honey, what happened? Who did this?"

I took a shuddering breath. "It was Stacey, baby. The police shot him."

He blanched and picked me up, carrying me back into the kitchen. He had me sit down at the counter and the paramedics got back to work, dressing my cuts, while he stood there looking helpless.

The officer came back in and said, "Miss Martin, we need to ask you some questions."

I nodded, but Danny held up a hand and said, "I know you need to talk to her, but she needs medical attention." He looked down and saw part of my ripped dress under the towel. His eyes got dark and his face turned beet red. When he spoke his jaw was clenched. "Jesse, did he—"

"No! No, I got away from him, and then the cops came in. How did you get here so fast?" I asked, bewildered.

He started to pull the towel away to see the extent of the damage. I grabbed it, not wanting any of them to see how bad things almost were.

"No, Danny. Please. I'm ok. But how—"

"The alarm company called my cell when the panic alarm was hit. They could hear everything going on, but they wouldn't give me any other information. I didn't know who was home. I called Patricia when I couldn't reach you and she said she'd just dropped you off. Fuck, honey, you're so hurt! I'm so fucking sorry I wasn't here." He hugged me gently, his hands trembling as he touched my back.

I held him in my arms, trying to reassure him I was ok. But then everything started to get to me.

"Danny, baby, I think I need to..."

When I woke up next, I was in the hospital. Danny was in the doorway talking to a police officer. He must have heard me stirring, because he was instantly at my side.

"Jesse, honey, how do you feel?"

I laughed, but even that hurt my head. "Like shit. What am I doing here?" I asked, confused. I didn't remember leaving his kitchen.

"You fainted, honey. They brought you here. You had to have stitches on your forehead, but your lip they thought would be okay without."

I touched my lip tentatively with my tongue. It was swollen, but okay. Danny looked a wreck. His eyes were bloodshot, and there was blood all over his grey t-shirt.

"You're going to have security from now on. You and Jane. I don't care if I have to post a fucking guard in front of the damn house."

I patted him on the arm. "Going to take self-defense, okay? It's okay."

He shook his head. "The police want you to give a statement when you feel up to it. I tried to tell them to fuck off, but they said that wasn't possible, and warned me they'd take me in if I interfered. Fuckers."

I giggled, reaching up to brush his hair back. "I can talk to them."

He kissed my cheek and leaned back with a grimace. "I can't kiss you anywhere! I'm so fucking sorry this happened. It's all my fault."

I shook my head, grabbing his face. "No, Danny. This was all about Stacey being desperate. He said he'd gotten fired, lost his apartment, hocked his guitar. He was looking for someone to blame. I'm just glad he didn't find you. He had a knife, Danny, and I don't think he would have been much for talking with you. At least I stalled him a little."

Danny just looked more pissed. "Fuck," he growled, stomped away from the bed, and kicked a chair into the wall. The officer looked into the room to be sure everything was okay, giving Danny a stern look. Danny took a deep breath and ran his hands through his hair.

"Can we come in?" Patricia, Julian, Bronson and Alex were at the door. The officer stopped them.

"Just a short visit, and then the detective needs to take her statement."

They nodded and then rushed into the room.

Patricia got to me first. "I brought you a change of clothes, Jesse. I'm so sorry! I should have walked you inside. What happened?"

I squeezed her hand. "I'm glad you weren't with me," I whispered.

"Did he hurt you, Jesse?" She whispered back.

I shook my head. "Just what you see. I was able to hit the panic alarm. The police were there in minutes. I'm fine."

She let out a breath and gave me a weak smile. "Thank God! I'm so sorry, sweetie." Patricia backed up so Alex and Julian could check on me.

"I'm all right, guys. I probably just went into shock, and that's the reason I fainted. I'm fine. He's not, though." I gestured towards my poor boyfriend.

Danny's face was pale. He looked as hollow as he did the day I met him. I didn't want him to be so upset. Bronson was talking to him, but he was staring at me.

"Okay, folks. Miss Martin needs to give her statement, so you'll need to step out. Mr. Black, that means you, too."

Danny frowned and ground his teeth. "I'm staying. I'm not leaving her fucking side again," he said through a clenched jaw.

Patricia spoke softly to him and his face fell.

"Sir, you'll need to wait outside. We'll leave the door open," the officer said, trying to let Danny know he understood.

Danny glared at him, then walked over and kissed my forehead. "I'll be right outside, honey. I'm going to find out how soon I can take you home."

I nodded. "Thanks, baby. I'm okay."

He nodded, squeezed my hand, and walked out with Bronson, who nodded to me as if he'd take care of Danny. I mouthed "Thank you," to him.

The officer brought in a striking female detective named Sandra Rowell. She was short, stocky, and dressed in a dark blue suit. Her light brown hair was pulled back in a severe bun, almost like I would wear for work. She had a scar on one eyebrow and looked like she could beat the shit out of anyone who crossed her. She just had that vibe about her. But with me, she was warm and encouraging. I needed that right now.

"Miss Martin, I'm sorry to have to do this now, but I need to know what happened so we can move forward with the investigation."

"It's okay, really. I'm feeling okay, just a little sore."

Talking was actually irritating the hell out of my lip, but I wanted to get this over with. I explained that Stacey must have been waiting in the bushes by the front door. It was all I could think of as to how I'd missed seeing him. I told her what happened inside once he put his hands on me. She grinned at me when I explained to her how I got him off me.

"Good for you," she whispered.

I smiled weakly and then told her how the officers came in and that one of them shot him three times. She nodded, her recorder picking up everything I said.

"Is he dead?" I asked, afraid of the answer.

She nodded. "He died instantly. Suicide by cop, unfortunately. At least he won't be bothering you all anymore."

I let out a shaky breath, and then thanked her.

She asked if there was anything else I remembered.

"He certainly had it in for Danny. It all started a while back. He was over at the house one day in June. He was drunk, and he threw me in the pool. Danny was furious. He had him removed from the house. Then, not too long ago, Danny ran into him at a bar and he started talking to Danny about me and, well…"

She waved off my comment.

"I can only imagine." She chuckled and turned her recorder off. "I can guess exactly what happened after talking to Mr. Black earlier."

I shook my head, but then a thought occurred. "Detective Rowell? I promised myself that if I made it through today, you know, um, if I was okay, that I would get some self-defense training. Do you have any recommendations?"

She laughed. "I already gave Mr. Black my card. I actually give private lessons on my days off. I'd be happy to come over and work with you and his daughter. He seemed insistent that she get some training as well."

"Thank you so much. I would love that. My dad taught me a few things when I was younger, but I didn't really feel prepared for something like this."

She smiled. "It's no trouble. I know how scary it is to be a victim of something like this. I also gave him the name of a therapist we work with that is great at helping victims deal with trauma. You might experience some post-traumatic stress, and I wouldn't want this to impact your life. You're a tough cookie, for a dancer," she said and winked at me.

Danny must have told her a lot about me.

"Thank you, Detective. I'd like to start as soon as possible."

"We will. In a couple of weeks or so, when you're feeling stronger. I'll see you soon." She walked out and Danny came back in looking concerned.

"You okay? Was it okay?"

I smiled at him, as much as I could. "It was fine. I like her a lot. Thank you for talking to her about the training. I want to do it. I want to be able to protect myself, and Jane."

He motioned for me to scoot over so he could sit beside me on the bed. I sat up and he wrapped me in his arms. I just breathed him in, desperate to get Stacey's stench off me.

"I just want to go home and take a shower with you," I murmured and I felt him sigh.

"Me, too, honey. I'm so sorry I wasn't there to protect you. I can't fucking believe I let this happen to you."

I jerked him around to face me. "Danny, if I'm not going to blame myself, you can't either, okay? This is not your fault. It will only make it harder for us to move on if you blame yourself. So stop. I just need you to hold me. And get me out of this joint!"

He laughed, kissing my cheek. I must have winced because he got that disgusted look on his face. "Your poor face."

I pouted, which hurt my lip. "How bad is it?"

He shook his head. "Well, you look like you got into a fight. What do you think? But you're okay, and he didn't...hurt...you?"

I shook my head, holding him close. "No. He tried, but my head-butt put an end to that. I'm pretty sure I broke his nose. Then he bled all over me. God, I hope he wasn't sick."

"We'll make sure they test you, and him I guess. You'll be fine. You have to be. God, to think I almost lost you, Jesse! I almost fucking lost you."

We held each other and cried for a good long while until the Mannings came in.

"Hey, Jesse. Here are some clothes for you. Patricia left them with us. She's going to pick up Legs, too, and bring her to her place. We called Nora, Danny, so she won't go inside. She's going to Connie's. We thought maybe the two of you could come back to our place tonight."

Danny looked at me to see if that was okay. "That would be great, guys. Thank you."

The doctor came back in, then, and Danny asked him about the blood test.

"We took a sample from Jesse when she came in and one off her attacker. We will let you know just as soon as the results are in. For now, let me just check your vitals, Miss Martin, and if everything looks good, you can go home."

He did a quick exam and he said everything looked good. "You're going to be pretty sore. You got yanked around quite a bit. You might want to wear a neck brace."

I shook my head. "I think it's fine. When can I get these stitches out?"

"Go see your primary physician in a few days. They shouldn't need more than a week."

I thanked him and his staff for taking such good care of me. He squeezed my hand and left. Danny came over to check on me and I laughed.

"We really know how to rock the medical visits, don't we, baby?"

He smirked and said, "Let's get you the fuck out of here!"

He kicked the Mannings out, said we'd be over soon, and helped me take off the hospital gown. He teared up when he saw the bruises on my arm and on my legs. He bit down on his lip and I squeezed his arm.

"Bruise easy, remember? It looks worse than it feels," I assured him. It really did hurt as much as it looked, but I didn't want him to beat himself up any longer.

"As soon as you're up to it, you'll start training with Sandra, and I'm going to have Bob start watching the house, too."

"Bob?" I asked and he nodded.

"He's my security guy. My bodyguard. I haven't used him a whole lot in the past few years, but he's going back on the payroll. Full-time. Anytime you and Jane go out, anytime I'm not home, I want him there."

I took a deep breath. "Baby, I'm tired. Can we talk about this tomorrow? Right now I just want you to guard my body."

He snorted and helped me into a loose fitting sundress, careful not to bump my head.

The Mannings lived in a huge house off of North Beverly Drive. It was understated from the road, but once inside, it was modern decor to the max. It totally looked like a bachelor pad. Julian let us in, hugging me gingerly, and told Danny to take his old room. Danny chuckled as he led me down the hall.

"That's right! I forgot you lived here."

He laughed, setting down his wallet and keys on the dresser. "You hungry? Bronson ordered from Mulberry's."

My stomach did feel pretty empty. "That sounds great right now. I haven't eaten since... What time is it?"

"It's after midnight," he said quietly. He walked over to where I was standing next to the bed, putting his hands on my shoulders. "If you want me to sleep in a different room—"

"What? No! Why would you sleep in a different room?"

He cleared his throat. "I just, if you were uncomfortable... I would understand."

"Jesus, Danny! He didn't rape me. I told you I'm fine, and I'm fine! I'll probably be a little more jumpy than usual for a bit, but I'm okay. Okay? Now will you please come take a shower with me? I just want to wash all of this off me. I'll probably want to burn this dress."

He nodded solemnly and took my hand.

The bathroom was attached to the room and had a door leading to the hallway. He got the water ready and pulled out a towel.

"Grab two towels. You're getting in here with me. There's blood on you, too."

He looked down at himself and grimaced. I started to pull my dress off over my head and he grabbed the bottom to help me. I didn't wait for him. I grabbed the hem of his shirt and started undressing him. He watched me as if I was going to break at any minute. I was determined not to, and determined that he was going to get on with normal life, too.

We showered and dressed in some sweats Julian had brought in for us. He was thinner than Danny, so they didn't totally fall off of me, but he was taller so I had to roll them up. The sweats Danny put on fit him really snug across his ass, a fact that made it difficult to keep my hands to myself. I kept touching him and he kept dodging my hands to get away.

"I can't help it! You are definitely not allowed to wear those in public. It's hard enough keeping women from throwing themselves at you without you putting your goods on display like that."

He burst out laughing and put an arm around me as we went out to join the brothers in the kitchen.

I smelled pizza as soon as we entered and my mouth started watering. "Oh, that smells so good," I moaned, accepting a slice from Bronson, but then I frowned. I couldn't bite into it. I looked at Danny with a pout and he laughed.

"Only you could make a fat lip look adorable and sexy at the same time." He got a fork and knife from Julian and started cutting my pizza up into bite sized pieces.

"Thank you, Danny," I said and he kissed my unmarked cheek.

Julian and Bronson had heard what happened already pretty much in detail. They apologized again for Stacey's behavior.

I made them stop. "Guys, he wasn't well. I'm just sorry for his family. Does he have any?"

They looked at each other and shrugged.

Danny said, "I'm sure Jerry knows."

"We told him what happened. The guy is blaming himself, too. He didn't want to fire Stacey, but the last time he was scheduled to work, he came in five hours late and they got into a huge brawl. He had to have him removed from the premises by security. Guess we should have known he was capable of anything."

I rolled my eyes and said, "Alright! No more blaming! I'm going to say this one more time. I. Am. Fine! I'm just a little pissed I can't eat my pizza the correct way."

Mulberry's pizza was New York style and meant to be rolled in half and savored.

Danny snickered. "I promise to take you back when your widdle wip is aw bettew." I pinched his side and he jumped out of his chair and scooted over to the fridge. He grabbed a beer from the door. My expression stopped him.

"Can you, um, not? I'm sorry. I just don't want to smell that smell tonight. It's kind of turning my stomach."

He nodded, understanding. He came back to sit next to me with a ginger ale and muttered, "But you're fine, right?" I narrowed my eyes at him and he held up his hands. "Alright! Alright! I'm sorry. I'll take your word for it."

Julian and Bronson watched the two of us like observers at a tennis match and then made disgusted sounds.

"Dude," Bronson said, "She's going to kick your ass."

Danny looked me up and down and said quietly, "I hope so. At least I'm going to make sure she can."

We finished our pizza and talked for another hour or so until I started yawning. Danny excused us and Julian followed us to bring us toothbrushes and toothpaste.

"You guys are welcome to stay as long as you need, ok? Jane too." We thanked him, I kissed his cheek good night, and we crawled into bed, too exhausted to do anything but hold each other.

Chapter - Four

Danny was up before me the next morning and I was glad for it. I was so damn sore, it took all of my energy to get to the bathroom and use the toilet. Everything hurt. I'd heard that adrenaline could leave all of your muscles sore, but I guess I'd also underestimated just how much Stacey had yanked me around. My lip was really sore, making brushing my teeth quite painful, and the bruising on my face looked freakin' fantastic! I had six stitches just about an inch below my hairline, and my whole forehead was bruised. I had two black eyes and my right cheekbone was bruised. My lip was less swollen, but the split inside was sore. I was so glad I hadn't had to have stitches there.

I couldn't stand looking at this mess anymore, so I went out to see if I could find Danny. I heard him before I saw him, sitting out on the back patio.

"I know, Jack, and I'm sorry...I didn't call last night because it was so late...I know. I'm sorry you had to hear about it on the news... Yeah, she says she's okay, but I don't know...You and me both. He's lucky he's dead or I would have made it much more painful...Yeah, I'm going to have Bob, my security guy, at the house when I'm not home and whenever she goes out. Maybe even drive her to work, too, if she doesn't fight me on it...I know, I'm so sorry. Please tell Lydia I'm sorry. I'll have her call when she wakes up...Thank you...Alright... Talk to you soon."

"I'm so sorry you had to take that phone call."

Danny spun around and stepped quickly over to me. I could tell he was relieved to see me, but it also caused him a lot of pain.

"It was on the news late last night and this morning. I already talked to Ivana and she's going to keep Jane out of the loop and at her house at least until tomorrow. Nora is a wreck and worried about you. She's just waiting for the police to clear the scene so she can get the cleaners inside the house. Patricia is going to bring us clothes later this afternoon if the police say she can go in. She knows to grab your medication. And Gloria called Patricia. She said for you to call her when you felt up to it. She was really worried about you." He looked closely at my face and then winced and shook his head.

"You're going to give me a complex if you keep doing that. Just pretend it's Jane's makeup job, please? I know I look terrible."

He shook his head, his hands coming up to cradle my face. "No. You look beautiful. It just looks like it hurts."

"It sure hurt to see it in the mirror. Jesus!"

He laughed and walked me into the kitchen to feed me. "Cosmo called. He was so fucking pissed at me, he said he was going to beat my ass when he sees me, and made me promise to have you call or else he's coming over."

I tried to stifle a laugh. "I'll get you off the hook with my other men. Just let me finish my juice."

Danny came around behind me and wrapped his arms around me, kissing the back of my head. "I hope you don't mind that I'm going to be all over you today. I just can't get it out of my head, Jesse. I could have lost you." His voice cracked.

I turned around on my bar stool and wrapped my arms around his waist, resting my head on his chest. "I'm sorry I scared you, Danny. There were a few minutes where I thought you might lose me, too. Thank God you have that panel right by the door. That saved my life. He got my phone away from me and the door was shut. There was nothing I could do except try to stall him until the police got there. The funny thing was, the officer that shot him was that guy I was telling you about, you know? The cop who kept hassling me? He recognized me right away and was super nice to me." Danny searched my eyes for signs

I wasn't being totally open with him. I cringed. "I'm sorry there was such a mess. I hope the cleaners can—"

"Don't even fucking worry about it. I hate that fucking room anyway. I think we should just get rid of all that shit, redo it. What do you think?" I laughed nervously and he cocked his head to the side. "What?"

"The first time I came over I thought it was a terrible room. So uninviting. The more I got to know you I hated it even more. It's not you. A lot of that house isn't you."

"I guess you're right. You're going to have to help me make it about us, honey. It's our place now."

I shook my head and sighed. "Danny? Can we talk about something?"

He pulled back and frowned. "Sure, babe. What is it?" He came around and sat on the stool next to me.

I took a deep breath for courage. Maybe with my face looking like this he wouldn't totally get mad at me. "We've talked a lot about getting married lately, and I'm really happy about that. But something has bothered me about being married to you and I wanted to talk to you about it."

He frowned and took my hands in his. "What is it, Jesse?"

Another deep breath for courage and I dove right in. "The first time you said to me 'what's mine is yours,' I kind of laughed it off. It bothered me. I don't think about it that way. Then when we started talking about marriage, and then I thought about it some more. Danny, if we get married, I think I should sign a prenuptial agreement. Your money is your money and I don't want anyone to think, especially you, that any of that is important to me."

Danny fought the urge to laugh, I could tell. I raised an eyebrow at him, trying to resurrect the teacher look. I managed to look ridiculous.

"I'm sorry, I'm really not laughing at you. But there's no fucking way we're having a prenup. You've made it more than clear to me and everyone else that you don't want anything to do with my money, so I don't think we even need to worry about it. Now is there anything else you've been 'thinking about' that you want to get off your lovely chest?"

I rolled my eyes. "Danny! I'm serious!"

"I am too! Don't worry, I'm not going to shove it down your throat, but I'm going to make sure you have an expense account for when you take Jane places, for gas, shit like that. Don't think I don't know you've been spending your own money on my daughter. That's going to stop, Jesse."

I blew out a breath, completely not happy with how this conversation was going. "Danny..."

He shook his head. "Mr. Bossypants is going to win this one. I don't care how fucking cute you look with that pouty lip. I've already failed in taking care of you. I'm not going to do it again. And I'm hoping you'll let Bob take you to and from work. He's going to be at the house—"

"No way, Danny! I do not need to be driven to work. If you want to have him drive Jane around, I understand, but I am perfectly capable of taking..."

I stopped. Obviously, in Danny's world, I wasn't perfectly capable of taking care of myself. I jumped up off the stool, needing to move. Danny watched me, cautiously. I shook out my hands and paced around the kitchen.

"Jesse, we don't have to talk about this now," Danny said softly.

I turned on him and tried to control my anger, but I wasn't very successful. "*We* are not really talking about anything! I'm talking at you and you're saying 'No, Jesse. No, Jesse.' How is that us talking about this?"

He took a deep breath and started pulling at his goatee. "I'm sorry, honey. I'm just trying to do right by you. I fucking love you, Jesse! I've told you over and over that I just want to take care of you like you take care of me. Please?"

The goddamned 'gimme look' was back. I figured I might as well just give up. I sunk down on a chair and put my head in my hands, wincing when I came into contact with my bruised-to-shit forehead.

"I shouldn't have even brought this up right now," I said, wishing I could have a do-over. Telling Danny I didn't want to be taken care of when I looked like a mugging victim probably wasn't the best idea.

Danny came around and knelt on the floor in front of me. "Jesse, you've been through hell. Why don't you just rest today? I promise you can yell at me all you want when you are feeling better. Okay?"

I groaned. "I don't want to yell at you, Danny. I just wish we were on more equal ground."

He said in his most serious voice, "If you come down here on the floor, we'll be on equal ground."

I couldn't resist playful Danny. I smiled and let him pull me onto the floor. There was a bright patch of sunlight right where he laid us down on the thick carpet and wrapped me in his arms. It felt really good. I let myself just relax into his embrace.

We spent the rest of the day being lazy at the Mannings'. I called my parents and Cosmo and assured them I was fine. Dad was proud of me for the headbutt, as I knew he would be, and he was very pleased to hear that I was going to be taking self-defense. Cosmo wanted to see me in the flesh to know I was okay, so Danny invited him and the guys over for dinner. I asked if the Mannings would be upset and he snorted.

"As often as they invite themselves over to my house?"

Patricia came late in the afternoon and brought me some comfy clothes and two of my new dresses, along with my undergarments and medicine. She said the police cleared the scene and Nora already had cleaners getting to work. Danny called Nora and told her to have them 'clear the damn room, rip up the fucking ugly carpet, and haul that shit away.'

"When Jesse is feeling better, we're going to redecorate that room. I'm thinking a home gym sounds great, complete with mats, punching bags, weights..."

I could hear her laughing on the other end of the phone. She wanted to talk to me so Danny handed me the phone.

"You alright, sugar? I'm so sorry," she said.

I set her straight immediately. "No more 'I'm sorrys' Nora. I'm really okay, I promise. I look horrible, but I'm hoping that it will be gone in a few days. Probably not by the time I'll see Jane, though. I'm afraid she's going to be really upset."

She assured me that she'd talk to her about it and for me to just rest. "Danny said you guys would be home for dinner tomorrow, so I'll make your favorite fried chicken."

I thanked her enthusiastically and we hung up.

Bronson had bar-b-que delivered and Cosmo and the gang arrived at the same time as the delivery guy. We were really lucky any of the food made it into the house. Cosmo was pissed when he saw me. He turned to Danny and I saw him clenching his fist. I got between them with my hands on my hips, ready to put an end to this.

"Cosmo! It's not his fault! This guy was nuts, all right? If Danny would have been there, we'd likely be planning his funeral right now."

That got the room quiet. Cosmo's face fell and he held out a hand to Danny, who shook it, his face with the disgusted expression again. Cosmo hugged me tight. I had to tap out as much from the smell as from pain. Cosmo only showered on Sundays, it was his thing, and today was Friday. He was such a handsome guy. It was really a shame. I wondered if he was still seeing Maria and what she thought about his hygiene routine.

We ate and the guys all sat around talking music. I lay on a couch with my head in Danny's lap. He ran his fingers through my hair gently. At one point his fingers got caught in a snarl and pulled. I tensed up, which hurt my neck. I had to squeeze my eyes shut to get past the moment. Danny could tell I was in distress. I tried to play it off, but it was icky. I excused myself and went to the restroom, where I promptly threw up my dinner. When I came back out, Danny looked really worried and told everyone he was putting me to bed. I said my goodnights, actually glad to be off the hook for entertaining guests, and Danny crawled in with me.

"Aren't you going to go visit?" I asked.

"Nope. My place is with you. Those fuckers can entertain themselves."

I chuckled and settled into Danny's side. "Thank you for taking care of me today," I murmured. He kissed an open spot on my forehead. It had taken some maneuvering and practice earlier, but he'd found places he could kiss me where it didn't hurt. He started to kiss them once more. I felt myself melt against him.

"I don't want to hurt you, honey. Maybe we should..."

I unfastened his pants and he groaned, his body going tense.

"No, we shouldn't wait, if that's what you were going to say. I need this," I said, my voice shaking a little. "I need you to make me feel good so I can forget the way he touched me." I felt Danny suck in a breath and then his arms came around me tight.

"Whatever you need, honey, you'll have. I'll give you whatever you want. Just please don't ever leave me. I don't ever want to lose you," he cried against my neck. He gently took my clothes off and kissed all of my boo boos. I made sure to point out the ones he may have missed.

When we were both naked and ready to go, I froze.

"Let me be on top, Danny. Just this time."

He sat back and let me switch places with him. "If you want to stop—"

I put my hand over his mouth and sank down, joining us in the closest way possible. We both cried out and I had to stay still for a moment. He was so gentle with me. It was the most tender lovemaking I'd ever experienced with him. When my energy started to flag, he pushed me over onto my side and entered me from behind. It was perfect. I didn't feel trapped, and Danny's whispers in my ear kept me grounded. I tried to fully relax, but I couldn't. Not this time. After a bit, Danny noticed I was getting frustrated, so he rolled me onto my back and lay next to me.

"Honey, I know it might take time for you..."

I slammed my fist down on the bed and cursed...then the sobs came. Danny held me through it all. My determination to be over it and move on wasn't enough to convince my body. I was going to need time.

I woke up sometime in the middle of the night feeling restless. I gently extricated myself from Danny's grip and used the restroom without turning on the light. I heard music coming from the room past the kitchen while I was getting myself some water, so I peeked through the door.

Bronson was playing an acoustic guitar quietly and staring out the window. He noticed me hovering and stopped, offering a smile. "Can't sleep?"

I shrugged. "Just antsy. What's your excuse?"

"The same. I'm like Danny. I don't sleep much." He gestured for me to sit across from him.

"I can't sleep. I can't sit still. I'm tired, but I don't want to go back to bed right now."

Bronson strummed a few more chords, and then spoke without looking up. "Shortly after Julian and I met Danny, I dated a girl who was a bartender at the Roxy. She was drop dead gorgeous and would never go out with anyone. When I say I dated her, she went out to dinner with me once, and I went back to her apartment after. She was a spitfire, you know? Full of spirit. I totally thought sex with her was going to be phenomenal and I was so ready to get it on. When I was ready to make my move, she freaked out. She started screaming and beating the shit out of me. I just held onto her and tried to get her to calm down."

He cleared his throat and played a few more bars before he spoke again. "When she looked up at me, she was absolutely terrified. I thought I had done something, but she was finally able to get a hold of herself and tell me that it wasn't me. Some jackass had attacked her in the parking lot after work one night and raped her. I never would have known. I never guessed. Anyway, we spent the rest of the night talking about it. She said she'd never told anyone and hadn't been with anyone since. She hadn't even called the fucking police, which pissed me off. It had been about six months and she thought she was over it."

I took a deep breath and asked, "Did she ever move on? I mean, did she get better?"

He laughed. "Yeah, she did. Unfortunately, not with me. She ended up falling for the owner of the bar, who was like twenty something years older than her, and they got married. She's had babies, the whole thing. I see her around every once in a while and I know she's happy now." He stopped and finally looked at me. "I don't know why I'm telling you this other than I know you're strong and you're going to get over it. But it's not going to just go away. So don't beat yourself up, you know? Try to just allow yourself to feel what you're feeling?"

I smiled at him and laughed. "Who'd have thought you'd be the one giving me sage advice?" He blushed a little and looked down at his guitar. "I'm serious, Bronson. Of all of you, I feel like I've probably talked to you the least. I'm seeing a whole other side of you tonight."

He smiled, strumming softly. "I know. Danny and I don't have the best track records when it comes to each other's ladies. You know what I mean? So I stayed away a little, probably. I respect the hell out of you, Jesse, and I love Danny like a brother. I'm just really sorry that this happened at all."

"Thank you, Bronson. But I mean it when I said it's done. Although…"

I paused. Thoughts of Stacey's shooting had been what woke me up. I wanted to talk about it, but I didn't want to tell Danny. "I don't know how to handle knowing he's dead, you know? That was my first time seeing a dead person, especially someone that I kind of knew? It was weird. Very unsettling."

He looked up at me and his blue eyes were darker than usual. "The way I look at it? It's better all around. He's not suffering anymore. You and Danny don't have to deal with a trial or anything. It's over. There's closure."

I nodded, relieved I had said something. "I am happy there will be no trial. I'd hate to have Jane go through all that. This is going to be bad enough. I'm so afraid for her to see me like this."

He nodded. "That's why I thought it would be good for you guys to stay here. Although, no offense, but it's going to take longer than a few days for those bruises to fade."

I rolled my eyes. "I know. I look terrible! How the hell am I going to go to work on Monday? My students are going to freak out and I really don't want to tell them everything."

"Do you have sick leave? Can you be out? I'm sure your boss will understand."

"I'll call her tomorrow. I don't want to think about anything else tonight." I pulled my knees up to my chest and exhaled loudly.

Bronson laughed. "I think we need to do something to take your mind off things."

I raised an eyebrow at him and he held out his hands. "I don't mean anything that will get us in trouble. Well, not you anyway." He set his guitar aside and stood up, stretching his back. He was in a t-shirt and sweats. I pressed my lips together to keep from laughing. He so didn't look the rock star when he was rockin' the sweat pants. He looked like a second string basketball player. Ok, maybe with long hair not quite a basketball player. Maybe a coffee house poet guy.

Bronson walked over to the far wall, which was covered with shelves holding pictures, knickknacks and books. Looking around the room, I noticed some tour posters, a couple of platinum album plaques, and pictures of his family. Holy shit! He even had his Grammy on the shelf! There were five or six guitars on stands in the corner and two couches in the middle of the room, facing each other.

"Aha! Just the one I was looking for." He pulled a large photo album off the shelf and brought it over to me. "Damning evidence from Blackened's early days. He'll be pissed at me for showing you this. I'm not even sure he knows I have it. I'm a total geek when it comes to saving pictures and memorabilia." He sat down at the far end of the couch, giving me space, and probably trying to be appropriate in case we were discovered.

I took the album from him, excited at what I might see. When I opened it I had to clap a hand over my mouth. It was a scrapbook, in essence, of Blackened's beginnings. The cover page had a publicity photo of the band, probably from when they first started in 1997 or '98. They were all posed together in leather and denim. Bronson and

Julian still looked the same. They were even dressed similar to how they dressed now, in black jeans, thick, studded belts with large buckles, cowboy boots, sleeveless shirts. Alex had longer hair and had no shirt on in the picture and was holding his drumsticks in one hand. Other than looking younger, they looked how I'd expect.

I could not, however, get over Danny! He wasn't kidding when he told me his hair was down to his ass. His red hair had waves and curls and so much blonde in it, it almost looked highlighted if I didn't know better. He was wearing black leather pants and a leather vest. No shirt. He was much thinner. His arms were really cut and tattoo-free. He looked dangerous in a way, but he also looked like such a baby. He had a long goatee and heavy silver rings on all of his fingers. My snickers increased as I turned the pages. There were shots of the guys recording in the studio with Ron, who looked much younger and thinner, not to mention he actually had hair back then as opposed to the dome look he sported now. But the shots on the tour buses and backstage really made me laugh. There was so much alcohol and so many girls all over them. It was comical.

"So now I have actual proof of the debauchery! You better hide these when Jane comes over. I'm not sure Danny's ready for her to see this stuff yet." There were pictures of Danny taking body shots off a scantily clad woman, the guys at a strip club posing with dancers, and Danny passed out in a bar somewhere with panties on his head.

Bronson chuckled. "Yeah, some would say 'those were the days.' We did have fun, but when we got serious about our music, we didn't have time for that insanity anymore."

I noticed as I got further into the album, about two years later by the dates on the pictures and other items stuck in there, there were no more half-naked women. I saw other changes as well. Danny with a couple of tattoos, Brooke on his arm at an award show, and a very pregnant Brooke posing with Danny and Alex, who both had their hands on her belly. The caption of that one said, "Countdown to 'Who is the Father?'" It was kind of not funny knowing the truth about Brooke.

"I think I like the earlier pics better," I grumbled and Bronson laughed.

"Yeah, me too. Brooke really put a damper on things. Poor Danny. He really tried to make her happy. The bitch." His angry tone surprised me.

"I've heard you and she were not huge fans of each other. Care to tell me why?"

He scoffed. "Let's just say that she tried to get between us. Before they were exclusive, she showed up at my house a couple of times. I wasn't really that interested in her, wasn't interested in Danny's leftovers, and she didn't like being told no. She turned around and told Danny I'd been stalking her, basically, which led to him and me getting into a huge brawl. It was almost the end of the band. He totally kicked my ass. But I think she realized her meal ticket was going to be gone if we didn't continue as a band. By then her career was stagnating. She's three years older than Danny, did you know that?"

I shook my head, a little shocked.

"She kind of lies about it. Not many people know. We were a huge success from the start. As soon as our album came out and went platinum, and the tours and shit... Danny came into a lot of money fast and she was close to broke. She did a few more decent films in the meantime, don't get me wrong. But if it wasn't for him, she'd have been a nonentity."

Another piece fell into place. I wondered about something. "Bronson? Danny said he thinks she's using. Is that something that was an issue before?"

He frowned. "I don't know. We were gone a lot and Danny didn't always share what was going on with us when we were off the road. It wouldn't surprise me. Nothing about her would surprise me."

I tried not to fuss at my lip with my tongue. My forehead was itchy from the stitches and my eyes were getting heavy. And all this talk about Brooke had me a little unsettled. I was nearing the point of finding out more than I really wanted to know, even though my curiosity wouldn't let me shut up.

"Jesse, can I say something?"

I frowned at him. "Of course you can."

He pulled his hair back and re-wrapped a hair tie around it. "I just hope you don't let Brooke get between you two. I know they've been divorced for a long time, but she still has a hold over him sometimes. About Jane. I just see how happy the three of you are together, and I know she's gone off to New York, or whatever, and is supposed to be getting married. Just don't turn your back on her, you know? She's manipulative."

I really appreciated him for saying that. It was nice to know that my hunches about her were correct. "I can see that. You're right, thank you. He and I have been through a lot and I don't intend to let anything else get between us."

He smiled slyly. "That's my girl. Now why don't you go back to bed? I can see you trying not to yawn over there."

I laughed. "I think you're right. Thanks, Bronson. For everything." He nodded and I stood. "Can I borrow some of these pictures sometime? I owe him a really good payback in the near future. I'm hoping he's forgotten and I really want to make it a good one."

He barked out a laugh and stretched his back. "Absolutely. There's plenty more where that stuff came from, too. Anything to make that dickhead squirm."

I said goodnight again and crept quietly down the hall. When I entered the room we were staying in, Danny was frowning in his sleep. I tried to slide in without waking him, but he grabbed for me, pulling me close.

"Jesse," he muttered.

I kissed him and he opened an eye.

"Oh good. I was dreaming you weren't here."

I snuggled closer and sighed. "I was up for a little while. I'm sorry I disturbed you. Go back to sleep."

He mumbled some more about loving me and keeping me safe. Poor guy. I knew he would do everything in his power to make that happen. I just hoped I didn't have to strangle Mr. Bossypants in the meantime!

Chapter - Five

Saturday morning Bronson suggested we all stay with them until the work on the house was done. Nora came over and cooked us all breakfast, and then the three of us sat down and talked over plans. Nora and I overruled Danny's plan to turn the whole living room into a home gym.

"Seriously, Danny. It's a huge room. What if you moved your office into the library and turn your office into an exercise room if you're so concerned? It's big enough."

He shrugged. "What do you think, Nora?"

She laughed. "Sounds a hell of a lot better than you turning that huge room into a sweaty, gross mess! I'm with Jesse on that one, and I think it would be good for her to have some room to work in the library, too."

Danny smiled at me, kissing me on my unaffected cheek.

Nora had cringed and gotten teary when she saw me. I assured her I was fine, a word Danny rolled his eyes at every time I said it.

"I know you'll be fine, sugar, but I hate what he did to you." She held me for a long time before Danny started whining that he and the boys were hungry. She grumbled at him, cussing under her breath. I knew he'd done it to save me from further inquisition when he winked at me behind her back. I so loved this man and was grateful for him.

Thankfully Nora had brought over the rest of my new clothes and a few more pairs of yoga pants. She brought Danny jeans and t-shirts, his usual wardrobe, and extra boxers because she knew I liked to steal them. This woman had to have been sent from heaven.

"Hey Danny? What about that collection of horror memorabilia you have in storage? That would be so cool if you turned your living room into a room like in the Munsters house or something." Julian was really excited and I could see a twinkle in Danny's eye.

He ran his hands through his hair and said, "I don't know, this is our house, now, and I don't know what Jane—"

"Jane will think it's cool, dude. You know that. She can scare the shit out of her friends. It'll be great! Remember when we took her to the Hollywood History Museum for that Halloween gig? She loved that." Julian obviously was partial to this idea.

Danny looked at me like he was afraid to ask what I thought. "Jesse?"

I laughed. "Sounds cool to me! Frankenstein is one of my favorite novels and one of the best films ever made."

Danny's eyes rolled back. "God, you are so the perfect woman for me." He leaned over and kissed me until Nora started to clear her throat.

Danny blushed. "I'm sorry. Nora, what do you think?"

She raised an eyebrow and squinted at Danny. "As long as none of that crap migrates into my kitchen I'll live with it. I don't have to go in there."

I laughed and Danny jumped up to kiss her. "Thank you, ladies. I've kind of missed my stuff. I had it in a rehearsal space we rented for a long time, but some of the other spaces got broken into and I didn't want to lose any of it. Maybe I'll call Nikki. He decorated Funny Farm like that. I know he did a lot of it himself, but I bet he knows people."

I gulped at his mention of Nikki's name.

"Maybe he'll even come over, Jesse. Will you be able to control yourself?" Such a joker. It was definitely payback time.

I narrowed my eyes at him and jumped up to chase him. He easily evaded me until he made the mistake of hiding behind Bronson. I hit the icemaker on the fridge on my way to him. Bronson moved aside, and I shoved the ice forcefully down the front of Danny's pants before he could get away.

"Ahhh FUCK! That's cold, honey! C'mon! You don't want shrinkage, do you?"

We all cracked up as he danced around, trying to keep the ice out of contact with his 'boys.'

"I guess you better not mess with her," Bronson said, giving me a wink.

I giggled conspiratorially.

Danny looked between us and frowned. "What the fuck does that mean?"

I rolled my eyes. "Nothing. I told him I owed you payback from the moustache episode."

Danny's eyes got wide. "Shit! I forgot about that." He sat back down at the table, cautiously, and looked at me with a frightened expression.

Nora rapped her knuckles on the table. "Now, back to what we were discussing. We'll need to have them empty the office, make space in the library, and basically you want them to rip up the entire living room, is that correct?"

Danny pulled on his goatee and started drawing on a piece of paper. "Yeah, and if we set up the library like this, Jesse and I can both have office space in there. And—"

"But Danny," I interrupted. "You need your privacy. I don't need to have any office space. I can just keep my things in a bin or a box or something...Why are you laughing?"

"Jesse, you're not going to live like a fucking hobo with your office stuff in a box. This is your house now, too."

Everyone got quiet. They all looked to me for my reaction. I was speechless.

I exhaled and said quietly, "Danny? Can I talk to you for a minute?"

He seemed to get that I was serious. He looked around at the others and Nora said, "We'll just give you guys a minute." She led the brothers out of the kitchen and I put my head down on my arms on the table.

"I'm sorry. I didn't mean…"

I held up a hand and he was quiet. We sat there like that for a long time. I finally lifted my head and reached for his hand on the table. I picked it up in mine and turned it over looking at his skin, his tattoos, his calluses, his scars. These hands had held me when I needed him, had made me feel tremendous passion, and were capable of making the most beautiful music. I was safe in these hands. I knew that. Why couldn't I just relax and let him take care of me? Because it was his hands that had worked so hard to earn all of what he had, not mine.

"I'm having a hard time," I started, and then I paused. I didn't know how to say what I needed to say. "I don't understand how you can just…Why, Danny? How can you just rearrange everything? Why would you just move me in and—"

"Because I love you. I want you to be my partner, Jesse. In everything. I don't need privacy from you. I need it with you, not from you," he said in a softer voice.

I cracked a bit of a smile and blew out a breath. "I just don't understand how it can be so easy for you to just do this. To take me in, move me in alongside you."

He shrugged and smiled. "Remember the first time I fucked up so badly with you? When we were sitting in the library and I freaked out about Jane?" I nodded, hating to remember that day. "The same could be asked of you. Why did you come back? Why did you stick with me all of those times I was such a jackass?"

"That was easy, Danny. Because I love you. Because even though you were being stubborn, I had to out-stubborn you."

He took both of my hands in his and rubbed his thumbs across my knuckles. "This is me out-stubborning you. Please? Don't say no?"

"Do I have a choice?" I laughed and stood so I could sit on his lap. "I hate being out-stubborned," I said, curling into his body with an exaggerated pouty face.

He sighed happily. "I'm so glad you've admitted it." I tickled him and he wiggled to get away. We toppled off the chair and I landed on top of him, tickling until he was howling. He wasn't trying to fight me off too hard. He let me have the upper hand easily.

When he was breathless, he finally called, "Mercy! Mercy, honey! God, I'm going to puke."

I pinned his arms out to the side and leaned down, nose-to-nose with him. "Promise you'll never call me a hobo again?"

He nodded. "Yes, just please, no more!"

I figured I'd take advantage of this opportunity. "Promise no more blaming?"

His smile was gone and he nodded, a determined look on his face. "I promise."

I brought my hands to his face and searched his eyes. "Promise you'll be patient with me? Never let me go?"

He smiled, his eyes full of love. "I'll never fucking let you go. Come here."

He kissed me deeply, being careful with my lip, which was much better today. I stretched out on top of him, enjoying his touch. We rolled over and he continued to caress me and kiss my neck. His hands roamed gently, careful of my sore parts. I craved his touch so much. I was desperate for him. He ran his fingers up my leg, sliding my skirt up as he did. I groaned as he found my core, found me wanting him. He touched me so slowly, so reverently, it took mere moments for him to bring me to my peak.

"Danny! Oh, baby, I love you," I sighed, my whole body a pool of desire for him. I couldn't believe I'd been able to reach orgasm just like that. Danny sure seemed to believe it.

He kissed me gently and whispered. "I guess it just took a sneak attack for you to relax. I'll have to remember this move for those nights when you are stressed." He kissed my neck and jaw until I was a quivering mess.

"There! Now, will you accept the alterations to the house that include taking care of your needs?"

"So not fair. But yes."

He smiled that devastating smile. "I fucking love you, honey."

"I fucking love you, too, you manipulative orgasm-giver!"

He barked out a laugh as he stood up, helping me to my feet, and we went back to our seats. He started drawing plans on some scratch paper, asking me questions as he went. The others slowly filtered back into the room.

"So it's settled," Nora asked.

Danny grinned triumphantly. "Yes, ma'am! I'm going to call Nikki and then I'll let you get to work making arrangements. Thanks, Nora." He kissed her on the cheek and she rolled her eyes.

"Yeah, yeah. I'm just glad we're getting rid of that ugly ass furniture in there. I mean really, who here liked all that metal and sticky leather?" I swear I heard crickets chirping.

"I guess that's your answer, Nora."

We all laughed. Danny pulled out his phone to call Nikki and I used this opportunity to call Gloria. Nora left to go pick up some clothes for Jane and bring her back here.

Gloria told me to absolutely take the week. "The kids will likely have heard about it and may ask you questions, but a week from now it'll be a little easier. I just want you well, sweetie. It'll all be here when you're ready."

I thanked her and told her I'd email lesson plans and request a sub. Before I hung up, she asked, "So what did Danny say about his test results? You both must be so excited!"

My eyes shot to Danny, who was still deep in discussion on his phone. "I haven't even told him," I whispered. "With everything that happened...I can't believe I forgot." I'd have to rectify that. I needed a plan. How could I break the news to him and make it special considering my damn face right now?

After hanging up with job number one, it was time to call job number two. The dance studio understood as well. My new classes had been going really well, especially with Jane there. She was having a blast learning a new form of dance. She thought it was way more fun than ballet. Danny made a point of picking her up so he could watch for a while.

The guys were getting close to wrapping up the first part of recording. Julian told me all the tracks were done and now it was time for mixing. This was apparently an arduous process, a time when tempers were often set off over which was the best take or mix. I still hadn't been over there. I thought since I was going to be off this week, perhaps I could finagle an invitation.

Danny came walking back in with a peculiar look on his face. "I just talked to Nikki," he said with a strange smile.

I frowned. "And what did he say?"

He laughed and sat down next to me, taking my hands in his. "He gave me the number of the decorator he worked with. He also said he'll shoot the album cover for us."

"That's great! I know you really wanted that." But Danny was looking at me funny and stroking his goatee. "What else?" I started to get nervous.

"Well, he actually asked if you and I would pose for him for one of his other projects." He raised his eyebrows and I really got concerned.

"You and I? What kind of project?"

He laughed and tugged at his goatee. "Um, how do you feel about posing nude, for him, with me?"

My face must have said it all because he squeezed my hands and laughed loudly. "I say nude, but we'll be sort of covered, or so he told me. Our private parts will be covered. What do you think?"

I was thinking all kinds of things, but none of them would form into a coherent response. "You and I, naked, in front of Nikki Sixx?" He nodded, looking hopeful. "I don't know what to say. What do you think?"

He shrugged. "I told him no fucking way was I putting your body on display for anyone. He promised we'd be covered. Frankly, I didn't really want my junk out there either, but that's not my main concern. He actually mentioned it the night we saw him at the Roxy, that he wanted to photograph me. But then he got a good look at you. He said he's been thinking of us since that night for this project."

My face felt hot. This was way too much to have to think about, especially right now. "Are these going to be public? I'd need to talk to my parents. And my job! Teachers get fired for this kind of thing. When does he need to know? I don't know, Danny."

He laughed and leaned over to kiss me. "I told him we'd need some time. I told him what happened, and he said he's so glad you're okay. He offered his bodyguard, his house, whatever we needed." There were so many people offering to help us, it made me feel cared about for sure.

"Let me talk to my folks and to Gloria. But what do you think?"

He shook his head. "I don't know. I told him he was crazy when he asked me. You, I totally get. You're more gorgeous than any model I've ever seen. But he said this project is kind of a fallen angel kind of thing and that I have the right look."

I giggled, covering my mouth with my hand. "He's kind of right about you. I can see that."

He laughed and then he winced. "He said I'd need to get a body wax. Can you believe that shit?"

Now I was cracking up. "Oh no! Not your gorgeous hair! I love running my fingers through your hair."

He growled a little. "Yeah, well, he said it would 'get in the way,' whatever the fuck that means."

I couldn't help but laugh. His expression was a frustrated, dig-my-heels-in kind of stubborn, and he seemed a little embarrassed.

"It'll grow back, baby."

He raised an eyebrow at me. "You like me furry?"

I laughed and ran my hand under his shirt, raking my nails through his chest hair. His eyes rolled back and he moaned. "Ah, shit, Jesse. That feels so fucking good."

I whispered to him just where else I'd like to run my fingers. He shivered, grabbed me up, slung me over his shoulder, and carried me to our borrowed room.

We emerged several hours later after making love, and napping, which was a first. Danny never napped. Then more lovemaking, showering, getting dressed, removing clothes, more lovemaking, and getting dressed again.

We were sitting in Julian's office in front of a ginormous monitor, looking at furniture and ideas for the new room, when Jane and Nora returned. She came into the room, looking nervous, and gasped when she saw me. She didn't run to me like she usually would. She actually clung to Nora's side a little.

"Hey, sweetie! I've missed you," I said and held my arms out for a hug. I glanced at Danny and saw him frown when she hesitated, but I wasn't surprised. She came over and hugged me tentatively. She squeaked when I pulled her onto my lap.

"Are you okay, Jesse?"

"I'm okay. I was a little sore, and I know my face looks terrible, but everything is okay."

She didn't seem to believe me. She hugged me again, hiding her face in my hair. I held her and stroked her back. Danny reached over and rubbed her back, too.

"I know it's upsetting to look at her face. It's killing me," Danny said seriously. I snorted and Jane popped up, frowning at me. Then she realized what he'd said and she giggled, too. It took Danny longer to get it. When he did, he shook his head.

"I can't even get you back right now! This is so not fair!"

Jane laughed, but then looked back at me with worry.

"I'm really fine. He didn't hurt me," I said to her, hoping she understood what I was trying to tell her. "I want you to do me a favor, though." She gave me her full attention.

"I want us both to take self-defense training. The detective I met at the hospital said she'd come to the house and teach us. Would you do that with me?"

She nodded vigorously. "Yes! Of course I will. I'm so sorry this happened to you, Jesse."

I thanked her, kissing her forehead. "Thanks, Jane. I promise I'm okay. Now, the next item of discussion is that your dad has decided to make some changes at the house," I said, gesturing to the computer.

Danny took over explaining what we were thinking of doing in the living room and her eyes totally lit up.

"It's gonna be so cool! I can't wait! Will it be done by Halloween? Can we have a big Halloween party?"

Danny and I looked at each other and shrugged.

"I don't see why not," Danny said and the two of them started planning the party. I sat back, feeling a little tired. My heart swelled with love for these two crazy redheads.

After they plotted for a bit, we got Jane settled into the room across the hall from us. She looked around at the modern furniture and it made me think of watching her check out the hotel room when we went to Los Gatos. Man, that felt like so long ago, but in reality it was less than two months. So much had happened! Of course, I could say that about the entire time I was with Danny.

Nora stayed to cook us dinner and then Connie was coming to stay with her. Nora, it seemed, was a little freaked about what happened and Connie didn't want her to be alone. Danny called the decorator and scheduled a meeting with her on Wednesday. We were going to go over to the house together then for the first time. Nora already had people coming to clear the room and put everything he was keeping in the garage. Some specialists were going to move the piano into the great room off the kitchen for the time being. I couldn't believe this was all happening.

So we camped out at the Mannings'. It was a little weird, but they really missed having Danny over and they made every effort to make Jane and I feel at home. We all missed Legs, though. Their backyard was a series of decks and not safe for our growing pup. Legs would stay with Patricia and Max until we could get home.

After dinner the guys had a jam session and played some of the new songs they'd just recorded. The Mannings had turned part of their home into studio and rehearsal space. It was cramped and loud, but they provided us girls with earplugs. Jane and I curled up together on a loveseat and Nora sat on the arm.

Their music was absolutely brilliant! When Danny sang the new lyrics, I felt my stomach tighten. Somehow he'd managed to spill our ups and downs into the most beautiful words. He sang of love at first sight, of the excitement of getting to know someone, loving one who's forbidden, the fear of losing the one you love, and even the thrill of a new lover. All of the songs were powerful and were a huge departure from what they usually sang about.

They played for about an hour and a half. Jane and I were enthralled the whole time. When they took a break, we took out our earplugs and she looked up at me, her blue eyes huge.

"I never knew they sounded so awesome! My dad is...Wow."

I giggled with her. "I know."

The guys sat in a circle facing each other. Danny's back was to me. They were talking in musician speak about the songs and which ones they might want to play live and which one should be their first single. Bronson tossed his hair back and took a long swig on his water bottle before addressing the group.

"I think Tuesday we should have Patricia and someone from the label come down and hear what we have so far. She wants to meet with us to schedule the first round of appearances and interviews."

Danny nodded and said, "Definitely. I think we're ready. And Nikki's ready to do the album cover as soon as we are. He also said he'd do some publicity shots for us if we want. Julian, are you going to update the website?"

"Already working on it. I've got some ideas for teasers. I was almost thinking we could drop hints or passwords in interviews that would unlock material on the website like photos, clips of the new songs, etc. What do you guys think?"

Danny stroked his goatee, deep in thought. "Maybe we could also do some scavenger hunts for clues to where we might make appearances? That could be fun. Some random places, like The White Stripes did in Canada on their last tour? Like post on Facebook thirty minutes before where we're going to be there? Dude, we could like show up in a parking lot where they're having a Food Truck Mafia!"

The guys laughed and seemed game for that.

Then Jane spoke up. "Dad, what about GeoCacheing? You know, leaving clues lying around that people can use their GPS to find and then when they find the right location, there's like autographed stuff? Some of my friends are into that."

Danny turned around and smiled at her. "That's a cool idea. We'd need to find someone who knows how to do that shit, though."

Jane hopped off the couch. "Well, I kinda do. I did some with my friend Sasha and her mom. We could work on it together."

Danny beamed at his daughter. He grabbed Jane and kissed her hard on the cheek, giving her a squeeze. "My daughter is a genius. Maybe we should make you our marketing guru! That's sure a helluva better idea than those clowns have ever come up with."

Julian said he'd help her put the info up on the website.

Alex laughed. "Remember that time they tried to get us to play that pothead music festival? That one up in Humboldt? They thought it would 'broaden our fan base?' I'm so fucking glad we didn't do that. Or the time they wanted us to be on an episode of Desperate Housewives? What the fuck was that all about?"

The guys swapped stories of lame ideas the label had come up with. Bronson laughed loudly and sputtered, "Remember the action figures? They wanted us to fucking be like KISS?"

Alex frowned. "I kind of liked those dolls. You guys shot that one down."

Danny was laughing but then he got quiet. "You know what I'd like to do? I'd like us to sing the National Anthem at a Giants game. Wouldn't that be so cool? I heard Metallica showed up once, had a whole themed night. I'd love to do that. But maybe we could do like Spring Training or something, where there's a smaller crowd of the diehard fans and then we could do like a show someplace after, in a club or some shit. I miss those intimate gigs. It's been a long time."

They all nodded and Jane asked, "Can you even sing it, Dad?"

He raised an eyebrow at her and then launched into the song a cappella. His voice was so powerful. I watched as everyone in the room broke out in goosebumps. When he hit the final high note, Julian and Alex started whistling loudly. At the end, Jane's jaw was on the floor.

"Daddy! How did you learn how to do that?"

He grabbed her and pulled her in for a kiss. "Practice! Now, why don't you grab that guitar over there. Let's play them our song."

Danny had taught Jane how to play "Smoke on the Water." The guys clapped along and Julian and Alex joined in quietly to provide the bass and drums. Danny sang quietly, his voice able to go from the National Anthem to Deep Purple without missing a beat.

The jam session went on and on. After Jane played she came back to the loveseat and leaned into me. In a few minutes she was fast asleep. Danny carried her off to bed. I followed them and waited in the hallway for Danny to come out.

He was grinning like a madman when he opened the door. He backed me up to the wall with an intense kiss. He pulled back and cradled my face. "I liked having you here while we played. What did you think of the songs?"

I swallowed hard. "It was kind of a shock. I had no idea..."

"I know it's really personal. I hope you're not upset."

I shook my head. "No, not at all. It's not like anyone else is going to know what it's about."

His smile fell a little. "But they will. I'm going to be doing interviews all over before the album comes out. They're going to ask. You gonna be okay with our relationship being out there?"

I paused before answering him. He backed up from me so I could sit on the bed. I wasn't sure how I felt about it. *Here life goes, taking another crazy turn*, I thought to myself. I looked at him and took his hands in mine.

"I don't know. Just how personal are we talking? I can only imagine my students might see or read an interview about you. I'm kind of concerned."

He tugged on his goatee a little. "I can see that. I guess I shouldn't talk about your flexibility, or that sexy mole you have on your lower back."

I pinched his side and he scooted back on the bed to get away from me.

"Ow! Fuck! Alright! I guess I really shouldn't talk about how you like to abuse me." I tackled him and straddled his chest, pinning his arms with my knees. "Oooo, I like this move, honey. Okay, fine. I will definitely not tell them about how much you like skinny dipping in my pool."

"Remember, I can always do my own tell-all interview," I said with a smirk.

He stopped laughing. "You could. I wouldn't stop you. But I'm only kidding. I hope you know that. I will only say that 'yes, I am in a new relationship, it's very serious, and she's the love of my life.' Will that be okay? I mean, if they really listen to the lyrics, it might give them other ideas..."

I leaned down and kissed him. "Just don't go into detail about our bedroom activities. Or my new bra size."

He pulled his arms out and cupped my breasts. "Mmmmm, no way. These are mine. I fucking love these. I loved them before, you know. Now they're just more kissable, and suckable and cuddleable."

"I get it. There's just more of me to go around."

He moaned. "Exactly."

"But you *can* tell them how excited you are that you passed the California High School Exit Exam and are officially a high school graduate."

He stared at me blankly. "What did you say?"

I bent down and rubbed noses with him. "You passed, silly. I told you you would! I'm sorry I hadn't told you yet. Gloria called me and told me the day everything happened. I—"

Danny flipped me over on my back. I was completely at his mercy. I'm sure he thanked me at some point. I was just distracted by his expert use of his tongue and fingers, and the way he contorted my body to get exactly where he wanted to be. I could barely hold on as he showed me with his body just how much he appreciated all of the hard work we'd done together, and were about to continue doing together.

When he finished inside me, we were both gasping for breath. He nuzzled my neck and fingered my necklace with the Teacher pendant that I never took off.

"I am so blessed to have you in my life, honey. Thank you for this gift of you."

I started to tell him we needed to plan a celebration, but he silenced me with his kisses.

"This is all the celebration I need. This and a fucking wedding reception. Everyone and everything else can wait, God dammit. I just want you." I started to protest, but he just had this way of taking over. Just like with everything else. This time I was happy to let Mr. Bossypants be in charge. He continued to be in charge for hours.

Monday and Tuesday the guys were in the studio. After I picked up Jane from school, we hung out at the Mannings' and watched movies. We spent time in their hot tub, ordered take out, and bummed around. It was probably no different from what the brothers did on a regular basis.

Wednesday afternoon Nora took Jane to the ranch while Danny and I prepared to go to the house and meet with the decorator. He worried about how I would feel going over, but Nora assured us the room was already gutted. The crew she hired moved fast. I was less worried than Danny, but I knew it would be weird for a while. I would feel better as soon as I started self-defense training with Sandra. I made a mental note to get her number from Danny.

We pulled up in front of the house and the decorator was already there. Her name was Megan, she was totally Gothed out, and had a very dry sense of humor. Danny tried to be his usual charming self. Her response was a blank stare. It was up to me to make this working relationship happen. She brought some samples and Danny brought pictures of his collection. That finally warmed her to him, and together they geeked out over his classic horror film collection.

"I have a better plan now," she said and grabbed him by the arm. She led him around the room pointing, talking colors and gesturing.

I watched from the steps, not quite frozen, but once again reliving the attack. I must have missed Danny speaking to me because he was by my side in an instant with his hands on my arm.

"Honey? Jesse! Are you okay?"

I shook myself and gave him a smile. "Sorry. Did you ask me something?"

He frowned, but let me off the hook. "Yeah, Megan asked whether we wanted to go leather or velvet for the seating. What do you think?"

I raised an eyebrow at him. "Velvet. Definitely."

His eyes dropped to my mouth and he seemed to be on the same page.

Megan assured us she would have the room done in time for a Halloween bash. I knew that would make Janey happy. Danny brainstormed all kinds of ideas to make Janey's friends squeal. He planned to enlist 'the guys' to make a haunted house for the kids and then afterwards, have a grown-up costume party. I was excited, too. He wanted me to invite Cosmo and the boys and even mentioned having them play at the party.

Having everyone over made me a little apprehensive. I couldn't help but think back to the disasters that accompanied each of the gatherings we'd attended so far. The pool party, the wedding reception...I decided I'd have faith.

Chapter - Six

We stayed with the Mannings until a week before Halloween while the house was being worked on. I really had fun getting to know the brothers better and they were absolutely accommodating. They didn't even bring random chicks home. Jane loved them and was having a lot of fun learning more about the early years of Blackened.

One night at dinner, I put on a slideshow for Jane with some of the tamer pictures Bronson showed me. Danny buried his face in his hands and groaned the whole time. Jane acted as though she was watching a car wreck. She winced, she sucked in her breath, and finally said, "Oh, Daddy…No. Just no. These pictures need to go away."

Bronson and I high-fived.

Danny moaned, "Touché."

School was going well for Jane, but I noticed she was spending a lot more time on her phone texting with her friends, I assumed, and she didn't always look happy. We spent a lot of time together, especially on the nights we went to the dance studio together. She'd take her class and then hang out in the office that was attached to the studio doing her homework. We talked a lot on the drive to and from, and I loved getting to hear about school from her perspective. She had a teacher she really didn't like and I had to bite my tongue when she shared stories about what happened in class. Part of the problem was that Jane wasn't used to hearing 'no' and this teacher sounded very strict.

Danny and 'the guys' finished the album a week or so before we moved back home and mixing took place then. I was able to go watch them, which was quite embarrassing. Danny chuckled at all my questions and my need to touch everything. I also got to watch him work with Cosmo and the rest of Greek Tragedy. He recorded four demos with them and had the same guys who were doing production on Blackened's album finish fine-tuning the Tragedy.

Going back to work was a challenge. Telling the story over and over could have been hard, but with every kid I told, I felt a little stronger and I used it as a teachable moment. I reminded them to be aware of their surroundings and encouraged them all to learn to protect themselves. I had a great idea that I could have Sandra come and do workshops at the school, so I got Gloria's permission. Starting mid-October, the staff and many of the students spent Saturday mornings learning self-defense. Sandra brought in a few of her police buddies, which was a great way for the kids to interact with cops on a positive level. I even brought Jane. The first time she was able to take down one of the smaller cops, she whooped and hollered with delight!

"See," Sandra told her. "You don't have to be bigger. It's all about using their weight and size against them. It's about keeping your head about you, like Jesse did, and not panicking when someone puts their hands on you."

Sandra became a great confidant for me during our weekly sessions. She let me vent and encouraged me to continue working out. "Dancing is great for your flexibility and your treatments are good for your health, but building some muscle will really help you with your RA."

I agreed with her so Danny added some more free weights and exercise equipment to his order for the "gym," which he wouldn't let me step foot in until we officially moved in.

"It's a surprise," he said. Little did he know I'd been working on a surprise for him, too. When the room was finally ready about a week before we moved in, he covered my eyes and walked me inside.

"Open your eyes, honey."

I gasped in shock. Danny had them turn the room into a dance studio. There were mats in one corner for our use, he'd had hardwood floors put in, and he'd had the walls covered with mirrors. There was even a warm-up bar along one wall. In another corner was a heavy bag and a weight bench with a free weight set and an assortment of foam rollers, balance balls, and medicine balls. It was perfect! I thanked him properly. Right there on the new floor.

We'd all really missed Legs during this time, so the day after we moved in, Patricia brought her home and we all took turns cuddling with her. It turned out that she was very much an Irish Wolfhound mix. She was now already five months old and over 60 lbs! She'd been super spoiled at Patricia's house because she slept with Patricia and her husband, Max.

"Dad, she can sleep with me! There's plenty of room."

Danny grumbled but allowed it, of course, once Jane put on the gimme face. Genetics. It was time, however, to do some real training with her. Danny was concerned that she'd be too much for Jane because of her size. Nora and Jane started taking her to training on Friday evenings. I was exhausted by that time of the week. Thankfully Nora assured me she had it under control.

Plans for the Halloween party were finalized and we were ready to go for Friday night. Danny and the guys got wigs and costumes so they could dress like KISS. The haunted house utilized a lot of Danny's props and he and his guys, along with Cosmo and the boys, had a blast scaring the pants off Janey's middle school friends. They loved it! The kids took turns hanging on to each other for dear life and went through it again and again. A lot of their parents stayed and enjoyed the food we'd had catered. I hung out with Rebecca and Patricia for much of the night. We dressed as witches in coordinated costumes. They helped me keep things rolling since Danny had given Nora the weekend off. She wasn't really into all the scary stuff, so she and Connie went on a three day cruise to Baja California.

The only trouble came when some of the boys were leaving. The kids were scheduled to leave by eight o'clock. Jane lingered talking to a tall, lanky kid with longish black hair who was dressed like... An emo band guy? At least I hoped it was a costume. Danny watched them with interest until the boy gave Jane an awkward hug. As he was walking towards the door, he said, "I'll kick you," with a bit of a smile. Danny tensed next to me and stalked towards the kid.

"Did you just say—"

Jane slid in front of Danny. "Daddy, this is Carson," she said slowly like she was addressing a small child. "He's a friend from school. He's going to message me on Kik. It's an app on the phone, remember? We talked about this? Carson, this is my dad."

The kid bravely held out a hand to Danny, who was doing his best to get himself under control. Bronson and Julian approached, followed by Alex. The four of them looming over this kid might have been scary under regular circumstances, but standing there in black spandex with giant wigs and boots on just made the situation laughable. Carson did a tremendous job of being respectful and not laughing right in their faces.

"It's a pleasure to meet you, Mr. Black. Thank you for having us over." Danny paused before shaking his hand. He grunted and walked away, at which point the boys all started murmuring excitedly and patting Carson on the back as they walked out the door.

"Eddie Haskell-looking little fucker," Danny said as he approached. I raised an eyebrow at him and was getting ready to scold him when he winked at me.

Jane went home with Sasha and Ivana. We hugged and said goodnight, then got to work cleaning up the little mess left over from the kid party and setting up for phase two. I was at the sink doing some dishes when I felt Danny's warm embrace from behind. "Think anyone would notice if we snuck off together, pretty lady?"

I giggled. "Yes, Paul Stanley. I think Danny, you know, my boyfriend, would be very upset." I turned in his arms. "Besides, I wouldn't want you to mess up that killer makeup." I brushed his wig back from his shoulders and nibbled his collarbone, which was at the perfect height since he had on ginormous platform boots!

"Damn, girl. Danny is one lucky fellow. You sure know how to make a man feel *goooo-wooo-woooooo-woooooooo-wooooo-hooo-hoood!*" Danny belted out a very Paul Stanley note and I heard laughing in the other room.

"Hey Gene," he called out to Bronson. "Let's get the stage set up! I'm ready to rock and roll all night!"

And we proceeded to do exactly that! By ten o'clock the house was packed. This time, however, I knew everyone, and it was very different knowing this was my house now, too. It still felt pretty surreal. Especially the office/library. Danny had bought me a matching desk and we moved the two desks together in the center of the room so we could both work and still make googly eyes at each other.

I made the rounds, talking easily with all of our guests. Cosmo's now-girlfriend Maria, whom I'd met the night we went bowling, was there and the two of them looked very happy. They had been getting pretty serious, apparently. It turns out he passed her tests and she loved the rest of the boys as much as I did. She kind of filled my spot as Wendy to their Lost Boys, which made me feel much better about being away. She was dressed as Elvira tonight and Cosmo and the boys were dressed as Dead Elvises. They had their equipment set up out by the pool and pretty soon, everyone was out there dancing to their covers of Elvis songs as well as classics from the Stray Cats, Jerry Lee Lewis and others. I danced with Maria, Rebecca, and Patricia until I was about to drop. Then it was time for KISS to take the stage.

I couldn't help but snicker at their ensembles. For all I knew these were genuine KISS hand-me-downs. They looked totally realistic. Danny looked so scrumptious in all that spandex. I could barely contain myself when he turned his back to the crowd and pranced around on his platforms! He stared right at me the whole time they played "I Was Made for Loving You" and "Love Gun." I did my best disco moves right in front of the stage, which had him really showing off his goods. When the song was over, he hurriedly called for a break before he picked me up, tossed me over his shoulder, and carried me into the house at a jog. All the blood had rushed to my head by the time we got back to the bedroom. He set me down hard once inside and slammed the door.

"Paul! I told you, I'm with—"

He kissed me so erotically that there was no way I could keep up the charade any longer. He pulled my dress up and ripped the lace panties right off of me. It didn't take much effort for him to free himself from the spandex pants. He pressed me against the wall and wrapped my legs around his waist. He never stopped kissing me as he thrust into me, hard. Out-of-control Danny hadn't made a showing like this in a long time, what with the house remodel and everything, and I was just beginning to realize how much I'd missed him.

Danny kissed and bit down hard on my neck. His stubble chaffed my face and added to my excitement. He wobbled a little and then cursed. "I'm going to break an ankle in these fucking boots," he laughed.

"We can't have that," I gasped, encouraging him to set me down so he could get out of them. It was strange to be looking so far up into his eyes! "Take them off," I giggled.

"No fucking way," he said, and carried me into the bathroom. He turned me to face the mirror and I laughed at the smeared makeup all over us. "There's no way I could have stayed out there in these fucking pants as hard as you make me." He grabbed my shoulders and angled me so he could thrust into me from behind. "I can't see you," he complained, and reached around to free my breasts from the stretchy, low-cut, wrap dress I had on. "This fucking dress has been driving me crazy all goddamned day." He thrust harder now, grabbing my hips for leverage. He had me breathless. He was hitting me so deep inside, my legs were quivering.

"I love it when something drives you crazy," I whispered. "Then I get to feel you like this." I pushed my hips further back to him and he stilled himself for a minute.

He pulled out and turned me around, lifting me up onto the counter. He dropped to his knees and proceeded to show me just how crazy he was feeling. I tried not to scream as he brought me to the highest peak, but it was hopeless. I just prayed the music was loud enough that no one would hear me. When I floated back down, he stood up and pulled me against him, his boots still making him a little too tall to get the right angle. He growled and turned me back around to face the mirror. We watched each other's reactions as he pounded into me from behind. He groaned louder and louder, and when he came, he bellowed, "FUUUUUUCK JESSE!" I tightened around him and reveled in the feeling of him loving me like this.

We stood there panting and shaking, unable to speak. "Goddammit, Jesse. I love you so fucking much."

I turned around and plastered myself against him, needing to feel his skin against mine. "I fucking love you, too! Now get cleaned up! I have a surprise for you and it's going to be here soon!"

He had a little kid grin on his face for just a moment. It relaxed into worry. "Honey, you didn't have to do anything. I'm so fucking happy right now, having you here, having our house done—"

I smiled and kissed him quickly. "That's great, but I'm serious! Get cleaned up, Paul. Otherwise Danny is going to find us."

He shook his head and stepped back to adjust his pants. "Jesse—"

"I know. I love you, too, and you can't know how happy I am, but I'm going to be happier in just a moment so hurry up!"

He grumbled as he fixed his makeup and his wig. I had to wash off the black and white paint he'd smeared all over me, which looked grey on my skin. I reapplied makeup and fixed my dress so it covered the girls.

"I'll meet you out there," I said, smacking his ass as I ran for the kitchen. It felt so good to be able to move like that and not worry about pain. The medication the doctor prescribed for my RA had me virtually pain free. I was even able to dance more without the pain and swelling I'd grown accustomed to. I was still seeing the acupuncturist and getting massages as well. I felt like a whole new person! It was such a gift Danny had given me. I wanted to give him something back.

When I entered the kitchen, Gene/Bronson hurried to me. "Is he coming? Everything's set up, our guest is in Nora's house waiting for me to come get him."

I squealed and did a little hop in my heels. "Fantastic! Make sure Patricia has her camera ready to roll. I do not want to miss a moment of this."

He left to go get things started and I waited for Danny, pretending to be busy with a tray of food. When he rounded the corner looking put together, I asked, "Hey babe? Can you please carry this tray out to the table? Rebecca said they needed more cheese."

He kissed me loudly on the lips and groaned before taking the cheese tray. "Anything for you," he whispered.

He could still floor me with that look and his words. I waited a couple of beats before following him with some waters for the cooler. The stage lights were turned down. Just the Tiki lights had the patio illuminated. Suddenly, a spotlight shone on the stage and a voice thundered from the PA.

"Daniel Adam Black! Please come forward!"

Danny stopped mid-stride and dropped the tray at his feet. Standing on stage in the spot he had occupied before our little tryst was his hero, Alice Cooper. I crept up next to him and whispered, "Surprise, baby!"

His eyes shot to me, wider than I'd ever seen them. "You did this?"

I nodded. "With Bronson's help." I gave him a push toward the stage and our guests cheered loudly.

"Daniel," Alice called. "Come here, son."

Danny grinned like a loon and trotted up to the stage, wobbling on his platforms. He pulled off his wig as he stood next to Alice and shook hands with him.

"I've been told you have created a new house of horror, and as the godfather of all that is creepy in this world, your lady friend and bandmates thought it fitting that I come and offer a blessing, if you will."

Danny looked at all of us and shook his head, blushing. "Thank you. That would make this whole thing perfect."

Alice nodded and raised his scepter. "Lead the way, Daniel."

He totally played it up as Danny walked down the steps next to him and led the way into the living room. We all followed behind as Danny showed off his collection of life-sized classic monsters, vampire killing kits from the turn of the century, human skulls alongside the skeletons of other creepy mammals, relics from horror movie sets, and the pièce de résistance, a full-sized guillotine Alice Cooper had actually used on stage during one of his early tours. Alice even let Danny "chop his head off," which led to Danny squealing like a little kid. He was so animated, so excited, and every so often he'd smile at me from across the room.

"Now I think this blessing will only be complete with a song or two."

Everyone screamed and Alice motioned for Danny to lead the way back outside. Once onstage Alice took the microphone again.

"There is one other reason my presence was needed tonight. Daniel, come here please."

Danny jumped up on stage and stood next to Alice kinda looking like a dopey kid. Alice put his hand on Danny's shoulder.

"Son, your teacher informs me that you have passed your exit exams and earned your high school diploma. That calls for a tribute!"

Bronson played the opening riff for "School's Out" and Danny started cracking up. I got several hugs from our friends and Danny stood at the front of the little stage shaking hands and hugging our guests. We all sang along with Alice while Danny's face turned redder and redder. Danny picked up his guitar when that song was over and they all played "Welcome to my Nightmare" and "I Love The Dead." When it was over, Alice hugged Danny and I couldn't hear, but it looked like he thanked him for having him over and must have asked about me, because then they walked toward me. I tried to breathe normally and not allow my freakout to show.

"Jesse, I would love for you to meet Mr. Vincent Furnier, best known as Alice Cooper."

He took my hand in his and kissed the back. "Thank you, Ms. Martin for inviting me tonight. I haven't had this much fun in years. Sadly, I must be going as I have an early flight to catch. Enjoy your new home."

I thanked him, I think. I tried to get those words out but it could have been "bless you," for all I know.

He smiled, shook hands with the guys in the band, and then was led out by his driver and a couple other people I hadn't seen.

Danny turned on me and picked me up off the ground in a hug. "That, honey, was an awesome fucking surprise."

I was just glad it all turned out. "Thank Bronson! He's the one who got in touch with him and ultimately got him to come."

He hugged Bronson and thanked him, too. Just not as intimately as he thanked me later, after everyone went home.

Chapter - Seven

A week later we were once again covered in makeup and body paint, this time in Nikki Sixx's photo studio. Danny and I posed suggestively and innocently for Nikki, but once Danny started kissing me, all bets were off. Nikki, his staff, and his girlfriend left us alone to let us play. It was almost as if Danny had pre-arranged it. Too bad he couldn't really enjoy it completely as he was itching like crazy from either the makeup or his hair growing back in. Either way, I suggested that we continue having our fun back home. He shook his head and held up a finger.

"There's one more thing I want to try." He trotted away from me for a moment, rummaged through his bag, and then trotted back over to the camera. He set the timer once again and walked over to me with a shy smile. He turned me so my back was to the camera, and told me to turn my head the other way. I did as he asked, giggling, and felt him tug on my hand.

"Jesse, you can look now."

I turned to find him on one knee… with a ring in his hand. I started to shake and my other hand flew to my chest. I didn't even hear the camera clicking, nor did I pay attention to our surroundings as Danny uttered the most precious words he'd ever said to me.

"Jesse, honey, please give me the most incredible gift you could ever give me and tell me you'll marry me."

I could feel my heart stuttering in my chest and my eyes filled with tears. I tried to speak, but all that came out was a sob. Danny looked worried for a moment but then smiled when I nodded vigorously. He stood and kissed me until I was breathless.

"Yes! Of course, yes, baby! Yes, I'll marry you!"

He pulled me to him and held me tightly to him, letting out a relieved breath. "Oops, I forgot something," he laughed and stepped back far enough to pull my hand up between us and slide the ridiculous diamond and platinum ring over my ring finger.

I gazed into his loving face and just beamed. "We're really going to do it?" I asked.

He frowned. "Of course we are! Damn, woman! I've been telling you I was going to marry you. Just been waiting for the perfect moment to give this to you."

And then I remembered the cameras and pulled him back against me. "And you got the whole thing on film, didn't you, you rat!"

He laughed and squeezed me so tight the breath left my lungs. "I did. Nikki was happy to help. He got his crazy pictures, and I got photographic evidence that you agreed to marry me. You can't get out of it now."

I threw my head back, laughing at his conniving. "I don't want out of it, Danny. But I hope you weren't planning on showing these to the family."

He shook his head. "No way. Only for you and me. Because that's all that counts, when you come down to it. Well, let's take a couple we can show Janey and Nora at least."

We moved closer to the camera and took several shots of Danny holding my hand against his chest, him kissing me with my hand showing off the ring against his cheek, and then finally of my hand resting on my shoulder. I cringed as I took a closer look at the ring. "Danny, this must have cost a fortune! You really didn't need—"

He shut me up with a kiss and shook his head. "Uh uh. No way. I found the perfect ring and you are not going to ruin this for me."

I knew he was only sort of playing. We'd had several arguments over the expensive things he purchased for me. He insisted. I ranted. He used the gimme smile. I caved. It was becoming our routine. He listened when he knew it was important to me, like when I told him I felt really uncomfortable having a security guard with me all the time. He acquiesced on that matter, but he'd pull the Mr. Bossypants routine if he thought I wasn't letting him take care of me how he wanted to.

After more kissing, more tears, more groping, and finally, more itching, we pulled on our sweats and tried to at least gather up the feathers we'd strewn all over the studio. Now, Danny really needed a shower, and probably some Benadryl. It appeared he was getting hives from the makeup.

"Let's just tell Nikki we're leaving," he said with a grin as we stepped out of the studio. Nikki's office was across the hall, and a note was tacked to the door.

"Assuming all went as planned, congratulations! I'll get you the prints as soon as possible. Go home and celebrate, and don't forget to add us to the guest list. Love, Nikki."

I rolled my eyes. "Did everyone know about this but me?"

Danny nodded, rubbing at his belly. "Yep. I told Janey and Nora first, then called your folks, then my mom, then Patricia, then the guys... Pretty much everyone knows. Thank God you said yes!"

I swatted his behind and he groaned. "Can you do that some more, like really fast? I'm so fucking itchy right now. I need to be scratched!"

"You poor man. Let's get you some Benadryl and get you home."

We stopped at the drug store and I was glad when Danny opted to stay in the car so I could get this over with quickly. I couldn't help staring at my ring. I almost walked into a pole! I found Benadryl tablets, some oatmeal bath packets, and several bottles of cream in case he needed more relief. I hurried to the car and found him squirming like crazy.

"I'm so sorry, baby! Let's get you home." I drove the Challenger as fast as I could without getting arrested for reckless driving. I got us into the garage and felt terrible as Danny hopped out of the car and jammed for the door. He stopped short in the doorway. I heard a female laughing as I approached.

"What happened to you, Danny?" As I stepped up behind Danny, I could feel the tension coming off him in waves.

"Brooke," he said in a tone that told me several things; he didn't know she was coming, wasn't happy she was here, but had a feeling why she might be. As we rounded the corner into the kitchen, her smile fell when she noticed me behind him, but didn't take on the bitchy look she usually got.

"Hi Jesse. I'm sorry to barge in. Nora let me in earlier. She left to pick up Jane and take her to ride Misty. I like what you've done with the place." She yammered on for a moment more as we entered the kitchen. She was actually being quite civil, but she looked like hell.

I took the bag from Danny and started getting him some pills and a glass of water. I handed them to him as he addressed her coolly. "I didn't know you were coming."

She shrugged and smiled sadly. "I didn't either. I have nowhere else to go."

I blanched at that and felt Danny stiffen. She glanced nervously at me and then at Danny.

"Danny, I'm going to take this stuff to the room and shower. You okay?"

He nodded and squeezed my hand before turning back to Brooke with his arms across his chest. I heard their low voices as I headed down the hall. God, what now?

I showered, dressed, and then waited for Danny to come in the room. I didn't want to disturb them. It was getting close to six, so I knew Nora and Jane would be home soon. I paced back and forth wondering just what the hell was going on. I felt like it wasn't my place to intrude. I heard the front door a few minutes later and knew the girls were back. I figured it would be safe to come out then.

I entered the kitchen and found Danny chewing on a fingernail, Nora angrily putting away groceries, and Jane hugging her mom weakly.

"I need to go shower and get this shit off me."

Nora looked up and frowned. "Danny! You've got hives all over!"

"I know. It's the body paint. Jesse got me some stuff. The Benadryl is already helping. I just need to get this off me."

Nora nodded at me and said, "You go on, then. I'm going to fix dinner. Brooke, are you staying for dinner?"

Brooke looked hesitantly to Danny, who nodded. "She is. Nora, after dinner, can you get the spare room made up, please?"

Nora's eyes shot to him in alarm. The look on his face stopped her from making any nasty remarks. "Sure."

Jane looked helplessly from me, to Danny, to her mom. Danny picked up on this and said, "Jane, why don't you go let Legs out of her dog run and play with her for a bit. I'll be out in a few."

She nodded and hurried toward the slider. Legs' happy yips sounded as Jane got to her cage. Inside, we silently waited for Danny to speak.

Brooke excused herself to use the restroom. She must have sensed that Danny wanted to talk to us without her present. Once she was out of the room, Nora turned to Danny with her hands on her hips.

He cleared his throat and sighed. "Brooke left Oliver. She came here because she doesn't want her manager to know anything yet. She wants to go to rehab and needs my help. I told her she could stay here until I can get her set up in a facility."

Nora cursed and turned back to her dinner preparations. Danny frowned at her and then looked to me.

I stepped closer to him and put my hand on his arm. "What do you need me to do?" I asked him softly.

He leaned down and kissed me quickly. "Can you go run me that oatmeal bath? I'll be there in just a minute." His eyes shot back to Nora as I left the room.

I met Brooke in the hallway. She was looking around with a smirk at the living room. "He finally got his house of horrors, I see." She turned to me with an embarrassed smile. "I'm really sorry to impose on the two of you. I don't mean to intrude. I just didn't have anyplace else to go."

I shook my head and my hand came up to push my hair out of my face, putting my new ring on display for Brooke. I really didn't do it on purpose, but her eyes grew wide, then narrowed.

She looked bitterly back at me and smirked. "I'll be out of your way soon. You can have my ex-husband and all of this," she said, gesturing to the great room, "to yourself."

I could tell she was upset. I steeled myself and refused to sink to her level. "It's fine. Do you need anything? Clothes or anything?"

She shook her head, irritated. "I have a suitcase. It's in the spare room."

I nodded. "Okay. I'll see you at dinner."

I turned and heard her huff. "Jesse," she called out. I turned around and took in her disheveled appearance, her limp hair, the bags under her eyes... I felt sorry for her. "Thanks," she said.

I smiled and said, "Whatever you need, we're here." That made her feel worse, I could tell. She slouched off to the kitchen and I went back to the bedroom to get Danny's bath ready.

He came in a few minutes later looking disturbed. He stripped down and got in the shower to wash off while I sat on the counter, watching and waiting patiently for him to speak. I'd learned that sometimes Danny needed some time to work things out before he spoke. If I'd known that this past summer when we had our first blow up, I might have been able to avoid several tense moments where I almost walked away from him.

After he washed he stepped over to me and looked to me as if he needed a hug. I opened my arms and he wrapped himself around me. He took several deep breaths before he spoke.

"Damn, if she doesn't have the worst timing. I should be making love to my fiancée right now." I giggled and ran my fingernails over his scalp. He sucked in a breath and closed his eyes. "Mmmmm, do that some more, all over."

I laughed and pushed him towards the tub. "In you go. Then you can tell me what's going on."

His shoulders sagged as he climbed into his giant tub. Once he sat back, I took another packet of oatmeal and rubbed it onto his hives. They were in the bands where the black had been, including across his face. My poor baby.

"I'm sorry, Jesse. I can't turn her away."

I shook my head. "No, of course not. I wouldn't ask you to."

He frowned. "She's the mother of my daughter. I can't just throw her out on the street, although God knows she probably deserves it. I'm so sorry. I hope it will only be a couple of days. I'm going to talk to Patricia after dinner and see if she knows of a place that is good about discretion. Brooke's worried about losing her role on this show. I guess she's really happy with it, but the hours were killing her so she started taking crank to stay awake and edgy or some shit, and now she's really sick. I swear, I'll get her out of here as soon as possible, okay? I don't really want her around Janey that much either." He rubbed at his head and closed his eyes.

"Shhhhh. It'll be fine. If Nora can't handle it, she can leave everything to me. I know she has a hard time with Brooke."

Danny snorted. "That's putting it mildly. Thanks for the offer. I may have to take you up on it. I don't want Nora to quit, and I don't need those two going at it in front of Jane."

He was so smart. I wrapped my arms around his neck from behind and kissed his shoulder and the back of his head.

"I fucking love you, Jesse. My fiancèe. The future Mrs. Black." I giggled. He turned and smiled deviously at me. "You will change your name, won't you? Jesse Black sounds so fucking sexy."

I stuck my chin out and smirked. "I'll think about it. I'll at least hyphenate. I'm the last Martin in my father's family. He might like it if I kept the name."

"Oh yeah? Whatever you want to do is fine. As long as I can call you Mrs. Black." I whispered in his ear just what he could do with me and he started breathing heavy. "Shit, Jesse. You can't say things like that!"

I heard Jane calling for me so I bit his earlobe and said, "Soak. Get the itchies taken care of, okay? I'll go hold down the fort."

"Goddamn, you are incredible. And I'm pretty smart for asking you to marry me."

I groaned as I walked back in the bedroom. Jane was standing in the doorway and she ran to me for a hug.

"Jesse," she cried, pressing her face into my chest.

I held her and stroked her hair as she cried. "I'm sorry, sweetie. Are you going to be okay with her here? For a few days?"

She nodded. "As long as you are here. Daddy leaves in two days with the band and I'm afraid to be alone with her."

I pulled her tighter, cursing when I remembered that Danny was leaving. The band had interviews with a couple of magazines and radio shows and appearances on the Tonight Show starting Thursday. They'd be gone for a week. I really hoped Danny got something in order before he left. Otherwise, we were going to have a long-term houseguest.

Dinner was tense, to say the least. Nora cooked, served, then fled to her house, choosing to follow the "if you don't' have anything nice to say" rule. I kept my mouth shut, Danny clenched his jaw, Jane's blue eyes were huge, and Brooke chattered nervously. I cleaned up so the three of them could talk. I gathered from their stilted discussion they were choosing to leave out the rehab part of the discussion with Jane. She excused herself early to go to bed and asked me to tuck her in. Brooke was wise enough to bite her tongue and just gave a pained smile when Jane kissed her good night.

"Jesse, it's so weird with her here," Jane said, sounding wrecked.

I braided her hair and scratched her back and told her to just focus on what she had control over right now. School. "Try to forget about it tomorrow, okay? When you come home, you'll have time enough to deal with it." I was really at a loss here. I couldn't imagine not being able to talk to my mother when I was Jane's age.

"Hey Jesse? Can I ask you something?"

I kissed her forehead and pushed her a little so she'd move over and make room for me. "You can ask me anything if I can lay down next to you. That photo shoot was pretty exhausting today."

Jane sat up and grabbed for my hand. "Oh, that's right! Daddy proposed to you. Did you say yes?"

I laughed and tickled her, causing her to lie back down, facing me. "I did say yes, you little sneak! You knew all about it, didn't you?"

She beamed. "I told him it would be romantic if he could get pictures of your face saying yes. I'm so happy!" Then her smile fell. "I just wish...Never mind. Jesse? If you had a friend that was doing things you didn't think were right, would you still be friends with her?"

Uh oh. "It would depend. I'm sure I would tell them I didn't like what they were doing, but I don't know what I would do after that. Is the person trying to involve you in this something?"

She shook her head. "No. I have told her I don't like it. She says I'm just being a baby and I should get over it."

I didn't know how much to push, but I wanted her to keep talking. "Do you want to tell me what's happening?"

She rolled onto her back and stared up at the ceiling. "It has to do with boys. Some of the girls at school joined this Kik conversation and were playing like truth or dare, but the dares were really icky stuff. Stuff I don't even know what they meant, but I know are sexual. Then there were pictures involved..." She shuddered and made a retching sound.

"Sounds like these girls are getting in a little over their heads. I think you are wise to stay out of it. I know how persuasive friends can be, though." I also knew a little about Kik since my students were using it. It had a photo capability similar to SnapChat, and kids were taking nude pictures of themselves and sending them to each other. They didn't quite realize that once a picture gets sent, you have no more control of it. A student I knew even had hers posted on Facebook and shared around until even the teachers at her comprehensive high school had seen it. It ruined her hopes for a modeling career, among other things. I was really worried about Jane being involved with any of this stuff, so I shared the story with her.

"See," she said, "that's exactly why I didn't want to get involved. But one of my friends started calling me names and trashing me to everyone else on the convo. Ugh! I hate it!"

I pulled her into a hug and kissed her hair. "I know, honey. Technology sometimes makes it so much harder to get through your teen years. If it makes any difference, I'm proud of you for not getting involved in something like this. If it helps, use your dad as an excuse. Tell them your dad checks your phone every night and will make you take Kik off your phone if you're misusing it. And that he reads all of your conversations. That ought to make them back off."

She giggled. "It would. I hate to make Dad look like a bad guy, but that would make my life easier. Okay. Thanks, Jesse. I love you! I can't wait until you're my step-mom for real."

Damn, this girl! The tears started and I sniffled a couple of times before letting her go, kissing her once more, and saying goodnight.

I could hear Brooke's shrill voice from the kitchen and I just didn't know if I should intrude so I went to the bedroom to wait for Danny. I must have fallen asleep because when I woke up next, Danny was sitting on his stool in the corner playing guitar.

"Hey," I said quietly. He put the guitar down and came over to my side of the bed. "Your hives look better, are you still itchy?"

He shrugged and put his head in his hands. "Jesse, I don't know what to say. We should be celebrating tonight, and instead, I've got this fucking…"

I sat up and crawled behind him, massaging his rock hard shoulders. I needed to call Connie tomorrow.

"Danny. We've been through this before. It's just a bump. We'll deal with this, and when we get past it, we'll celebrate." I kissed the side of his neck and felt him relax substantially.

"Thank you so fucking much for saying that. I'm so afraid of losing you, honey. I don't want to do anything to fuck this up."

I wrapped myself around his back and rested my head on his shoulder. "Just keep talking to me, okay? And be cognizant of Jane. She's really wigged out by Brooke being here. While I know she's got to learn how to deal with her eventually, having her staying here is a strain on her. She was okay when I tucked her in, but she's—"

"God, I know. Poor baby. She's been through so damn much. Fuck. All right. I called Patricia and she's going to come over in the morning so we can get Brooke taken care of."

Thank God for Patricia. If anyone could fix this, she could.

"Okay. Tomorrow's Wednesday, so I've got work, then I'll pick up Jane and take her to the ranch and meet you back here for dinner. You leave Friday, right?"

He exhaled a stream of curses so graphic I barked out a laugh. That got me a small smile.

"Yeah. Fucking New York. I think we're back Monday or Tuesday, then home for a couple days and then we're heading to London for interviews and a couple of shows, then back…" He tensed up again and I kissed his neck again.

"Babe, we'll get through it, okay? I love you."

He turned and pulled me to him to kiss me sweetly. "I fucking love you, you fucking gorgeous woman. It's killing me to not be inside you right now, but I just… Dammit. I don't know what's more of a boner-killer…These damn hives or having my fucking ex-wife down the hall! This whole situation sucks big hairy donkey balls." He pouted so adorably. I couldn't be upset.

"Well, I hate to be more of a boner-killer, but I have an OB-GYN appointment on Friday and I wanted to talk to her about permanent birth control."

Danny's face fell. He cradled my jaw in his hands. "Oh, honey. But you're feeling so much better. Can you wait? Like, see how you're doing? You're so young and…"

I smiled at him. "I'll just ask her about it, okay? I won't make any decisions yet."

He knew me so well now. He knew to not push me, but I could also tell that he wasn't ready to be done with this conversation. I couldn't imagine adding a baby to this mix.

We talked for a bit more and fell asleep in each other's arms. He felt so good there, I was beginning to dread the part of his life that was going to have him travelling and being away from me.

Chapter - Eight

I was in such a hurry the next morning to leave for work that I forgot to take my medication. I knew I'd have enough time if I jammed home on my lunch hour, so I let Gloria know that I was going to be gone. When I pulled up, I was surprised to not see Patricia's car. I figured she must have already left. I went in and checked the kitchen first and found no one, so I figured they must be outside. I hurried down the hall, checking my watch to be sure I had enough time. And I heard giggling. Female giggling. Then I heard Danny's voice. *What the—*

"Come on, Danny! You can't tell me you don't miss it."

My stomach turned to acid. I couldn't make my feet move.

"I do. But things are different—"

I came around the corner to see Danny in a towel in the doorway of the bathroom. He must have caught the motion out of the corner of his eye.

"Jesse! What are you doing here, honey?" He acted completely innocent, just confused. I tried not to hyperventilate.

I stepped further into the room and saw Brooke sitting on the settee next to the closet, thank God, and fully clothed. She, however, had a knowing smirk, as if she knew exactly what I was going to think of this scenario.

I pushed past Danny and into the bathroom. "I forgot my medication," I muttered and grabbed for my pill tray. Danny stepped up behind me and tried to pull me into a hug, which I resisted. "I'm going to be late getting back. I'll see you later." I couldn't get out of there fast enough.

Danny was faster. "Hey," he called out from the doorway. I turned and glanced back down the hall. "I love you," he said, sounding a little unsure. I shook my head and raised an eyebrow. "What?" he asked.

I rolled my eyes. "I'll see you tonight." I slammed the door behind me and ran to my car, running out of time. I dialed Nora and put it on speaker.

"Jesse, what's up?" she answered, sounding concerned.

I groaned. "It's probably nothing, but I just ran in to grab my meds and found Danny in a fucking towel and Brooke sitting in the room with him. Does he not get it!?"

Nora cursed. "No, he most certainly does not. Don't worry. I'll head in there and create a diversion. I'll let him know in no uncertain terms that he's being a jackass."

I thanked her and downshifted as I hung up and flew back down Sunset. I prayed for no traffic. My phone started buzzing as I pulled into the lot at school.

you ok?

There were so many reasons I wasn't okay. Texting was only going to make things worse. I went into my classroom. I dropped my phone into my file cabinet so I wouldn't be distracted, and had only seconds before my first afternoon student arrived.

Two hours later school was over and I grabbed my things. On my way out I felt buzzing in my purse, so I pulled out my phone. Danny had texted me ten times. The messages ranged from 'are you mad' to 'I'm sorry' to 'please fucking answer me, I'm freaking out,' to finally 'Jesse, you're scaring me, fucking answer me!'

I drove over to Jane's school and arrived in time for her to get out of her after school music club. She'd decided to join this year and was playing her guitar with some other kids. I texted her that I'd arrived. She came out moments later, smiling, with two other kids. She waved to them as she neared the car. She seemed so grown up. She'd changed so much since I'd met her just a few months ago. She put her bag and guitar case in the trunk of my car and hopped in.

"Hey, Jane! Have a good day today?"

She nodded and immediately started texting. "I did have a good day, and I took your advice. Sasha and I are both babies now and it's awesome. We started our own nerd version of truth or dare on Kik and our dares are totally nerdy."

I laughed. Leave it to this girl to make me feel better and be nerdy at the same time.

Jane had a lot of homework and asked if we could skip the ranch tonight. I agreed, although I was not looking forward to the reception I'd get at home. We pulled up in the driveway and Jane took off running into the house. I took my time gathering my things from the trunk, again, not in any hurry. Apparently I was taking too much time. Danny came looking for me.

"Hey," he said, looking irritated.

"Hey," I said, closing the trunk.

He stood there with his hands on his hips. "Why didn't you answer me?"

I sighed. "And say what, Danny? That it was pretty awful walking in on you in your towel with Brooke in your bedroom? That's not something I wanted to text."

He looked confused. Then pissed. "You didn't actually think something was going on, did you? After everything we've talked about? After—"

"Danny, it was just weird seeing her in your room."

He crossed his arms over his chest. "Our room, you mean."

I nodded, dropping my bag down. "In our space. With you in a towel. I didn't know what to think. I mean, I didn't think you... I know how you feel about...I just... It was icky, okay?"

Danny looked down at his feet. "Yeah, you're right. I'm sorry. We had just been talking. I went for a swim and then I needed a shower. She was just sort of following me. I didn't even think—"

"I know. You wouldn't. But she did. She gave me a look, Danny. She wanted me to think something was going on. I'm sorry, I know she's in a bad way, but—"

"No. You're right. I should have... I just don't think of her that way so I wasn't thinking about it. I'm sorry. I won't have her in our space again." He stepped forward hesitantly, touching my waist.

I shook my head when the gimme smile made an appearance. "You're unbelievable," I said against his lips as he claimed mine.

He pressed his body against me. That tether between us pulled like crazy. I wanted him so bad! I didn't care that the whole neighborhood could be watching.

"Danny," I whispered. "As much as I'd like to continue—"

His tongue plunged into my mouth and his hands tangled in my hair. "Don't talk. Don't say anything about anything. Just fucking kiss me. Let me just pretend for thirty more seconds. Just thirty more seconds." At the end of that thirty more seconds I was ready to divest him of his clothing and—

"Danny! Patricia's on the phone," Nora called from the front door. He groaned and pulled my hips to him one last time.

"Fuck, I want to taste you so bad right now. This fucking sucks! Coming Nora!"

I giggled, "Or not."

He bent down and picked up my bags before jogging into the house. I trudged behind reluctantly.

"Jesse, can I talk to you for a minute," Nora said.

I followed her out onto the back patio where Jane was playing with Legs. She turned her back to them and spoke in a low voice.

"I can't take it, Jesse. I'm going to stay at Connie's until she's gone. I'll tell Danny when he's off the phone with Patricia, but I wanted you to know. I cooked all day, so there's plenty of food for you guys in the fridge and freezer. I'm sorry to leave you like this, but I'm going to sock her in her pretty little mouth if I have to spend one more minute with her."

I snorted out a laugh and shook my head. "I don't blame you. We'll be fine."

She hugged me and went inside to talk to Danny. I sat down next to Jane and gave Legs some ear scratching.

"So Nora's going," Jane said, looking sad.

I nodded. "Just for a few days." I brushed her hair back.

Jane gazed up at me with the saddest expression on her lovely face. "You think my dad would let me go stay with Sasha? At least for the weekend?"

I sighed, thinking that was probably a good idea. Without Danny here this weekend, Jane would only have me as a buffer between her and Brooke, who came out just then.

"Hey, Jane! How's school?"

Jane immediately turned sullen teenager. Brooke sat on the lounge chair facing Jane and tried to engage her in conversation, but Jane was down to one-word answers. This was a nightmare. I didn't want to leave Jane alone with her, but I needed to pee like mad.

"I'll be right back," I said.

Jane's eyes shot to mine and I did a little pee pee dance to show her why I was leaving. She laughed a little and went back to petting Legs.

Brooke wasn't going to let things lie. "Oh, Danny's dressed now. You'll find him in his office this time."

I raised an eyebrow at her, glanced at a surprised Jane, and hurried into the house before my bladder burst, feeling the need to take deep cleansing breaths.

I heard shouting from down the hall. I hurried to the library door and found Danny and Nora facing off.

"I don't give a fuck if she's the Queen of England! I'm not waiting on her! I don't work for her, and if you keep making a stink, Danny Black, I won't be working for you!"

I rushed to intervene. "Whoa, whoa, what is going on?" I could not let Danny screw things up with Nora. No way. "Danny, I think it's a good idea—"

"What the fuck do you want me to do, Nora? I'm doing the best I can!"

Nora crossed her arms. "Enabling that wench to keep messing with your daughter and fucking up your relationship is what you're doing. It's up to you, but I'm not staying. Either you give me leave, or I'm quitting!"

Danny looked like he'd been slapped in the face. "I can't believe… Fine. You do what you have to do." He turned on me, furious. "You leaving, too?"

I blanched. "No," I said calmly. "I'll stay with Jane. I can handle it. But Jane asked if she could stay at Sasha's this weekend. I think it might be a good idea if Brooke is still going to be here."

He exhaled like a defeated man. "You're probably right. I'm sorry, Nora. Please, go stay with Connie. I'm sorry…"

She stepped forward and hugged him briefly, uncomfortable with the whole crying thing she was trying not to do.

"I'm sorry, too. I'll be back when she's gone." She turned and started for the door. "But Danny, I meant what I said. Don't let her ruin your life again." He gazed at her for a long time and then nodded. She was gone. I was left with a very emotional Danny.

"What happened with Patricia?" I asked him, praying she'd come up with a solution.

He shook his head. "We found a program for Brooke, but she can't start until Monday. I'm gone until then, so Patricia said she'd take her Monday morning. I'm afraid that leaves you here with her for the weekend."

Great. "Okay. We'll make it work."

He pulled me into his arms and kissed me. "Thank you," he whispered. "I don't know what I did to deserve you, but I promise I'll make this up to you. Once this is all said and done, let's start talking wedding plans." His eyes twinkled at the thought, but the worry lines on his face told me he had way too much on his plate to be thinking about any of that.

An hour later, Danny put dinner together for us and we had another tense meal. Nora was gone, Jane was brooding, and Brooke appeared oblivious to the commotion she was causing.

The guys came over after dinner and they all greeted Brooke coolly, especially Bronson. The guys set up their instruments in the great room off the kitchen and practiced for their performance on the Tonight Show, opting to play their soon-to-be-released single "Teach Me." It was a not-so-veiled reference to my relationship with Danny and I loved hearing it, usually. Not with Brooke in the room.

When they finished, Jane and I clapped. Brooke laughed. "I like it! Just wait until he writes the 'I hate you' songs, Jesse."

The room went quiet and Jane stood up quickly. "I'm going to bed," she announced. She stopped and kissed my cheek and then walked out the door. Danny frowned at Brooke and took off after Jane. I moved to finish the dinner dishes and the guys started packing up. Except Bronson.

"Brooke, you need to learn to quit fucking with people's lives. You know? You are so fucking lucky Danny took you in. I would have put your ass on the street where you belong."

I heard Alex curse under his breath and I fought the urge to turn around.

Brooke laughed. "Bronson you never did have any manners. I'm bored. You guys still sound like shit." She stood and walked out the door, smacking into Danny's shoulder on her way by.

"What the fuck was that about?" he asked.

I heard Brooke call out, "Your little friends seem to think I'm causing problems." Danny looked back to her, into the room, and then to me. I gave him a sad smile and shook my head.

"You need to get her out of this house, Danny." Bronson slung his guitar case over his shoulder and walked past Danny. "She's a fucking disease."

Julian gave Danny a bro hug, followed by Alex, who said, "Call me if you need anything."

Danny looked confused, upset, frustrated, angry...I wished I could make him feel better. He stared at me from the doorway, helpless.

"Want to join me out back?" I asked quietly.

He followed me through the slider. We sat on the sofa in front of the fire, which he turned on. It wasn't freezing, but it *was* November, and the air was quite chilly. It was close to eleven and the city lights twinkled brightly in the valley below us. Danny looked pensive. I sat with my back to the arm of the couch and pulled him back to rest his head on my chest. I cradled him with my arms and legs, knowing he needed to be grounded tonight.

Danny started to talk a couple of times and then stopped. I grazed my nails through his super short hair and across his chest under his shirt. He gave up on trying to speak. Instead, he rolled over and pulled me under him. In seconds he had my panties off from under my skirt and his pants undone. He gazed into my eyes pleadingly.

"I need you, Jesse."

I smiled, knowing exactly how he felt. For a little while I did what I could to ease him, to love him. I wanted him to feel as safe as he made me feel. Well, before Brooke showed up. I tried to keep those negative thoughts out of my head and surrendered my consciousness to the passion Danny brought out of me. He made love to me slow and tender, his entire body quivering. He whispered to me the whole time how much he loved me and needed me, and begged me not to ever leave him.

At that I stilled him with my hands on his face. "Baby! I'm not going to leave you, okay? We're okay. I love you. We just have to get through this."

He pressed his forehead to mine and moved more insistently within me. "I fucking love you, Jesse," he cried and then groaned when he came. I held him close to me, wishing I never had to let him go.

We stayed like that for a long time, and when it was time to go to sleep, Danny carried me to bed. He acted really cute, but I knew he was worried. I didn't want him to be worried. Then I would worry and we certainly didn't need that.

Danny took Jane to school the next morning. He and Brooke were planning to take Jane to the ranch after school and then grab dinner. Danny asked me to call Ivana and ask about Jane spending the weekend with Sasha. Ivana suggested we meet for lunch and I agreed, thinking it would be a welcome change from the drama at home.

Ivana and I had had lunch a couple of times and even gone to the movies once without the girls. It was nice to be able to talk dance with someone who could relate. She was completely understanding about the current situation, even though I didn't tell her about Brooke's issues, and was happy to have Jane for the weekend. I arranged for her to take Jane home with them Friday and bring her to school on Monday.

That left me with the proposition of having a weekend alone at the house with Brooke. Ugh.

I texted Cosmo to see what he and the boys were up to Saturday night, figuring I could escape over there for a little while. He hit me back.

Jinx's birthday bash, baby. You should come.

Even better. Thursday night I helped Danny pack, giddy to be seeing his performance wardrobe. Brooke and Jane watched movies in the theater, giving us a few minutes alone.

"I wish I could pack you in my suitcase, honey," Danny said as he closed up his bag.

I had to admit, he was much more efficient and neat than I ever was when I packed. Then again, he had more practice.

"I do, too. Except I have a date Saturday night. Damn. Sorry, babe. You'll have to go without me."

He tackled me on the bed and attacked my neck. "A fucking date? It better not be a hot date."

I moaned as his hands got busy. Then I smacked him. "Danny! We can't. I have to go to the lady doctor tomorrow, remember? No funny business!"

He frowned. "Really? You can't?"

I shook my head. "Nope. It's prohibited."

He lifted up my shirt and pressed kisses into my belly, making it very difficult to deny him. "Damn. But honey, you're not going to do anything, right? Just get checked? Because I've been thinking a lot about us and our future. I think there might be room for one more little red haired Danny? Maybe?"

I smiled down at him and shook my head. "You and that damn gimme smile. Let me see what the doctor says, okay? I want to give you everything you want, baby. I'm just..."

He pushed up to kiss me and ran his hands over my hair. "No pressure. I told you how I feel. I just had a dream the other night. You had this sexy pregnant belly and damn, I woke up so hard for you."

I rolled my eyes. He was so crass, but he was so mine. "You say the sweetest things. I love you, baby. I'm sorry we can't make love."

He crawled up next to me and unfastened his pants with a smirk. "You got a dentist appointment?"

I was sad to say goodbye to Danny Friday morning. This was the first of many times he was going to be gone. I hoped I could stand it. We hadn't been apart much since I started working with him six months prior. Six months! Crazy! I couldn't decide if that was a long time or a short time for all the insanity and happiness we'd experienced. I looked down at the gorgeous ring on my finger and smiled. I hoped we had many more good times to come.

I went to my doctor's appointment in the afternoon and luckily she was on time. Waiting at the OB-GYN is the worst kind of torture. Luckily, I really liked my doctor. She was young and blunt.

"Bottom line, Jesse, is do you want to have kids or not? According to research I've read, folks with RA actually tend to have a decrease in their symptoms while pregnant and it's not always passed along to your children. Now that you've gained weight, I think you'd be fine. You may have to adjust your meds, but I'd okay it if you wanted to."

My expression made her laugh.

"Was that not what you wanted to hear?"

I shook my head, waiting for the oxygen to get back into my lungs. "I'm just surprised. I hadn't ever thought I would find someone to marry, much less have kids with. We just got engaged and now babies? I might have a heart attack!"

Dr. Lewis chuckled. "No hurry. You've got plenty of time. You're still a baby and he's not over the hill or anything, is he?" I told her he was just thirty-six. She shrugged. "Why not? With your dancing ability and his singing talent? Your kid might be a true triple threat!"

She gave me a clean bill of health and told me to come back and see her if and when I was ready to get knocked up.

I left the office feeling a little light-headed from lack of food and too much to think about. Danny texted me that they'd landed and were settled in at the hotel. He had the Tonight Show taping and two interviews to do in the evening. Saturday morning more interviews and a photo shoot for Rolling Stone were scheduled, and then they were going to be on Saturday Night Live as the musical guests. Sunday the band would be doing a live performance on satellite radio along with an interview. I was going to be sure I was in front of the radio to listen. I couldn't believe this was their life! Patricia was travelling with them and promised to keep me posted with pictures and videos.

When I got back to the house, Brooke was outside by the pool sleeping. I opened the slider and stepped out. Legs barked from her pen. I shushed her, but Brooke sat up.

"Oh. Hi Jesse. I wasn't sure if I should let the dog out or not." Legs ran over to her patch of grass to pee and then wandered around the small lawn area. I went and sat in the chair next to Brooke's.

"Are you hungry? I can heat up some dinner for us."

She waved her hand lazily. "You don't have to take care of me, Jesse. I don't want to put you out."

I shrugged. "I was going to eat something myself. It's no big deal."

She rolled over and looked at me. Really looked at me. "I didn't mean to cause trouble for you. I know it's awkward. I didn't have any place else to go." Her blue eyes, so much like Jane's, filled with tears. I felt terrible. No matter what she'd done in the past, she was hurting.

"I understand. I just hope this program is helpful for you. Have you ever had to go before?" Awkward was me trying to talk to my fiancé's ex-wife about her drug use!

She shook her head. "No. And I haven't had anything since I've been here, I swear. I just need some time to, I don't know... I'm a mess, Jesse. I thought going back to acting would help, you know? Get back to work? But I haven't done television before and the shooting schedule was intense. I was up nights and days in a row, working eighteen-plus hours. It was crazy! I saw a doctor there who prescribed me 'stimulants.'" She laughed humorlessly. "Right. Just call it what it is. I was taking meth for Christ's sake. Then I just got so tired, and then we went on hiatus... And Oliver," she rolled her eyes. "I don't know what the hell I was thinking. He's such a douche!" I laughed at her language, not expecting her to talk like that.

"I'm serious," she continued. "I couldn't be around him and his douchey friends any longer! I've used douches that were less douchey than him!" At that I cracked up. I couldn't help it.

"Douchey sounds terrible. And gross. And quite vivid. Listen, how about we go eat something. Then you can tell me more about Oliver. Or not. Or..."

She smiled at me. "Thanks, Jesse. For not making this weird. I'm sorry I was such a bitch. Last night, before. I just...Yeah."

I wasn't quite sure what to say so I just smiled. "It's okay. I'm not always Ms. Personality."

She just sighed and nodded, like she was coming to terms with something. "I'm glad Danny's marrying you. You're good for him, you really are. And I thank you, you know, for being there for Jane when I couldn't. I guess I'm not cut out to be the mom of a teenager."

I stood up and she followed me into the house. I got out two servings of dinner. I chose the pasta with tomato cream sauce stuff that Nora made because it was my favorite. I heated hers, and then mine. She sat at the counter and I stood facing her, eating my food.

"Brooke, can I ask you a question?"

She shrugged. "I don't see why not, since I seem to be in a sharing mood."

I snickered, not sure if that was a go ahead or her cautioning me to watch what I said. "I was just curious, why would you say you're not cut out to be the mom of a teenager? I mean, I know they're difficult, but what changed for you?"

She pondered my question while chewing her food. I could sometimes see glimpses of the movie star in her, like now, when she made eating pasta look like an Academy Award winning performance of high drama. When she finally spoke, I had to shake myself out of the little trance.

"I guess it was when I realized she didn't think I was perfect anymore. I don't know. Jane is the greatest kid, you know? I didn't have to even try to make her love me. She just thought I was the best mom ever. Then, when we started to fight, I realized I couldn't keep up the charade anymore, that anything I did was going to tarnish her image of me. I don't know. I guess I was just tired. I never had to do anything and all of a sudden I'm failing at the whole motherhood gig because I don't want to hang out with her and her moodiness. I don't know. I know it sounds awful. I just think some women aren't cut out to be mothers. I never had a burning desire to be one. Danny wanted kids, so I went along with it since he didn't ask me for much. But I didn't get the fulfillment from it I thought I would. I love her. Don't get me wrong. She's amazing. She's kind of too good for me."

What a sad, sad woman! The fact that she said the last part was the only thing that saved her in my mind. She was right. She may have given birth to Jane, and probably wasn't the world's worst mother, but Danny definitely got the credit in my mind for making Jane the caring, wonderful person she was growing up to be. I was grateful she was in my life. Screw Brooke if she didn't want to be her mother. I'd be proud to be step-mother to such a sweet girl.

"I guess I understand," I finally said, thinking my expression likely gave my thoughts away.

She pushed back from the counter. "Thanks for dinner. I'm going a little stir crazy in this place. I think I might go out for a while. Would you mind dropping me off at my mother's?"

I didn't think she was supposed to be going out, but I wasn't her keeper.

"Sure, I guess. I thought you didn't want her to know you were here?"

She rolled her head around on her neck and stretched her back. "I talked to her earlier and filled her in. She's just glad I'm taking care of things."

I blew out a breath and then said, "Okay. I'll just go grab my keys."

I texted Danny to let him know what was going on, but he never got back to me. I knew he was busy. I had a bad feeling about this, but if I didn't take her, she could always call a cab, and then who knows who would see her? Or where she'd really go?

It turned out her mother lived in Beverly Hills, not too far from where she used to live with Jane. She didn't say much, just fidgeted a lot. She and I were about the same size, but she was shorter than me by about two inches. And had larger breasts, by a lot, even with my new cup size.

I pulled up to a large ranch house just as the last light left the sky and stopped the car.

Brooke looked off in the distance. "Thanks, Jesse," she said in a quiet voice.

It reminded me of the tone she had when I called her from the hospital months ago to tell her Jane had had an accident at the horse ranch... And that she was cutting herself. I didn't know this woman very well, didn't really want to, but I wanted her to get her shit together and be a mother to her daughter. I didn't want Jane to have to pay for Brooke's bad decisions.

"Are you coming back to the house?" I asked her.

She nodded slowly. "Yeah. Tomorrow sometime, or whenever I get sick of my mother. Don't worry. If you aren't there, I've got a key." She climbed out and moved slowly toward the front door.

The way she carried herself made me think of Jane and how she looked the day we went to pick her up in New York. Part of me felt sorry for Brooke, like maybe her mother was no picnic either. But that was a small part. The rest of me was just short of disgusted.

I stopped and picked up some food and toys for Legs and was looking forward to a long cuddle session with her tonight. If Danny and Jane were off without me, Legs and I were going to have a sleepover!

Saturday was the first lazy day I'd had in forever. Legs and I slept in, went for a walk late in the afternoon at Griffith Park up by the observatory. Then we picked up a hot dog at Pink's for an early dinner. It was a great day and I was really looking forward to my evening with the boys. I thought I'd bring Legs with me so they could see how big she was getting. She was already over eighty pounds and growing bigger every day.

I pulled up to my old apartment complex close to seven and shook my head. It was still as shitty as ever. Strangely, I missed it sometimes. Danny's place was fantastic, but this place had so much life to it. Too much at times. I looked in the back seat at Legs and shook my head.

"Don't worry, girl. We're just visiting." I also figured I could use her as my excuse if things got too crazy. I could say I needed to take her home.

The party was already in full swing. Johnny handed out drinks and Sam manned the grill.

"Hey! Jesse's here!"

I hugged Jinx and wished him a happy birthday, handing him a card. His jaw dropped when he saw my hand.

"Whoa! Guys! Get over here! Black popped the question!"

All of a sudden I was surrounded by sweaty, smelly guys all trying to grab my hand from each other. Legs woofed protectively and Jinx looked down in shock.

"Holy shit! Is that Legs? What the hell have you been feeding her?"

I bent down to give her a scratch. "She's mixed with Irish Wolfhound. The vet said she's likely to top out over one hundred twenty pounds."

He looked over at Johnny, his eyes wide. "It's a good thing she's living with you. She's going to be a beast."

Cosmo came out then, shirtless in a pair of jeans. His long, curly hair was pulled back in a hair tie, he was freshly shaved, and he looked as though he'd just hopped out of the shower. His eyes lit up when he saw me. He made his way over to give me a hug.

"Jesse Baby, I've missed you," he said quietly.

I smiled up at him and he kissed my cheek.

"Dude! Look at this rock." Jinx stuck my hand in Cosmo's face. He blanched, then took it gently in his to examine it.

"It's beautiful, Jesse. Congratulations." He kissed my cheek again and hugged me, giving me an extra squeeze. When he stepped back, I detected a hint of sadness in his eyes.

I frowned. "Where's Maria?" I asked him, hoping to deflect any deeper conversation.

He shrugged. "Not sure. She and I parted ways. I guess the Tragedy was a little too much for her."

Shit. I was hoping that wasn't the case. "I'm sorry, Cosmo. Are you okay?"

He shrugged and sighed exaggeratedly. "I will be. I always am. I survived you leaving, so I guess I'll be fine."

I rolled my eyes and elbowed him. He noticed Legs. Then did a double take. "I can't believe it. She's huge!" He got down on a knee and Legs licked him affectionately.

I thought back to the afternoon I came and got her. That was back in July. He hadn't seen her in four months! He took my hand in his and I followed him back into his apartment. There were some familiar faces sitting around the living room so I said hello. The crowd seemed a little mellower than they used to be, and I was thankful for that.

Cosmo asked me what I was drinking. "Just water, thanks." I sat down at his dinette set in the kitchen and Legs sat obediently next to me. Cosmo put down a bowl of water for her and then took the other chair. We talked for a long time about the band, about Danny, about Jane... He asked me where everyone was.

"We had a little unexpected guest show up and throw a wrench into things. Jane's at her friend's for the weekend. Nora's staying with her sister. Danny and the guys are in New York. They're going to be on Saturday Night Live tonight."

"Really? Hey Jinx! Turn on the TV. Doesn't SNL come on earlier here?" He looked at the schedule and saw that the show would be on at nine, which was in just a few minutes.

Cosmo kicked some people off the couch so we could sit closer and watch. "So, unexpected guest?"

I looked around and spoke quietly in his ear. "It's Brooke. She's been staying with us this week. I guess things were not going well in New York." He nodded like he understood completely. "I dropped her at her mother's house yesterday and I'm not sure when she's coming back. I felt a little weird about leaving her, but I wanted to see you guys and I didn't feel like I could tell her no."

He smoothed his hair back. "She's a grown woman. Dealing with an adult who makes bad decisions is not a good time, baby. When is Black coming home?"

I sagged a little. "Monday sometime. He leaves again a couple days later." I sighed loudly and he put his arm around me.

"You're going to be fine. You just might have to take care of yourself, ya dig? Like borrow some of Jinx's porn collection."

I snorted out a very unattractive laugh. "Uh, no thanks. I think I'll survive."

"I don't know. Ladies left unattended can get, you know, frustrated. I'd hate for Danny to come home and find you—"

"I'll be fine, Cosmo!" I slugged him in his arm. This felt so much like old times.

I was leaning back into the couch when all of a sudden Sam shrieked, "LOOK JESSE! They're on!!!" He cranked up the sound on the shitty TV and there they were.

Danny wore black jeans and a black button down with the sleeves cut off at the shoulder. His smile was cocky and he was throwing off major sexuality. They launched into their new release, which had a complicated hook at the beginning. They sounded good, but it wasn't quite as thrilling as having them play in Danny's living room. Our living room. It was still so surreal, and here I was wearing Danny's engagement ring. I must have had a silly grin on my face because they guys all started razzing me.

The music pulled back at one point and it was just Danny voicing over a heavy bass line that grew and grew. He gripped the microphone in both hands and stared right into the camera. It was like he was staring right at me, singing to me. It was crazy! This song was one of the ones he wrote about us and it got a little explicit. I felt my face flush thinking about the specific night he was singing about and thought Cosmo just might be right about needing to take care of things.

When their performance was over, the TV got turned down and the music turned back up. The guys asked me when the wedding would be. I told them I had no idea, that it all happened so fast.

"I promise, you'll all get an invitation."

Another round of hugs and it was time for Legs and I to go home. I walked her around downstairs so she could go potty before we headed home. Cosmo stayed with me and lingered as I let her into the back seat.

"You sure you're okay, Cosmo?" I finally asked him.

He smiled and pulled me into his arms. He felt safe to me, like hugging a brother. "I'm fine, baby. Just tired. I'm ready for this band to take off, ready for something to happen. I can't keep partying with these guys forever. I'm thirty years old, man. I thought I'd be happy just lounging around this shithole all my life, but working with Danny, seeing there's a chance for us to go somewhere? I want it. I'm just sorry I realized it too late to be with you."

My stomach dropped a little. It was so much easier with Cosmo as my friend. I didn't want him to hurt. "I see great things happening for you. You're so talented, Cosmo. You're such a good man. I'm sorry if you're hurting."

He shook his head, looking embarrassed. "It's cool, baby. I think it was more the idea of you, anyway. I mean, I do love you, but I just see how supportive and loving you are with Danny and I want that, too."

I smiled up at him. "I want that for you. You just have to be selective. These little girls who hang out here aren't looking for a man like the real you. That's why I hoped it would work out with Maria. Maybe it's not too late?"

He shrugged. "Don't worry about me. I'm cool. You just be careful. I don't like you up in that big house all alone. Set the alarm, dig? And text me when you get home."

I kissed his cheek and he hugged me to him once more. "Take care, baby." He waved as I climbed in and drove off.

I saw in my rearview mirror that he watched as I drove away, his hands in his pockets. Needless to say my visit ended on an unsettling note. It took forever to get home and I was yawning as I pulled into the driveway. There were lights on, so I assumed Brooke was back. I groaned and turned around to give Legs a scratch. "You gotta hang out with me, okay? Don't leave me alone with her." Legs let out a sigh and I laughed. She was so expressive. I loved her so much.

The door was unlocked and I heard laughing from inside. I started to get the chills and Legs growled low in her throat. I kept a good hold on her leash and told her "easy." Brooke was in the living room with a couple of sketchy looking men. One of them was kissing her neck. She looked really out of it.

"Brooke," I called.

She noticed me and then rolled her eyes. "Oh, hi Jesse. This is Carl and Mike. Guys, this is the future Mrs. Black."

One of the guys, Carl I guess, was helping himself to Danny's booze and had a cigar lit. I cringed at what they'd been up to while I was gone.

"Brooke, can I talk to you?" I asked and started walking toward the kitchen.

Mike stepped away from her and blocked my way. Legs growled at him as he reached down to pet her. I yanked her back before she bit him.

"Whoa, now. No need to get feisty there, puppy. We're just having a good time. Why don't you come have a good time with us?" He fingered my hair on my shoulder and my stomach lurched as I jumped away from him.

I started to shake, but I wasn't about to let him know how scared I was. "I want you to get out of my house," I said firmly, not really sure where my courage was coming from. "Both of you. Brooke, your friends need to leave."

Neither of the guys looked ready to leave. I threw back my shoulders and loosened my grip on Legs' leash. She was really growling now, her hackles were all up.

"Jesse, we're just having some fun. Come on," Brooke said.

I shook my head. "Either they leave now, or I'm calling the police."

She stumbled trying to get to her feet. Carl came around and caught her around the waist.

"Come with us, Brooke. We've only just gotten started." He reached around to grab her breast and she pushed him away.

"I don't feel so good." She wavered once more and collapsed in his arms.

He laughed and laid her out on the couch. "Perfect."

I was beyond furious. This was NOT happening in my house!

I stepped over and punched the silent alarm on the keypad and yelled, "You two better get the fuck out of here. Now! The police are on their way. I'm more than happy to show you the fucking door." I let go of Legs' leash, but she stayed by my side, guarding me. I stepped into a defensive stance, ready to put my training to work.

Mike stepped closer to me and sneered. "How cute! Did you take a kickboxing class?"

He reached for me and three things happened. I delivered a punch to his throat, I kneed him in the nuts, and Legs lunged at him, snapping and snarling as he hit the ground. Carl hurried over and pulled a groaning Mike up from the floor.

"Jesus, lady! We were just trying to have a good time. We're out of here."

He dragged his friend out the door and I slammed it behind him, locking it tight. I slumped against the wall, the adrenaline too much for me. I felt like I was going to hurl, but I needed to check on Brooke.

Legs didn't leave my side as I made my way over to the velvet couch. Brooke was passed out cold. I turned her on her side in case she vomited and I sat with my head in my hands trying to get my breathing under control. Legs nudged me with her nose and I hugged her tight.

"You are the best dog in the whole world, girl! Thank you, my sweet puppy."

She licked my face a few times for good measure. I jumped when I heard pounding at the door. I hurried to open it once I checked the peephole. Legs never left my side. I grabbed her leash and held her back as she barked like crazy.

"Ma'am, we received an alarm from this house."

I exhaled, grateful once again for Danny's alarm system. "Yes, please come in. I came home and found some men in my living room and they didn't want to leave. I think we need an ambulance, though. My fiancé's ex-wife is passed out and I don't know if they drugged her or not."

Legs was going crazy, so I pulled her back before she bit the good guys.

"Do you know if there's anyone else here?" the officer asked.

I froze. "Oh my God! I don't know! I just assumed it was the two of them. Can you check the house, please?"

One of the officers checked on Brooke and then called for an ambulance. The other officer took off down the hallway. Once he checked all the rooms, he came back out and told his partner that all was clear.

"Ma'am, it looks like some of the drawers in your room may have been disturbed. Can you please come and check it out?"

Legs and I hurried down the hallway and into our closet. I gasped and got teary when I saw that my top drawer was opened.

"Oh no," I breathed. The pearls that Danny gave me when we went to visit his parents were gone from their gift box. I teared up, devastated to lose such a precious gift. Thankfully, none of Danny's things were missing. His drawers were all intact. The officer said he'd take a police report for the items, but he'd need information from Danny when he returned.

I sat on the steps going down to the living room and held onto Legs. I heard my phone buzzing from inside my purse.

"Jesse? Are you ok?" It was Patricia. "The alarm company just called me."

The second line buzzed at the same time and I saw Danny's name. "I'm okay, Patricia. Danny's on the other line. Let me answer." I put her on hold and picked up.

"JESSE! Oh, honey, are you okay? What the fuck happened?"

I exhaled and finally felt like I could breathe normally. "I'm fine, baby. I got home with Legs from Cosmo's house and Brooke had a couple guys—"

He started swearing and shouting.

"Danny! Listen, I'm fine, but Brooke's passed out and I don't know if they drugged her or if she's... I had them call an ambulance. I know she didn't want anyone to know—"

"Too fucking bad! What the fuck was she doing bringing losers into our fucking house? That's it! That's the last fucking time I ever help her out of a jam. I can't fucking... Oh shit, babe! Did anything happen? Please fucking tell me you're alright!" He was breathing hard.

I could tell he was completely distraught. I tried to reassure him. "I'm fine. Neither of them touched me. You can thank Legs and the self-defense training for that. One of them probably won't be walking right for a while, though."

He let out another round of curses. "I'm so sorry, Jesse. I never should have let her stay. I can't believe— God, I love you, honey. Let me call Patricia and see if she can get me a flight home."

"No, Danny. It's okay. I'm okay. I know you have to work. Patricia's on the other line."

He cursed. "No, she's knocking on my hotel room door. Hold on." I heard him put the phone down, shout a few more f-bombs, then I heard Patricia's voice. When he picked the phone back up, he said, "Jesse, I'm coming home. I'll be back tomorrow. The guys can finish the interviews without me."

I tried to argue, but he wasn't having it. My phone buzzed again. This time it was Cosmo. The police officers were trying to talk to me and the paramedics were coming in.

"Danny? I gotta go. Do you want me to go to the hospital with Brooke?"

He swore loudly. "Fuck that! No. I want you to stay put. Tell them to call her fucking mother. Fuck, I'll call her fucking mother and tell her to get her ass over there. Brooke's her problem now. I'm done." I tried to calm him down, but he kept ranting.

"I gotta go, I love you," I whispered and then hung up so I could deal with all of the emergency folks who were staring at me and trying to suppress a giggle at the sight of me holding the phone away from my ear. One of the paramedics approached me.

"Ms. Martin? We're going to take Ms. Jones to Cedars Sinai so we can evaluate her. Did you see anything she took?"

I shook my head. "No, I just came in and found her with the guys, although one of them was acting like…"

It turned my stomach and I knew I couldn't hold back. I ran for the bathroom, Legs hot on my heels, and I hurled violently. I had really not missed this.

When I got myself under control, I stepped back out and told them calmly what I thought was about to happen. They said they would take care of her. I thanked the officers for coming out so quickly. They had Brooke on the gurney by this time, and were wheeling her out the front door. I gave the officers further descriptions of the two men and they said they might need me to come down and meet with an artist to do a sketch if Brooke couldn't identify them by name. I told them I understood and wrapped my arms around myself, the evening's activities taking their toll.

"Do you have someone we can call?"

Just then a car came screeching up to the house and I heard shouting. Cosmo came running up the walkway and took me in his arms.

"Jesse, baby, are you okay?"

Jinx, Sam and Johnny were right behind him, ready to protect me.

The officer gave me his card and said, "If you think of anything else, or you need us, don't hesitate to call."

I thanked him again and went inside, the boys right behind me.

"You never called to say you got home okay and then you didn't answer your phone, so we came. Are you okay?"

I nodded, the tears finally flowing free. I gave them the abbreviated version and they walked me over to the couches in the great room.

"Jinx, can you take Legs out back, please?" She didn't want to leave my side. He had to really coax her.

"It's alright, girl," I called out to her. She finally went with him.

Cosmo sat next to me and I curled up to his side, my head resting on his shoulder, while Sam and Johnny got me water to drink and settled on the other side of me.

"We'll stay until Danny gets here, baby. I'm not leaving you alone."

I smiled up at Cosmo, who was furious, and felt my body finally relaxing. He coaxed me into lying down with my head on a pillow on his lap and I was out in seconds.

Chapter - Nine

Shouts woke me the next morning and I was totally discombobulated. I shot up off the couch and ran to the foyer. I saw Danny wiping blood off his jaw and the boys holding a very pissed off Cosmo back.

"Your drama keeps getting her into these messes! You need to clean up your shit before you even think about marrying her."

Danny shook his head. "I know, alright? Don't you think I know that? Fuck, that's a mean right hook you've got there." I hurried to his side and he enclosed me into his arms. "Honey, I'm so fucking sorry."

I frowned over at Cosmo. He shook off the guys holding him and walked back into the great room. He was back in seconds with his wallet and keys.

"Cosmo," I called to him, but he stomped out the door. I let go of Danny. "Give me a minute." He nodded, rubbing his hand down his face. "Cosmo!" I hurried to catch up to him and when I did, I grabbed his arm. "Hey," I said.

His expression was pained as he looked down at me. "Jesse Baby, I can't stand the thought of you getting hurt. It pisses me off that you keep suffering for his bullshit. I'm sorry I hit him, but dammit!"

I put my hand on his chest. "Cosmo, I appreciate you staying with me last night. I'm sorry I took you away from your party."

He exhaled harshly. "It's fine. You know I'm always here for you. It just...You scared me last night. I don't like this feeling. I wish you were still home with us where I could watch out for you, but I know you've moved on. Just, please? Please be careful, baby. With him gone..."

"I will. I promise. No more Brooke. No more being alone here. Just, no more hitting him, okay? I kind of love that face of his."

He smirked, not quite laughing. "Tell him I'm sorry."

I raised an eyebrow, giving him my teacher look. "Why don't you come tell him? I don't want you to leave on bad terms."

He nodded, shoved his hands in his back pockets and followed me back in the house.

I left him and Danny alone and grabbed the other three to follow me into the kitchen. "How about breakfast?"

They all grunted and sat at the bar. I got some eggs and bacon going, making sure I didn't burn the bacon or undercook the eggs. Jinx grabbed juice for the others and Sam helped me serve up the food. Danny and Cosmo came in a few minutes later and they both sat down looking grim. I served them both plates and they ate without talking. This was not exactly the homecoming I expected from Danny. The tension was killing me.

"Guys, I'm going to go shower. If you're gone before I get out, thanks again." I hugged and kissed all the guys, taking a little longer with Cosmo. I looked to Danny, who was frowning and moving his food around on his plate.

"Danny?"

He looked up at me, looked to Cosmo, then back down at his food. "I'll be there in a minute."

Dammit. Well, I'd give him a few minutes to stew and beat himself up, and then he was going to have to deal with me.

I showered and dressed in a t-shirt and a pair of Danny's boxers, my favorite outfit, and waited for him to come in. Ten minutes later he dragged himself in and stopped in the doorway. I held my arms out to him and he just stood there. After a minute, he walked over to the foot of the bed on the opposite side from me and sat down with his back to me. *What?*

"Jesse, I think it would be better for you if—"

"Danny? Please just come here and hold me. You're tired from your trip and—"

"Jesse, I think you should move out. I'll set you up in a place. You will be safe and away from all this—"

"Daniel Adam Black!" That got his attention. He turned to look at me, his disgusted look on his face. "Don't you dare! You promised me—"

"And look how good I've been at keeping my promises! I promised I'd keep you safe and I brought this shit into our home. Twice! No. Goddammit, it's been three fucking times now! I'm not good for you, Jesse."

I groaned and stood up, stomping around in front of him to make him look at me. "Damn you, Danny! You need to get over it right this minute! What the hell did Cosmo say to you?"

He shrugged and looked down. "Only the truth. This is no kind of life for you. You deserve better."

I rolled my eyes. "Don't try to tell me what I deserve or what I need! I'm a big girl and I make my own decisions. I knew exactly what I was getting myself into when I moved in with you. We've had some bumps in the road, sure, but you promised me and I promised you that we'd work this out. Did you forget about that? And contrary to what Cosmo might have said, I was in just as much potential peril living in the apartment complex with him. He needs to keep his big mouth shut. Just you wait until I see him, that interfering, manipulative Neanderthal!" I heard a sniffle from Danny. He was trying not to laugh.

"You're scary when you're mad," he finally said, wiping tears from his eyes.

"You have no idea," I said, pushing him onto his back. I crawled on top and straddled him. "I'm tired, I'm angry, and I just want to make love to my fiancé, who I haven't even been able to properly celebrate with, and now he's trying to throw me out. Well, you can forget it, you obstinate, aggravating, pain-in-the-ass—"

He interrupted me by sitting up and trapping me in his arms. His kiss was desperate, his cries urgent. I wrapped my legs around him and pulled him as close to me as possible.

"Don't you push me away, Danny Black! I fucking love you, you jackass!"

His deep brown eyes met mine and held. "I'm sorry, Jesse. I was just so scared."

I held him to me and we just rocked for a moment. I took a deep breath. "Please, Danny, if you don't want me, don't—"

"Jesus, honey, I'm so fucking sorry. Of course I want you! I'm just a really big jackass. I'm sorry! Don't listen to me. Please don't leave. I need you." His pleas continued as he undressed me.

I needed to be close to him just as much. When we were naked, I didn't hesitate to take him inside of me. We both groaned as we clung to each other. He cried. He begged me to stay. He made love like a dying man using his last wish. I yelled at him some more, he apologized some more, and when we'd both exhausted ourselves, we collapsed together in a heap and fell asleep.

Hours later I rolled over to find Danny on the phone. "Thank you. Yes, I'll let her know. I will." I sat up and put my hand on his back as he hung up. "That was Brooke. She called to apologize to you and to let me know she'd be going straight from the hospital into treatment. She spoke to the cops already and gave them whatever information she could. The doctor told her she was drugged. She's so lucky you came home when you did." I rubbed his back and he exhaled harshly.

"I'm glad, too. I wouldn't wish that on anyone. But Danny? They stole the pearls you bought me. I'm so sorry!"

He cursed and then turned in my arms and just held me to him. "I'll buy you new ones, don't even fucking worry about it. Are you okay, though? You sure? I promise, no more. She's not stepping foot in this house again."

I frowned. "Danny, that's not exactly realistic. She will have to see Jane somewhere and it's better if it's in a safe place where you have control, right? Just no more overnights, please?"

He nodded. "I guess I better call Nora. Sonofabitch. How the fuck am I going to make this up to you both?"

I giggled and reached down between us. "I know what will work for me. I don't think this will work for Nora."

He definitely made it up to me many times that afternoon.

By evening he was taking and making calls to smooth over this latest disaster. We ate the food Nora cooked for us while he plotted his apology to her.

"Jesse, let's take her to Spain. Let's just fucking go. I'll be back from London just before Thanksgiving. Can we go then?"

I shrugged, taking a bite of chicken. "Why are you asking me? I'm just along for the ride," I said with a wink.

His expression was dead serious. "I'm asking you because I want to marry you in Spain."

I set my fork down and swallowed hard. "You want to get married. In Spain. In two weeks." I stood up from the counter and staggered over to the sink for a glass of water. I drank it down before turning around to face him. He looked nervous as hell. "Don't you think you have enough insanity going on right now? You really want to throw a wedding into the mix here? In the middle of touring and releasing your album?"

He stared at me for several seconds and then shrugged. "Yep! I'd take you right now, but we need Jane, and I still have to get back in Nora's good graces. That's going to take me at least a week. Plus, I need to let Roland know." He stood from his seat and just slayed me with his sexy swagger. When he got to me, he slipped his arms around my waist and pulled me against his naked chest. His lips quirked up in a delicious smile.

"Did I mention Roland is an ordained minister in the Universal Life Church? He's married lots of people." He ran his finger under the strap of my cami. Damn him and his powers of persuasion.

"You don't say." He pulled the strap down and nibbled my collarbone. "But what about our families?"

He brushed the stubble from his cheek against my shoulder, causing my already unsteady legs to go liquid.

"If you want your parents there, I'll fly them there. Roland lives in a fucking castle. Plenty of room."

I was quickly covered in goosebumps, clinging to him for support, and ready to buy whatever he was selling. He pulled my hair back and kissed me deeply, his tongue making luscious sweeps that had me panting. Before I knew it, I was naked and propped up on the counter like a damn Thanksgiving turkey.

"You actually expect me to make a decision while you are—Ah! Danny!" I felt him growl against my navel.

"God damn, do you know how long I have wanted to eat in this kitchen? I have missed," he nibbled lower, "my," and lower, "fucking," I cried out as he found his meal, "kitchen."

I could barely stand the attention he was giving my most sensitive erogenous zone. He continued to carry on in between licks and sucks about "perfect counter height" and "correct placement of drawer pulls," as he hooked my heels on said drawer pulls. I moaned so loud. I was completely out of control while he was absolutely in control. Master of his fucking destiny.

"OhhhhhhmmmmmyyyyyGOOOOOODDDDD DANNY!" What was left of the tension in my body after my eventful week flowed out in waves of supreme pleasure.

Danny stood before me and licked his lips groaning, "Mmmmmmm….My favorite dessert. Jesse with cream sauce." I burst out laughing and leaned my sated body against his.

And that's how I was persuaded to get married in Spain, to Danny, on Thanksgiving. My parents agreed to let Danny fly them. My mother cried when I told her, as much because her baby was getting married as the fact that she'd finally realize her dream to visit Europe. Danny's wedding gift to me was to send them on a 21-day cruise throughout the Mediterranean after the wedding. He and my father talked and that damn manipulative fiancé of mine convinced Jack Martin to quit his job

and move into a bungalow in the Los Feliz neighborhood with my
mother and go to work for Danny after their cruise. Danny had Patricia
set the whole thing up. She'd already bought the house at Danny's
request. He and I had seen it one afternoon while driving around and
he fell in love with it. We sent pictures to my parents and my mother
loved it just as much. Patricia hired movers to take care of everything
on both ends. I was deliriously happy about their move. I even spoke to
Mom about working at the studio part-time. She might not be able to
dance anymore, but she could certainly teach.

Once again Danny was making all of my dreams come true. The
only snag in this whole plan was Jane. Danny's beautiful, but troubled,
daughter was having a terrible time in school. She'd had detentions for
talking back to her teacher, had cut class, and was failing English. I
talked to her about it, but she'd just cry. Danny took her to see her
therapist so they could talk about it together and he found out that her
English teacher was always bringing up Brooke and asking questions
about her. It was Grace Manning all over again. Danny asked me to go
to the school with him and Jane to meet with the principal and this
teacher. The meeting did not go well.

"Mr. Black, your daughter needs to understand that she must be
respectful to her teachers, whether she agrees with them or not."

Danny tried very, very hard to control his temper. "Mrs. Temple, I
agree with you. But at what point does the teacher show respect for the
student's privacy? Honestly, what happens between Jane and her mother
is none of your business."

The principal, if I read her correctly, appeared to be on our
side. She sat back and only spoke up to referee a couple of times.

"Mr. Black. Students have to earn my respect and frankly, with
Jane's lack of skill and effort—"

"Look, woman! I've had about enough of you bad-mouthing my
fiancé's daughter! As a teacher, I am beyond offended at your high-
handed methods. Jane should be treated with respect. Period. As should
all of your students. And as for her skills, I can attest to the fact that she
reads way beyond grade level, and her effort? I have spent hours with

her working on the asinine assignments you give out! Do you have any idea how horrifically awful they are? How boring and unchallenging? And—"

"Ms. Martin, thank you. I think what would be best for all involved here would be to move Jane to a different English teacher. I will speak with the guidance counselor, Jane, and you can pick up your new schedule tomorrow."

Danny gripped my hand tightly under the table and I felt my face get hot as I stared daggers into this poor excuse for a human being.

"Thank you, Principal DiPaulo. We appreciate your time. I promise you that Jane will be on her best behavior and will try her best in this new class."

Mrs. DiPaulo smiled gently at Jane. "I'm sure she will. I look forward to reading your end of the year writing portfolio. I loved your poetry last year." She winked at her and then turned her attention to Mrs. Temple.

"Mrs. Temple, please remain here. I'm going to see the Blacks out."

I couldn't help but narrow my eyes at the beastly woman. It was all I could do to not stick my tongue out at her. When we got to the front of the school, Mrs. DiPaulo shook hands with us and gave Jane a hug.

"I'll see you tomorrow, young lady," she said with a proud smile.

I stalked towards the car, furious at that teacher's behavior. I may have been mumbling under my breath. When I got to the passenger door of the Challenger, I turned to find Danny and Jane trying desperately to hold back their laughter.

"What?" I hollered at them, still fuming. Jane snorted first, I think, and then they were bent at the waist, roaring with laughter until spittle flew from their lips. Jane caught a case of full-body-racking hiccups. I put my hands on my hips and felt my teacher face coming out.

"She said 'ass'," Danny snickered and Jane howled.

"Really, Jesse, is 'assnine' even a real word?"

I narrowed my eyes at them both and tried to be serious. It was a losing battle. "I can't believe you—"

Danny held up a hand and bent further at the waist, trying to catch his breath. "Don't, please. I can't take any more!"

I rolled my eyes and a giggle slipped out. Jane rushed over and gave me a big hug.

"Thank you, Jesse. It means a lot that you would stand up for me."

Righteous indignation flowed through me and I started to berate that sad sack of a teacher again, but Danny wrapped us both in his arms.

"Can we please just go get some ice cream? Or dinner? Whichever? I'm fucking starving."

Chapter - Ten

The fairytale wedding was to take place in Southern Spain near the town of Granada in four days. Roland Curtis was delighted we had chosen to have him marry us at his home. I had so many reasons to be nervous it was ridiculous. We weren't doing this fancy, just plain and simple. I decided to just wear my other crocheted dress that I'd bought before the last wedding. Easy. No muss, no fuss. We were set to fly to Spain in two days. That was the plan anyway. Then Janey got sick with mononucleosis, Nora threw her back out, grabbing the pancake griddle off of a high shelf, Legs got into some chocolate and had to spend the night at the emergency vet, and to cap it all off, some assholes broke into the studio and stole three of Danny's guitars. While they were trying to get away, they plowed into the Challenger and totaled it. To put it mildly, we were a mess.

"Fuck this fucking clusterfuck! All I wanted to do was marry my fucking fiancée on Thanksgiving and all of this fucking shit gets in the way!"

Danny was edgier than I'd ever seen him. I tried to stay out of his path the eve of our departure as he called Patricia and had her cancel everything; our flights, the car, the photographer, the pet-sitter...I felt awful for Jane. She blamed herself.

"Janey, you can't help being sick! You can't travel like this, sweetie. You know? When things like this happen, I always believe there's a reason. Who knows? Maybe our plane would have crashed, or someone would have gotten hurt, or for crying out loud, maybe I would have toppled off the cliff behind Roland's castle and dragged your father with me to a watery grave!"

That got Jane to laugh.

"Nothing has changed. Your father and I still love each other and we will get married when the time is right. All right? So no more worrying."

If only it was that easy to calm Danny. His "dick" persona was back. He bit everyone's heads off, with the exception of "his girls." I took over Nora's duties and giggled while they all ate my horrible cooking with gracious smiles over their grimaces.

"I know it's awful, I'm sorry. You don't have to pretend like it's good."

Danny was the first to snort. "Honey, you know I love you and I could care less if you can cook. But this? It tastes like ass. Like warmed over ass with a side of dead, rotting flesh."

I'd tried to pan-fry some steaks since I was less confident in my grilling abilities. Apparently the use of some sort of marinade or spices would have helped. It was all so intimidating.

Nora wiped her mouth and washed down her steak with some milk. "Jesse, maybe you should come to cooking class with me. Never mind. I'm not sure even cooking classes could help this. Sorry, sweetie, you should stick to dancing."

I barked out a laugh, but then Jane slammed her hand down on the table, startling us all. "You guys are so mean! Jesse tried hard to..." she broke off into a coughing fit.

I stood to rub her back. "Jane I'm not upset at all. I feel awful that you guys are eating this. I promise, I'll stick to Mac 'n' Cheese from now on."

She was not convinced. She defiantly continued to eat the disgusting meat while Danny and Nora continued to come up with colorful adjectives for how bad it was.

After dinner, Jane went to take a bath and Nora went to her cottage to take some pain medication and wait for Connie to arrive. Danny and I retired to the library and he turned on the fire. He was still angry. I could see it in his every jerky movement.

"Baby, come sit with me. Let me rub your shoulders."

He stopped in the middle of the floor with his hands on his hips, his shoulders bunched up. "How can you be so calm about this? Aren't you upset?"

I patted the couch next to me for him to come sit down. He hesitated before finally slouching and stomping over to the couch with a pout that would have rivaled a toddler's. I climbed up onto the back and had him sit on the cushion in front of me. I placed my hands on his shoulders, but I could barely get any purchase through his rock-hard stress.

"I'm very disappointed, just like you. But I just feel it in my gut there must be a reason we're here. For some reason we weren't meant to go to Spain right now and I'm ok with that. We'll go when we can arrange it."

"Yeah, but Roland is starting a new film and will be on location for the next few months. He won't be able to get away to marry us. And then the tour... Christ, I just want to get married!" He kicked his heel back against the couch and I paused my hands.

"I don't want you to take this wrong, Danny, but why are you in such a hurry? Aren't you happy just being together?"

He turned to face me and his expression was all over the place. "Of course I'm happy! I just want to prove to you that you're it for me. I just want it official. I don't want anything to take you away from me."

So that was it. He was feeling insecure. I pulled his face close to mine and kissed him with my eyes open. "Nothing is going to take me away from you. I don't need a piece of paper, or a wedding, or even a ring to make me feel bound to you. I love you, Daniel Adam Black. You're it for me. I'm certain of that. But it sounds like you aren't convinced?"

He exhaled a huge breath and dropped his head in his hands. "I guess because I felt this way before and—"

"And she left you. I know. You have all the reason in the world to be worried, but you don't have to. I know it will make you feel better to have that marriage license, but it doesn't change anything for me. Does that make sense?"

He turned and buried his face in my lap, his arms encircling me. He held me like that for a long time while I ran my fingers over his scalp. He sighed deeply and I felt the tension ease in his back. "You never told me what happened when you saw the lady doctor," he said against my thighs, so it came out a little muffled.

"The lady doctor? That's right! It's been a little crazy."

He lifted his head and gazed up at me. "So what did she say?"

I shrugged and continued lightly scratching his back. "About what?" I decided to play dumb. Danny narrowed his eyes at me.

"You know exactly what! Wait…She said yes, didn't she!" I tried my hardest to look innocent.

"Yes to what?"

Danny growled and pulled on my hips. "C'mon, Jesse. Don't tease me. What did she say about having a baby?"

I sighed and looked up at the ceiling. I answered him in a non-committal tone. "Oh that. Hmmm. She might have said it was okay, if I wanted to. She said you weren't too old." I pressed my lips together to keep from laughing.

"Are you fucking with me? Are you? Jesse?" I couldn't help it, a giggle slipped out. "She said yes? SHE SAID YES!!!" He buried his face in my crotch and shouted into my crotch. "SHE SAID YES! WATCH OUT, UTERUS, YOU'RE GOING TO SEE SOME ACTION!"

"Danny!" I should have known he'd freak out.

"Now we have even more reason to hurry the fuck up and get married!" He shoved his face back in my crotch and I fought desperately to get away from him. He yanked me off the couch and onto the floor with him. We rolled around wrestling for a bit until he had me pinned beneath him. His sly smile was making me nervous.

"Danny, please. She said we could, that it would be safe, but I'm still nervous, okay? And all this insanity? Let's just take some time to think about it, okay?"

He kissed me softly until I melted into him. In my brain, I knew I shouldn't relax, but he just had this way—

"I'll give you a reprieve...Until after the wedding. Then I'm throwing your fucking pills away."

My eyes popped open and I gawked at him. I should have known.

"You'd seriously do that, wouldn't you, you manipulative—"

More kissing. When would I learn?

I felt a yawn building up, so I tapped his shoulder. "Let's go to bed, baby. Tomorrow is Thanksgiving and I know tonight's dinner sucked, but I want to cook that turkey."

Danny pushed up and looked alarmed. "Please let me cook the turkey, honey. You can help with everything else, I promise. I just don't think I can take it if the turkey tastes foul. AH HAHAHAHA get it? Fowl?" He fell apart laughing. It was so infectious that I lost it, too.

I dragged him by the arm down the hall to the bedroom while he continued to throw bad puns at me. I shushed him. "You're going to wake Janey, you goof!"

The laughter subsided, however, when we got to the bedroom. He became quite intent on practicing his babymaking skills. I'll admit the fact that he was so excited about it had me considering the possibilities. I had so many things to be thankful for on this holiday.

Thanksgiving morning Danny was up before me and I heard him singing all the way in the kitchen. I hurried out there to see what I could do to help and found he had everything under control. We talked for a while before Jane trudged out. She said her throat was better and apologized again for causing us to not get married.

Danny swept her up into his arms and spun her around. "Beautiful daughter, nothing on earth will stop me from marrying Jesse. Nothing. I'm just going to have to put on my thinking cap and find a way to sweep her off of her feet and create another magical matrimonial mission."

"Lord, last night was the puns, this morning it's alliteration?"

He wiggled his eyebrows at me. I just knew I was in trouble.

We spent the day being lazy and watching movies in the theater. I was grateful Danny had a handle on the cooking because I was feeling pretty worn out from having to be the one in charge the past couple of days. We ate dinner early and were just sitting down to watch another movie when first my phone, then his, started buzzing. We looked at each other with concern

"JESSE! It's Cosmo…"

I didn't even hear the rest of Jinx's words. I flew out of my seat and ran for the bedroom. I dressed quickly and was just grabbing my purse when Danny ran in behind me to get his wallet and keys.

"Just let me tell Nora and we're out of here."

Danny drove the Range Rover like he would have the Challenger, which made for a harrowing ride to the hospital. We rushed into the ER to find Jinx and Patricia waiting for us.

"He's still in surgery. When the ceiling collapsed, it trapped his leg. They said he should heal from that just fine, but they're concerned about the burns and the amount of smoke he inhaled."

Slowly the story unraveled that the guys had been partying pretty hard the night before and Sam and Johnny hadn't slept. They'd been hanging out with a new group of guys who had them experimenting with stimulants of some kind. They'd been up all night and got the brilliant idea to try to cook a turkey. They put it in the oven without covering it and turned it on high. They left while Cosmo was in his room sleeping off his alcohol stupor from the night before. He didn't wake when the fire started. The alarm malfunctioned. Jinx was in my old apartment and his alarm went off just as the fire broke through the wall of the two units. Jinx barely got out with his life. He ran into Cosmo's apartment without thinking and was dragging him, unconscious, from his bed when the bedroom ceilings collapsed on both units.

I hugged Jinx tight while sobs racked my body. I couldn't believe my worst fear about that place came true. "I'm so glad you're okay," I whispered to him.

He had burns on his arms and face, but other than some mild smoke inhalation, he would be fine. Cosmo? They just couldn't tell us yet.

Danny sat with me and held me while I cried. Jinx held my hand and Patricia did her best to find out what was going on with Cosmo. She made sure Cosmo's family was contacted, so shortly after we arrived, the room was filled to the brim with shouting, crying Greek relatives.

"You must be Jesse," a striking woman in her fifties approached me with a sad smile. "I am Sofia Grammatica, Cosmo's mother."

My heart dropped. She looked like a shorter, more feminine version of her son. I pulled her into a tight hug.

"I'm so sorry," I whispered. "I'm sorry I wasn't there."

"He's a grown man, my dear. He made his choices. I just hope my son recovers from this."

She introduced me to several other family members who were alternately shouting angrily at each other and the hospital staff. I got the gist of what they were saying: It was time for Cosmo to get rid of that place, they should have let it burn to the ground, he needed to give up his nonsensical dream of this rock n' roll business...

I wanted to tell them all to go fuck themselves, that my best friend was in there and they needed to back the fuck off, but Danny held me to him and wordlessly warned me to bite my tongue.

"Jinx, do you have a place to stay," Danny asked quietly.

He shrugged. "I hadn't really thought that far ahead."

Danny put his arm around him and told him he'd be coming home with us. Jinx, I had told Danny earlier, had no family in the area. He was a runaway, just like Danny had been all those years ago. He was a hard worker, driving the delivery van for Cosmo's uncle's florist and gourmet food business. For the past four out of the five years I'd known Cosmo, Jinx had been part of the family, my little family. Now I was feeling even guiltier about leaving them.

Danny gave me a squeeze when the doctor came in to let everyone know Cosmo's status.

"He's going to be fine. He's waking up now. His lower leg was broken in two places and we had to set it with pins and rods, but it will heal fine. The burns on his back and neck should heal well. Most were only second degree. He's going to probably be the most angry about us having to cut his hair," the doctor joked.

"His hair?" I squeaked out. Oh no! That was so much a part of Cosmo.

"He'll be here for a few days so we can monitor him for infection, but he should be fine to go home soon."

Cosmo's mother thanked the doctor and followed him out into the hall. Jinx and I hugged each other.

"I don't know what I would do if he didn't make it," Jinx said, trying to hold back his tears. Jinx was normally such a joker. I knew he didn't handle this kind of stuff well.

"You'll stay with us," I reminded him. "We'll go over and get anything we can out of the apartments when you're well enough."

We waited until Cosmo's family had a chance to see him and then his mother approached us again. "He would like to see you, Jesse." She took my hand and I let her pull me up.

Danny motioned for me to go ahead. He was kind of supporting Jinx, who had fallen asleep against him. Poor kid. I followed Mrs. Grammatica down the hall and into the last room. Tears burned my eyes along with the many hospital's smells. Cosmo's eyes were closed as we approached. He coughed a couple of times and looked as though he was in pain. I took his hand gently in mine.

One of his eyes popped open. "Hey Jesse Baby."

I leaned over and kissed his cheek. He grinned, but it quickly turned into a grimace as he coughed again. "Don't try to talk. Your throat is a mess."

He nodded, and then both hazel green eyes opened wide. "I'm so glad you weren't there, baby. I—"

"I'm not! If I was there, this wouldn't have happened!"

He shook his head at me and put his other hand, the one with all of the needles and tubes in it, over mine. "No, baby. It's my fault. I should have gotten rid of those clowns a long time ago. It's just escalated since you left. They are totally out of control. I'm just damn lucky Jinx was next door. That guy…" He trailed off and took a deep breath, which brought on more coughing.

"You need to rest, Cosmo. We're taking Jinx home with us. You're welcome to stay when you get out…"

"Thanks, baby, for taking care of Jinx. I might go home. Or not. I don't know how long I can hear it from my uncles."

I knew he had a lot of reality to face when he was feeling up to it. I assured him Danny and I would be there for him however we could. He squeezed my hand and closed his eyes again.

"I'll come back tomorrow, and the next day and the next day until they finally let you out."

He grinned with his eyes closed. "Thanks, baby." He drifted off and I was glad for it.

I felt shaky when I thought about losing my best friend. I watched him sleep for a few moments before I went back to the waiting room and found Danny and Jinx talking quietly.

Danny stood and hugged me tightly. "I guess this was your gut feeling," he said quietly in my ear. I wanted to cry, but I was exhausted.

"Let's get you two home," Danny said to Jinx and I.

We said goodbye to Cosmo's family. His mother thanked me for coming and I told her I'd be back to see him the next day.

Jinx seemed reluctant to get in our car.

"Hey," Danny said quietly, putting his arm around Jinx. He spoke quietly to him and I watched Jinx nod a couple of times. They came to some sort of bro agreement and Jinx climbed in back. When I slid into my seat, I reached for Danny's hand and gave him a grateful smile.

We got Jinx set up in the spare room and Danny gave him some clothes to change into after he had a shower. Jane was filled in on what happened and she agreed to help take care of him. Danny called Patricia and they brainstormed ways they could help with this situation. Patricia had heard from the fire marshal. Everything was lost. All four units in that building were totaled. The rest of the complex survived relatively unscathed with just some smoke damage externally. It seemed that his uncles already had it under control. They had a cleaning crew coming the next day.

I spent the weekend visiting Cosmo in the hospital and shopping for Jinx at Danny's insistence. It seemed he'd taken Jinx under his wing. He got him to try to talk to his parents, who lived in Missouri, and they were thankful for the call. Danny said they seemed like nice people, but had no way of helping their son.

Cosmo was released to go home the next Wednesday with his parents. I arrived to visit just as they were getting him into the wheelchair to go home.

"Hey Jesse Baby! You're a sight for sore eyes." He may have spoken in his jovial way, but he looked miserable.

"You okay, Cosmo? Are you in a lot of pain?"

He shrugged and asked his cousin to give us a few minutes. "I'm in emotional turmoil more than in physical pain. I'm going to hate not having my own space, but it seems I'm going to be at the mercy of my mother and aunts for a while." He rubbed at his shaved head with a frown.

"Your hair will grow back, Samson," I joked.

He tried to smile, but I could tell he wasn't feeling it. It didn't reach his eyes. "I know. I just feel naked, and I'm not just talking about my hair."

He didn't possess his usual level of mystery and swagger. His confidence was hiding somewhere behind doubt and misery. I pulled up the chair next to his wheelchair so I could be on his level.

"Cosmo, I'm going to tell you what I told Janey about the wedding. Everything happens for a reason. Us missing our wedding happened for a reason. This fire, as awful as it sounds, happened for a reason. You have to look at it that way. Maybe this means there's something better for you?"

He looked out the window and I admired his profile. With his hair gone, he seemed much more stark and serious. His hazel green eyes had a far-away look to them under his thick, dark lashes.

"You might just be onto something with that, baby. I needed a kick in the ass. Getting rid of Sam and Johnny is my first priority, then selling the complex. My uncle already said he wants to buy it from me. I'm going to get a house where I can really focus on my music. I'm hoping Jinx will be on board. I don't want to lose him. I owe him my life and I intend to drag him along with me and see this through. Something is stirring. I can feel it. I need to embrace this opportunity, and I intend to. As soon as I'm back on my feet..." He trailed off like he was making plans in his head.

"We've got Jinx under control at our house. He told Danny he's going back to work this week, but I think Danny doesn't want him to."

Danny had been talking to Patricia about getting him some work doing music. He was an incredible bass player. It would be good for him to get a break. He worked so hard.

"Something is stirring. I have no doubt," he said in a really cryptic way. Maybe he wasn't as fragile as I had first thought. Or maybe it was the painkillers.

I gave his hand a squeeze, knowing his cousins would be back soon. "Is there anything I can do for you?" I asked.

He brought my hand up to his lips and kissed it gently with his eyes closed. "You already have. So when is the wedding going to be now? Spain would have been so beautiful. It's a shame you had to postpone."

We'd already been over this. I would have been devastated if we were gone when all of this happened.

"I have no idea. I think I finally convinced Danny we don't have to have a plan yet. Let's get through Christmas, for crying out loud, and his tour season next spring. Nowhere is it written we have to get married right now."

Cosmo laughed and gave my hand one last squeeze before letting go. "I don't know, baby. If I were Black, I'd lock you up until I had that certificate signed, sealed and delivered. Trust me. I already know what it's like to lose you." His laugh was incredibly forced.

I raised an eyebrow at him and he held up his hands in surrender. "I know. I'm just saying I wouldn't want anything to take you away from me if I were him." His eyes focused so intently on me, my breath caught in my chest.

This fire, the whole experience, it changed him. Cosmo on a mission was definitely going to be a force to reckon with. I just hoped he directed that force in a positive way.

His cousins came barreling back into the room fighting over who was going to push him out. Cosmo just gave me a sly smile and a "see you soon, baby," as they headed out the door. I watched them go and felt grateful I hadn't lost my best friend, although the Cosmo I watched leaving that hospital room was a new man.

Chapter – Eleven

Life was very busy, and a little lonely, with Danny on the road. The band toured the first three weeks of December. Danny came home exhausted. He spent the first two days resting his voice, hugging on Janey, and watching me longingly. At night... Well, if I'd thought he was a beast before. He was insatiable. I had to tap out a couple of nights. He took it pretty well. Mostly.

"But honey, I've only got two weeks, and Christmas is in a few days and... CHRISTMAS! Let's get married on Christmas! I'll have Patricia—"

"Danny," I sighed. I'd only just started my own break from teaching and I just wanted to sleep. I'd been trying to sleep before he woke me at two a.m. to apparently plan our wedding. "Let Patricia rest. Let's just rest. Jane's been really tired. I'm still trying to get Jinx to rest, but he's not only working, he's visiting Cosmo every day and they're working on music. We have enough chaos. Give me until after Christmas, please?"

He pouted. "Fiiiiiinnnneeee. But I want to marry you, honey! OH! We're going to be in Vegas for New Year's! Is it too cheesy to want to get married in Vegas?"

I glanced at him over my shoulder. He was leaning over me with eyes all crazy. I rolled onto my back and his hands started to roam.

"Danny! Babe. I gotta get some sleep. We were up all night last night and I had to get up early to—"

"I'm sorry. I am. I just can't keep my hands off you. Do you know how many times I thought of you in those fucking hotel rooms?"

I did, actually. He'd texted me in the middle of the night at least four times during the last leg of the tour. They'd played dates in major cities on the East Coast before coming home two days ago. They had two sold-out dates in Vegas planned for the 29th and 30th.

"Vegas? Really? What about Jane?"

He shrugged. "Nora can stay with her for a day or two after. Shit. I forgot to tell you. Nora's going to Spain after all. I'm sending her for Christmas. Patricia will stay with Jane. It'll be fine. It's perfect! We have the two shows before, we'll get hitched on New Year's Eve, and then we'll just stay for two days after that and have a little mini-honeymoon until I can take you somewhere nice. I don't think we leave on the bus until like the second week in January.

A bus. Ugh. "You guys will be careful on that bus, right? You guys have a good driver?"

He smiled at me wickedly and used those big, talented hands to position me right where he wanted me. I loved it when he manhandled my hips.

"I'll be fine. We're safe. We have an excellent driver. So Vegas. I can dress like Elvis, and you can—"

"What? Are you still trying to—Ahh!"

Danny was on his knees. He'd yanked my hips up to where my ass was pressed against his thighs and entered me in one thrust. He pulled me tight against him.

"Come on, baby," he pleaded, slipping into a very King-esque drawl. When he started singing to me, I knew I'd do whatever he asked. He slid a hand up my spine lifting me to face him. "Come on, honey. Come for me," he panted, then resumed his singing.

He was in such good shape that he kept up his rhythm without missing a lyric. I collapsed against him and let him continue to move me against him. He was so powerful, our lovemaking so raw. He made my body sing for him. He continued to emulate The King while I exploded in rapture over and over. He was relentless in his ministrations. It wasn't until I bent down and used my teeth to tug on his nipple rings that I felt him start to tremble. I'd learned that if I wanted to get any sleep, I sometimes had to resort to these tactics. Not that I didn't enjoy him thoroughly. I just needed to get rest so I could continue enjoying him. My reward was watching him completely lose himself inside me. He'd learned to kiss me as he came to muffle his screams. Most of the time.

"Please, Jesse. Please," he moaned as his body ceased its trembling. His hands cradled my face. His eyes implored me. "Please say yes."

That damn gimme smile. I rolled my eyes. "Fine. I'll marry you in Vegas. But I want a Priscilla bouffant hairdo then! You have to find me someone who will pile all this stuff up on my head until it's the biggest damned beehive you've ever seen."

He laughed heartily, his hands caressing my back. "Whatever you want, honey. I fucking love you so much. I can't wait to be married to you."

Chapter - Twelve

Danny called Patricia the next morning and set the wheels of chaos in motion. She called me directly after hanging up with him to ask me if I was ok with all of this.

"Frankly, I don't know. He kind of…He, um, sort of… Well, he kind of asked me under duress." The other end of the phone was silent for a few beats.

I heard her sigh. "Jesse, if you aren't up for this—"

"No! I am. I want to. I just…I don't really want to make my parents come to Vegas. They just got back from their trip and are trying to settle into the new house and Dad's new job." Danny and I insisted they go ahead and take their scheduled vacation even though there was no Spain wedding. They'd had a wonderful time and my mother glowed with excitement when we picked them up from the airport.

"Give them a call. See what they think. I'll hold off the beast for a few hours."

We laughed together for a while. I hated to admit it, but I was starting to get excited about the idea. Spain would have been breathtaking and beautiful, but Vegas…I hadn't been there since my dancing days. I'd done a couple of shows there. I just remembered there wasn't a lot for me to do because I was underage at the time. Now? I'd heard about the spas, the shows, the food…

I called Mom next and she was tickled.

"A Vegas wedding! That man of yours, Jesse. Of course we'll come. Then why don't you let us take Jane home afterwards? We'd love to have her for a few days. She hasn't spent the night over here yet, and last time you guys were here, I noticed her eyeing our spare bedroom. She gave that whole room a once over like she was—"

"She does that. Alright. If you guys are sure. I, um, believe it's going to be a themed wedding." I filled her in on Danny's plan and she laughed out loud.

"Oh, can I make your father dress up, too? He does a great impression of Elvis's pelvic—"

"MOM! I don't need to hear about his pelvic region!"

We spoke for a few more minutes and I told her Patricia would likely call her with travel arrangements soon.

Vegas. And I'd finally get to see a Blackened show! I managed to get that added to the plan once Patricia assured me that The Joint at the Hard Rock would be a fine place for Jane to see her father rock out. When I told Jane, she squealed with delight. She frowned a bit when I told her about the Elvis theme for the wedding. Danny won her over with his gimme smile and it was a go. He also promised, we'd have a proper reception at home once they finished their winter tour at the end of February. They'd be off for the month of March, play the festivals in April and May, and then head to Europe in June. I tried not to think about it or I would freak out.

I went to see Cosmo before we left and told him of Danny's crazy plan. He listened intently, but his smile was faked. It was probably better he wasn't up to coming. I wasn't sure how much more he could take of my happiness with Danny. I promised him we'd send him pictures and video. He assured me he'd be fine. Later on I talked to Jinx and he assured me he'd stay with Cosmo. Jinx also graciously agreed to take care of Legs while we were gone.

Brooke was still in her treatment program, but she'd been calling Jane every Sunday. The first few conversations were very brief. At least they were starting to communicate. Danny and I watched Jane closely after their conversations. The day before we left they spoke and afterwards, Danny got on the phone with her and told her our plans. When he hung up, he seemed off.

"Danny? Did that go ok?"

He shrugged. "I guess. It was a little weird. She cried and said she loved me and wanted us to be happy. What the fuck did she have to go and cry for? I'm just going to chalk it up to her being a mess in rehab."

I hoped he was right. Bronson's warning to me months ago was still fresh in my mind.

Nora, Jane, my parents, Patricia and Max and I all flew together in a private jet to Las Vegas on the morning of Blackened's first show. The guys went a day early to supervise all of the setup and, I found out, to plan a surprise bachelor party for Danny after the show. Bronson promised me it would be tame and told me not to worry.

"He'd kick our asses if we hired, uh, professionals. Nah, we're just going to take him to a club we know and listen to some good music." He filled me on some embarrassment he had in store for Danny. Bronson apparently had some things to get him back for.

We took a limo from the airport to the Hard Rock, which was off the strip. Danny and I had a two-room suite we shared with Jane. My parents and Patricia and Max also had suites on the same floor. Jane and I geeked out over the décor.

She wandered around looking at the pool table, the furry pillows, and the bar. "Daddy, I don't think this is a kid kinda room."

"I hope they cleaned up all the condoms," he stage whispered.

Jane shouted at him. "That's disgusting, Dad! Ew! Just stop!" She stomped off to her room and I had to tame my beast.

"You better behave! You also better get going. You guys have sound check in an hour and you need to—"

He pulled me into an embrace and bent me back in a dip. He kissed my neck and attempted to make his way down the front of my dress.

"Daddy!"

He pulled me up quickly and did some kind of weird dance moves before scooting over to Jane like Angus Young with his guitar. She balked and started to turn back into her room.

"Oh relax, babe. I'm just excited! Aren't you excited?"

She nodded, looking fearful. "You are so weird."

Jane and I had dinner with my parents at the Hard Rock restaurant across the parking lot from the hotel before the show. Dad was looking forward to seeing Blackened play. It was surreal hearing him talk about music and getting "pumped" and "stoked" for some "kick-ass rock 'n' roll." I was waiting for a "far out."

After dinner, I wanted to freshen up before the show, so I left Jane with my parents and went up to our room. As I exited the elevator, I heard raised voices.

"Are you fucking kidding me? Now? You're going to—"

"I'm sorry, Patricia. I knew you wouldn't understand."

"Then make me understand! You don't just walk out after ten years with no explanation!"

I had turned the corner and there was no way to escape detection. I gave them a nervous smile. Max was really red in the face. Patricia was red all over. I could see her chest heaving as she fought back tears of anger.

"I, uh, was just coming to freshen up. I'm sorry."

"Oh, it's almost time! I've got to get to the venue." She turned on Max with a fury I hadn't seen from her before. Not even when we had our Melrose Showdown with Her Hungarian Highness, as the incident had been dubbed. "We will continue this later." She turned on her four-inch red heels and stomped towards me, one plump curl bouncing under her chin. She threw her shoulders back and smiled at me. "I'll see you downstairs. You've got your passes? You're ready?"

"Absolutely."

She was back to business, but I made a mental note to check in with her later.

I changed into some jeans with blingy stuff on the butt that Danny really liked, and a matching black tank I'd picked up earlier from the hotel shop. I still didn't have much in the way of rocker wear. I did, however, have my black cowboy boots that I was dying to slip into. I left my hair down and applied just a little bit of makeup around the eyes and smeared my lips with sparkly, dark pink lip gloss. Then I giggled. I was going to see my boyfriend's band play. What kind of bizarre world had I landed in? That I was marrying into? In less than forty-eight hours!

The show was beyond amazing, beyond anything I could describe adequately. All four of "the guys" rocked their hearts out on that stage. The Mannings often seemed reserved to me when we hung out, but not on stage. Bronson prowled around like a dark shadow to Danny's fire. Julian threw off so much sexual energy, it was a miracle that more bras and panties weren't thrown, or that more of them didn't spontaneously combust. Alex was a major clown behind the drum set. He smiled the whole time like he was the happiest kid on the playground. These four men, who had become so important to me, were larger than life. I thought maybe they'd seem like strangers up there, but their personalities were just amplified, uninhibited. Bronson and Julian sang backing vocals frequently, which I guess I hadn't realized since the times I visited the studio, they were done recording. I loved the way their voices supported Danny's, just like they were always there to support him in life.

Jane and I watched the show from the side stage, while my parents sat in the luxury box reserved for guests of the band. Patricia flitted around back and forth between the box and backstage, making sure everyone had what they needed. She was on top of everything, but I was still worried about her.

I couldn't see Danny interacting with the crowd much from where we were standing. I guess I'd been worried he would see all of those women out there and decide I wasn't enough. But it wasn't really like that. He did catch my eye a few times and he grinned bashfully, as though he was worried about what I was thinking. The rest of the time I mostly had a view of his backside. And oh what a backside! Completely in his element, he was the epitome of male beauty and sensuality. I couldn't wait to get him back to our suite.

Jane loved the show. She rocked out next to me, singing along to all of the new songs. She was still learning their back catalogue, thanks to Brooke, who wouldn't let her listen to his music. She'd even learned to play a couple of the new tunes on her guitar and sang along. The first time Danny heard her sing one of his songs he shivered. Later he told me it freaked him out how much she sounded like him and wondered if she would want to start singing. He wasn't quite sure how he felt about that. But watching her having so much fun, I was beginning to see a future with music in it for our little Janey.

Ours! Oh! The wedding. I got lost in thought for a bit thinking of all the things we still needed to do for the wedding and kind of missed the rest of the set. The next thing I knew I was being swept up in a pair of strong, sweaty arms.

"I can't fucking take you being over here," Danny said close to my ear over the din of the crowd that was still shouting for more. "Let me do this encore and then I'm going to make you come so many times tonight, you'll likely lose feeling in your legs." He set me down hard and backed away, licking his lips.

"Ok, that was soooo gross."

Oh my God. Jane. "Oh, honey, I'm—"

"No. Don't be sorry, just, GOD, does he have to maul you like that? And he's so… ew!!!"

I totally laughed, feeling a little relieved she hadn't heard what he said. Then she'd really think he was "ew." The band played two more songs and then bowed together on stage. Danny pulled off his shirt for the encore, making it all the more necessary to fan myself. I couldn't even remember what songs they played when I tried to think of it later on the phone with Nora. My parents were brought backstage and they took Jane with them. That left me alone with the band and the crowd that was beginning to form of people who wanted a word, an autograph, a picture or a handshake.

Danny was super gracious to everyone, but his eyes let me know he already had me undressed in his mind. I could almost feel his hands on me as I watched him sign a young guy's t-shirt on his back. All the times he shook hands with people I imagined those hands playing me…

"Jesse, can I go over some things with you for tomorrow?" Patricia was standing next to me with her phone out and her calendar pulled up.

I shook myself. I'd been close to a fucking orgasm just from watching my fiancé. What the hell was wrong with me? Was this what I had in store for the rest of my life with him? Sign me up!

"Huh? I'm sorry. I—"

"I know. He fills out a pair of jeans well. Anyway, I need to take you and Jane to get fitted for your dresses tomorrow. Bronson is taking care of all of the guys for me, thank God. Then tomorrow night we've got the show and then the guys are going out afterwards. Did you want—"

"God, no. I need sleep. I don't think I've had a full night's sleep since..."

"He got back from tour. Got it. Don't need to hear the details." She was being sarcastic, but not really humorous.

This was not the same woman I'd grown to consider my close friend. I knew she wasn't right.

"Patricia? Are you okay?"

"What? That? In the hall? That was nothing. I'm fine. Totally fine. I'm on this. We need to get your dresses, then I wanted to get you into a spa to get pampered and get your nails done while your parents take Jane to see Cirque du Soliel."

"Oh! You were able to get them tickets. I know they'll love it."

Patricia nodded and went back to flipping screens on her phone. "Alright. I've got some things to take care of, so you get your ass back to your room and tell him I said not to keep you up all night, got it?" She kissed my cheek and stormed off.

Oh no. I was so shaken with worry for her that I barely paid attention to the conversation on the way back to the room between Danny and Jane.

"I really liked the way you guys changed up that bridge on 'Shelter' and the chorus on 'Fly' was so cool the way Uncle Bronson and Uncle Julian sang those dueling parts while their guitars harmonized."

"Jesse?" Danny tugged on my hand hard. "Honey? Are you with us?" My ears were ringing a little, but this time I heard him.

"Were you talking to me? I'm sorry."

They looked at each other and laughed out loud.

"Uh, you have the room keys," Jane snickered.

I narrowed my eyes at them. I was used to them ganging up on me by now, but I couldn't let them get away with it.

"Excuse me! I was just so engrossed listening to you accomplished musicians." I made fun of them a lot, especially now that she was getting to be quite proficient and showing very promising talent on the guitar. The two of them together… Overwhelming.

"I'm going straight to bed after I shower. Uncle Alex hugged me and got sweat and God knows what else on my new shirt. I can't even!"

Danny took that moment to rub his sweaty hair all over her back, causing her to squeal and run to her room. He laughed and called out "I love you" to her closed door. She answered back that she loved us. At least I'm pretty sure that's what she mumbled.

Then, I was in trouble. Danny made good on his promises. I could barely walk when I woke up.

The next morning Danny ordered a huge breakfast delivered to our room and everyone came over to eat. We all talked about the show and the day's plans. The guys had sound check again and they needed to get their outfits lined up for the wedding. This morning would be the last time I saw Danny until the wedding the next day. My stomach was doing jackknives and three-sixties and all manner of extreme sports. I thought I was hiding it pretty well, but Danny pulled me aside before he left.

"Honey, you look terrified. Are you okay with all of this? I know, Bossypants and all that shit, I kinda forced the fucking issue."

"I'm not going to lie. I'm scared to death. It has nothing to do with you. It's more like, will I trip and fall on my face? Will I put the ring on the wrong finger? Am I even going to be able to speak coherently?" I gulped hard and spoke in a low voice. "Am I going to be able to make you happy? Keep you happy? Will I be enough for you?" I offered a weak smile.

Danny pulled me into his arms and kissed my hair, heaving a big sigh. "I worry about the same things. Will I be able to protect you? Will I be able to be everything you need? Will you still need me, will you still feed me when I'm sixty-four?"

I pinched his side. Hard. "OW! Fine, I'm just saying I know what you mean and I think the answer to all of those questions is yes. Yes, we'll be happy. Yes, it's going to be tough sometimes, as we've already seen plenty of, but we can make it. We will make it. I fucking love you, Jesse Martin Black, and I'm going to spend the rest of my life loving you."

His gimme smile looked different to me this morning. He seemed different. It was like now that it was really happening, that we were in the place where we were going to be married and everything would be ready, he could finally relax. I thought having the show tonight would help calm him down a bit. He really got into a zone when he performed. Maybe because he was in his element.

"You can't call me that yet," I teased. It drove him crazy every time I corrected him.

He rolled his eyes and kissed me once more. "Fine. But I'm going to say it over and over once we're fucking married. Hell, I think I'll even get it tattooed! Damn! That's a great idea!

All I could do was shake my head as he shouted to Bronson that they needed to find a tattoo parlor after the show. "I'm getting my woman's name tattooed on me."

"Danny!"

It was useless. He was on a roll. About an hour later the guys cleared out to go take care of their stuff and it was time for Jane and I to go get fitted for our dresses. I had a picture of what I wanted and Patricia said she knew a private collector who would have the perfect dresses for us. Danny and I lingered in the doorway, just staring at each other.

"I know you'll be at the show, but I'm going to miss being with you tonight. Do we really have to follow that rule?"

"Yes, we do. There's enough unorthodox activity around us already. Let's at least observe a few wedding dos and don'ts, shall we?"

He cursed wedding conventions under his breath before kissing me one last time. "I'll meet you at the altar, baby," he drawled, curling his lip just like Elvis.

"Have a great show. And a great party. You guys have fun."

He hesitated for a minute. "You sure you okay with it? I could come back here... I'm sure I'd enjoy myself a helluva lot more." His hands started getting frisky so I pushed him out into the hall.

"Go! I love you," I said, holding my pendant to my chest.

He grabbed the leather cuff on his arm and said, "I fucking love you, Jesse."

Eight hours later I dragged a groaning and moaning Jane back to the room. "I'm so glad this is going to be over tomorrow. No offense, but if Patricia made me try on one more dress I was going to throw up on her shoes!"

I tried not to giggle at her incessant complaints. I knew she hated shopping. At least she enjoyed the spa. "I know it was terrible for you, and I'm sorry you missed the Cirque du Soleil show, but I'm so grateful to have you as my Maid of Honor."

She turned to look at me then from where she'd plopped on the couch and she beamed at me. "Thank you for asking me, Jesse. I love you." I hurried over to her and we hugged for a long time. "Just don't make me do this again. At least not for a while."

She went into her room to get ready for the concert that night and I took a moment to calm my heart down. It had been pounding out of control all day from the moment I first saw myself in 'The Dress.' Oh, it was perfect! It was a replica of an actual dress Priscilla wore. It had a loud black and white floral pattern, an A-line hem that hit me incredibly high on the thigh, and a boatneck collar that I knew would show off my Teacher pendant just perfectly. I opted for knee high white go-go boots with a heel that would make me taller than Danny. I knew he wouldn't mind. I couldn't wait to see what he came up with for clothes. Him and the rest of the guys.

I showed my mother when they came to pick us up for dinner and she laughed. "You're getting married in that crazy thing?"

"It's perfect, don't you think? You have met my fiancé, haven't you?"

She rolled her eyes. She had been concerned about Danny in the beginning, but learned to love him like everyone else in his life. She just worried about me. I don't think she completely trusted him, and that was hard. I trusted him as much as was humanly possible. We'd been through so much together. I had to trust him. To not trust him would mean living a miserable life worrying about what he might be doing when I wasn't with him, which could be a lot of the time.

I had to admit, while I was lonely when he was on the road, having that peaceful time to myself without the insanity he brought into our lives was kind of a reprieve. I didn't prefer it to the monster that was Danny, but it was necessary for my well-being. Like the trust.

We ordered room service again because Jane was so tired she'd fallen asleep for a bit. When she woke, she just wanted something quick. It was weird for me to be spending this kind of money and charging it to the room, but I figured I'd let Danny have his fun for this whole wedding gig. When we got home, I'd start being difficult again.

Watching the show from the luxury box was even more surreal than being backstage. It was hard to accept the fact that I was going to be marrying the guy on stage. My heart was still racing, and it didn't help watching him strut around the stage. A few times he slung his guitar back and moved about the stage interacting with the crowd. The screaming was so loud, the women so crazy for him… Could I really handle this? As they wrapped up the show, I asked my parents if they'd take Jane back to the room for me.

"I just need to see him," I said to my mom.

She smiled, a knowing look on her face. Jane was yawning so big. I knew she wouldn't complain. I made my way to the entrance backstage and showed my VIP badge. They let me back without questioning me and I prayed I could find the area where we met up with the band the previous night. As I turned a corner, I saw Danny leaning against a wall talking to a woman. He was leaning in close and smiling that handsome smile. I couldn't see her hands. I kind of saw red for a moment and lost control of my feet, which marched me right up to the two of them.

"Honey," Danny said, grabbing me around the waist and yanking me to his side for a sloppy, sweaty kiss. He smelled like beer. Guess they were starting the party early.

"I just…" I ran out of steam. I stared at him like an idiot and couldn't say anything.

He gave me a confused look and then turned us around. "I was just talking about you. Jesse, this is Sammara Gunderson. Sammara is from Feedback Magazine. She's the reporter I told you about that's going to do the feature on me. Sammara, this is my fiancée."

I looked down on this curvy woman. She was about my age with short, black hair in a stylish bob, and pale skin. Her eyes were kind of spooky, as if she could *see* things. Danny squeezed my side, hinting that I should actually take the hand of the woman in front of me.

"I'm sorry. Hi. It's nice to meet you," I got out, feeling like a complete heel.

"No problem. I know you guys have a lot going on. Danny, I'm going to find Patricia and set up our dates, okay? Thanks for the show. You guys sound even better than on your last tour, and I didn't think you could top that. Glad the surgery worked out."

He shook hands with her and she said goodbye to us. "Goddamn, that was sexy. You came storming up here like you were ready to throw down and protect your fucking property. I fucking love that, honey."

I pushed away from him, embarrassed by my behavior. "I don't know what I was thinking."

"You saw me with another woman. I get it. Don't you think I want to break the legs of every guy I see you talking to? Do you know how hard it is to watch Cosmo put his hands on you? Fuck, Jesse. I totally trust you, but you're so fucking beautiful. It's rough, man. I'll tell you that." He approached me slowly, sliding his hands around my waist.

"I just…Wow. I'm such an idiot. I know you would never—"

He shut me up with a passionate kiss, the kind that made me want to wrap my legs around him and never let go. He turned my back to the wall and deepened the kiss, so much so that I was ready to tell the guys to go fuck themselves, that I was taking my man back to the room with me. But Danny pulled away.

"If I don't stop…Jesus, honey. I want you so fucking bad right now. That's just going to make it that much sweeter tomorrow night. Look," he said, pulling out his phone. "It's eleven thirty. We're getting married at two o'clock tomorrow. That's just fourteen-and-a-half hours from now. I can wait if you can." He leaned down a little to make eye contact with me.

He was so... He was everything to me. And we were getting married.

"That much sweeter," I whispered. My heart finally calmed. This was happening. We were getting married. "Okay. You go have fun with your boys. I'm going to get some sleep before the beauty brigade shows up in the morning. I'll see you at two o'clock."

"It can't get here fast enough," he said against my lips before pulling away.

We watched each other as he backed down the hall away from me. I gave him a finger wave and he clutched his chest in mock pain. When I couldn't see him anymore, I finally turned to head back to the room. I figured as wrung out emotionally as I was at that point, I could sleep like the dead.

Incessant knocking at the door woke me the next morning. Shit! It was after ten. I'd totally overslept. I pulled on a robe and ran for the outer door to the suite.

"Finally," the woman said as she pushed past me with her roller bags. "First Patricia doesn't answer her phone, then you make me wait in the hall."

I had one pissed off hairdresser in front of me and no Patricia. "I'm sorry. I thought Patricia would be here. Please excuse me for a minute," I said, feeling out of sorts. I saw there was fresh breakfast laid out so I figured she'd been here. I frowned. "Help yourself to some food," I slurred, then walked over to Jane's room.

"Janey, sweetie. Wake up. We overslept." Jane sat up with a start. Her red hair was all over the place.

"Where's Patricia? I thought she was coming to wake us up."

I was already headed out to find my phone. I picked it up and skimmed through the "I fucking love you" texts from Danny that seemed to get drunker and drunker as they went on. But no messages from Patricia. I called, straight to voicemail. I texted. Nothing.

"Young lady, I need to get going on that hair of yours or there will be no wedding. Get that dress on. You're not pulling it over my 'do!'"

I did what Francine ordered, mostly out of fear, and prayed Patricia would walk through the door soon. I took a quick shower, keeping my hair from getting wet, then I dressed in my black satin undergarments I wore the night of the dinner party at Danny's parent's house, figuring he'd finally get to appreciate them. I left the garter belt off, but I'd picked up a black garter. It was barely covered by my dress when I walked. No hope in hell when I sat down.

Maxine raked the brush through my hair, then proceeded to tease the shit out of it until it was about nine times its normal volume. She used so much hairspray I thought I'd have a chemical burn. Her assistant rolled in shortly after and got to work on my makeup. Dramatic black eyeliner and false eyelashes were applied after some thick foundation. Pale pink shimmery shadow and matching frosted lipstick finished off the look. Jane stumbled out and gasped when she saw me.

"Holy... Wow! Is that really what women looked like back then? Because OH MY GOD is my dad going to shit a brick—UH! Sorry. I mean he's going to be so surprised."

She and I cracked up, but Maxine wasn't about to let us start having fun. It bothered me that Patricia still hadn't called or showed up so I walked over to the room phone and called her room. Finally, someone picked up.

"Max! Hi, it's Jesse—"

"She's gone," he said, cutting me off. "She, um, she came in and found... She's gone. I don't know where." He slammed the phone down.

"What the hell?" I instructed the hairdresser to get started on Jane and then called my mom. "Patricia is missing. Can you come sit with Jane and then you can go next? I need to find her."

She said she and Dad would be right over. I texted Danny what was going on. I threw my flip-flops on and was out the door with just my phone in my hand.

I searched the hotel from top to bottom when finally she called. "Jesse," she croaked. "Jesse, I'm sorry. I can't do this." She sounded terrible!

"Do what? Sweetie, where are you?" I stopped in the middle of the casino floor and looked around. Where the hell could she be?

"I left last night. That bastard. After ten years... Ten years! And he does this? I didn't need to see that."

"Patricia," I was starting to lose her to tears again. "Please tell me where you are. I'm coming to you."

She sobbed some ugly sobs on the other end of the line, and then pulled herself together. "I'm on the Strip. Bally's. I'm getting drunk and then I'm going to blow all of his fucking money on craps, and NO ONE IS GOING TO STOP ME!" She hung up on me.

Holy shit. I dialed Danny.

"Honey, what's going on?" He sounded like I'd woken him up. Good. That meant he slept.

"It's Patricia, baby. Something bad happened with her and Max. I'm going to Bally's to find her." I burst through the front doors and went outside. I hailed a cab and climbed inside. "I'm going after her. You just make sure everyone gets where they need to be, okay? Keep your phone handy." He started to protest as I hung up.

It only took a few minutes for the cab to arrive. "Oh no! I forgot my wallet! I'm having a bit of an emergency here. See, I'm supposed to get married and our coordinator is missing and—"

"Jest go, young lady. Leave the fare at the front desk for meh." The little old man smiled at me, only a little fiendishly.

"Thank you, so so much!" I got out of the cab and froze. It was fucking December 31st in Vegas. There was snow on the ground. I was in flip-flops and a short dress.

"Motherfucker," I cursed as I fled toward the doors of the Sports Book at the back of Bally's. I slipped and slid my way up the walkway, teeth chattering as I got inside. I hurried over to the craps area, ignoring the looks I was getting from people.

"SNAKE EYES, BABY! DADDY NEEDS A NEW SEQUIN DRESS AND PUMPS," I heard over the din of people. A large crowd was gathered around a table near the center. I elbowed my way through the people and gaped at what I found.

There, in all of her drunken glory, was the beautiful red-haired Patricia. But not the all-business, kick-ass-and-take-names Patricia. No. This Patricia had her hair down, was wearing just a slip of a black dress, the one she'd worn to the concert last night because she was planning on having Max take her out afterwards. She had kicked off her heels and one of her straps was hanging down. Her ample bosoms were dangerously close to making a public appearance.

"Patricia," I called as I approached her.

Her eyes locked on me, but it took her a minute to recognize me. "Priscilla," she shouted, then grabbed me into a hug. "You look amazing! Where's Elvis?" She snorted loudly and cackled. "He's probably getting blown by some drag queen. OOPS! Sorry! NO, that would be MY husband." She laughed hysterically as she threw the dice again.

The crowd all cheered, which I guess meant she did something right because money started changing hands and bets were placed on the table. The casino guy slid the dice back over to her, his eyes catching mine in warning.

Shit. "Sweetie, why don't we just collect your winnings and go talk somewhere? You can tell me what happened."

She pushed me away from her and stumbled, then got back to work with her dice, blowing on them and kissing her hands before throwing them down the table. More screams and cheers.

"Dammit! No, I am not leaving this spot until I lose all of his fucking money! I'm not about to let him blow it on cheap men wearing dresses nicer than the ones in my closet." She hiccupped and stumbled again.

A casino manager approached us with security. "Ma'am, you're going to have to step away from the table," he said sternly.

Patricia raised an expertly drawn eyebrow at him and stepped back into her shoes. "But I'm not ready to leave yet, SIR." Then she turned towards the table, reached in, and scattered the chips everywhere, taking out people's stacks on the ledge. She barreled through the crowd whooping in victory towards the doors leading to the Strip.

All eyes landed on me. I gave a nervous laugh, and hightailed it out of there, trying desperately to catch up with her. As drunk as she was, she could still run pretty damn fast in heels.

I caught up to her on the sidewalk, where she was laughing hysterically. She slipped on a piece of ice and started to go down, but a nice older gentleman caught her.

"You're so sweet," she said, kissing his cheek and leaving a red smear in her wake. He laughed and shook his head. Patricia then turned and started down the street mumbling under her breath about rhinestones and hairnets.

"Patricia! We've got to get out of this cold," I said through gritted teeth. I grabbed her arm and pulled her into the next hotel, Planet Hollywood. "Let's just sit down and you can tell me what happened."

"I don't want to sit down." She threw off my arms and stormed over to the roulette table. She yanked open her black purse and rained money down on the table. "Put it all on black," she hollered, laughing loudly. The guy at the table looked nervous and I saw him make eye contact with security.

Double Shit. "Patricia, we really have to—"

"Alright, ladies. Let's take a walk." Before I could get a word out, four burly guys in suits had each of us by the arms. They dragged us out of the casino area and through a semi-hidden door. Patricia fought them off as best as she could, but these guys were strong. I knew I was going to have bruises and my heart sank as I realized that yet another wedding was not going to be happening.

"We don't allow working girls on the casino floor. You two must be new in town or you would have known that."

Patricia stopped fighting and just burst into more hysterical laughter. I tried desperately to explain, but the casino security guy wasn't listening to me. They carried us through some back doors to a waiting patrol car. Then I really dug my heels in.

"You're making a terrible mistake! We're not—"

"You have nothing on you, unless you carry your ID in your g-string," the guy said, patting me on the ass before shoving me head first into the patrol car. Patricia was likewise dumped in and she landed on top of me, ass in the air. The guys made some more lewd comments before the patrol officer got into the car and started to pull away.

I shoved Patricia off of me. She was now bawling loudly. "Officer," I said as calmly as I could. He ignored me. I tapped on his glass gently.

"Ma'am, back away. I don't want to have to taze you."

What the fuck was going on here? I could see on the dashboard that it was one forty-five. I'd lost my phone somewhere along the way and Patricia's purse was back at the roulette table. Danny was going to have a complete cow! I slumped back in my seat and felt tears well up in my eyes.

I don't even remember how long it took to get to the police department. When the door opened, I looked up at the officer and said, "Can you please let me speak to—"

Patricia took that moment to empty the contents of her innards all over my beautiful dress. She heaved and heaved into my lap as I held her hair for her. The cops scrambled for towels or something to clean us up with. They slid on rubber gloves and grabbed garbage bags before yanking first me, then Patricia unceremoniously out of the back of the car. Some tech guys went to work cleaning up the mess. They left me a puke-stained, tear-streaked mess.

"I'm sorry, Jesse," Patricia moaned. "I'm so sorry I messed up your day. Danny's going to fire me, and he should. I have ruined everything for you, for him, for Blackened—"

"What did you just say?" One of the cops stepped closer to us and handed her a tissue. "Did you just say Blackened?" I looked up at the guy. He was a tall, lanky guy who looked a little young to be a police officer.

"She did. She's their manager."

He broke into a huge smile. "That's awesome! I just saw them the night before last. They were amazing! So you two aren't prostitutes, then?"

I shook my head. "Nope. Not at all. I'm actually a teacher." I lost my balance with Patricia leaning against me and the guy caught me before we all fell, getting covered with puke in the process.

"I'm sorry," I said, feeling totally dejected.

"If you'll just call the Hard Rock and ask for William Tell, you'll reach Danny. He'll clear this all up—Oh! Shit, Jesse! They're already at the chapel. Never mind."

"Ma'am, I am sorry this all happened. Is there someone we can call for you?"

As he spoke to me, the earth just crumbled out from underneath me. I landed in a heap on the ground, covered in vomit, freezing my ass off, and still not Mrs. Danny Black.

Chapter - Thirteen

We flew home from Vegas the next day. The police finally agreed to not press charges on Patricia for making a scene at the casino. Danny had to pay a huge amount of money to cover my ruined dress, the hairdressers, the bill for the hotel room, where Maxine and her assistant proceeded to order a bunch of food, clean out the minibar, take some "souvenirs" from Danny's tour gear, and generally wreck shop. Luckily Mom had taken Jane back to their room to wait everything out. Jane cried when we told her the wedding was off.

When Danny arrived to pick us up at the police station, I could barely look at him. I felt so disgusted by the whole event, but I was nowhere near as wrecked as Patricia. Danny slept in Jane's room that night, while Patricia and I cleaned up in ours and I held her while she cried late into the night.

See, the night before, after the show, she'd gone back to her room to grab Max, but he wasn't there. He'd left her a note saying he was sorry, but he couldn't live the lie any longer and he wanted a divorce. Patricia went out in search of him with no luck. She returned to the room in the wee hours of the morning and found him in the most graphic of positions with a male dancer from one of the drag shows. It was pretty clear the lie he was living was that he was really gay and he wanted to be with other men. Patricia railed on and on about how she should have known when he begged her to go with him to see Barbra Streisand, or when he insisted on getting a membership at that exclusive gym in West Hollywood. She was beating up on herself, which I tried to stop, but then she howled about how she'd ruined everything for us when Danny was her best friend and she was so ashamed...

I let her run out of steam and then I crashed hard. In the morning light she had back some of her business sense. She held a meeting with the band and told them they should fire her. When they absolutely refused, she said she was going to take some time off. She apologized profusely to my family and to Jane before leaving on her own. She planned to rent a car and drive back, said she needed time to think. Max had cleared his things out of the room and was long gone.

Danny and I hadn't spoken much. He had the disgusted look on his face every time I tried to apologize. The flight was short and quiet. The limo ride was even quieter. Danny held my hand, but didn't speak.

We got a surprise when we arrived home. Nora had returned, but had a guest with her. It seemed she and Roland's current personal assistant had more than hit it off. She took one look at our faces, introduced us quickly, and then took Jane with her to her cottage so Danny and I would have some time alone.

He carried our bags to our room and set them gently inside. I sat down on the edge of the bed and put my head in my hands.

"Did you want some food? Do you want to sleep?" He walked over and sat next to me, leaving space between us. I stared long and hard at that space.

"Danny, I don't..."

"You don't have to say anything. I'm the one who's sorry. But seriously? How the fuck was I supposed to know that Max was going to get a blow job from a drag queen? I mean, come on! I've known the fucking guy as long as I've known Patricia. When I see him, it's going to be really fucking hard not to put some dents in his skull, that's for sure. It was just shitty timing, I guess."

He had a half smile on his face. I turned to face him.

"Please call me Jesse Martin Black or Mrs. Black or something to let me know that you're not mad at me and that—"

"Jesse! How could you even... Son of a..." He took me in his arms and stroked my hair as I cried on his shoulder.

"I wanted you to carry me across the threshold when we got back! I wanted to go down to DMV with our marriage license and change my name! Why, dammit?"

"Shhhhh, honey. It's okay. It's going to happen. I promise you we're still getting married. We kind of have to now. Look."

Danny lifted up his shirt and across his left pectoral was tattooed in beautiful script "Jesse Martin Black." An infinity symbol was interwoven through the letters. It was still angry looking because he'd just gotten it done, what, two nights before? Was it two?

"Oh, babe! You did it." Seeing it tattooed there just made me cry harder. He held me and kept whispering silly things to me about how Max was going to hate all the shit he'd have to go through to become a drag queen. When he used the term "tucking," we fell back on the bed together and I let myself just breathe him in.

"You promise we're going to get married?"

He nodded against my hair. "You bet your gorgeous fucking legs we are. Just…No more Elvis. And no more Vegas. I don't want to see that fucking place for a long fucking time!"

We agreed to come up with a new plan…Later. After we'd rested, after Patricia was back and feeling better, and after the tours were over.

Chapter - Fourteen

2014

The new year sure came in with a roar. But after Vegas, we slipped back into life like nothing had changed. Danny gave up his obsession with getting married, but thankfully he didn't give up his obsession with getting busy with me. We had so much fun when he was home from tour. I was grateful. I worried he would mope. I worried the other shoe would drop. It took a while for me to stop flinching every time the phone rang.

Things had definitely changed, though. I rarely saw Nora. She and Amalia spent most of their time out and about or holed up in her cottage. She still cooked and took care of business, but I missed our chats. One night towards the end of March, Nora sat down at the table where I was grading papers.

"Jesse? Can I interrupt you for a bit?"

She never really talked to me like that. I was already nervous. "What's up?"

Jane had gone to bed with Legs an hour before. I was just trying to get my work finished so I could enjoy Spring Break. I put everything aside and folded my hands in front of me.

"Amalia wants me to come to Spain with her. Roland will be home for the next six weeks before he starts his next film. I want to go." My heart jumped a little. How was I going to make it without her? We had a nice little rhythm, her, Jane, and I. Sure, Danny was coming home, but...

"Is this for good, or..."

"I don't know. We want to have a commitment ceremony. We want Roland to officiate it."

"Oh, Nora." I jumped up from my seat and wrapped my arms around her.

She laughed and cursed my crazy-ass tears. "I'm not going to be gone forever. Calm down. We might split our time between here and Spain."

"It's not that. I'm just so happy that you are happy. Nora, I just want you to be happy." She smiled at me and I was taken aback at how much younger and carefree she looked. Love had quite an effect on her.

"I just don't know what to do. I don't want to leave my home, my family, you guys…This is the hardest decision I've ever had to make. But she can't be here full-time, not yet. I know our marriage could happen, but then there's a green card, and—"

"Nora, weren't you the one who told me to go with my gut and do what felt right? You love her. Do you have any doubts about that?"

She shook her head and her eyes welled up. "Not a one. I know it's been fast, but she gets me. We're just. Yeah. Happy."

"Yeah. We'll be fine. We'll miss you like crazy."

We hugged for a few more moments before she pulled away and collected herself. "I can recommend someone to come in and cook, you know, so you guys don't starve."

I swatted at her, used to being the butt of this joke. "We'll be fine. We'll figure something out. I suppose you and Danny will need to sort things out."

Her smile slipped a little. "I hate to disappoint him."

I knew what she meant. "He'll get over it. Your happiness comes first."

She thanked me and kind of scooted out of the room before she really started to cry. I hated that she had to choose like that. Once it sunk in, though, I kind of started to panic and my heart felt heavy.

Danny came home two days later and the two of them had a heated conversation. He was disappointed but did a good job of hiding it. He was more concerned with whether or not this woman was going to be good to her. He told her he wanted her to keep her cottage there for at least the rest of the year, until she'd really made a decision. He wanted her to have her home to come back to if things didn't work out.

Amalia didn't talk much to us because of the language barrier. She was painfully shy as well. She was younger than Nora, perhaps by a decade or more, and was breathtakingly beautiful with long dark brown hair and huge brown eyes. She cooked for us a couple of nights and Danny raved about her paella. Alex was there that night and had a very intense conversation with her in Spanish, which I had no idea he could speak so fluently. Later on he reassured us that he felt this woman was the real deal and that she truly loved Nora. That made Danny feel better about the situation. When they left in mid-April, we gave them a good send off. We'd all pretty much come to accept her absence as possibly permanent. Except Janey.

Janey didn't talk much in those last two weeks Nora was home. She asked to go to the ranch more so she could be with Misty, and she avoided being alone with Nora. She barely talked to me except to fill me in on her school adventures. I worried how she would handle Nora's absence. They were so close. I hated that another person was leaving her, but she needed to understand that this was a part of life, and that Nora wasn't going to be gone for good. I got my opportunity to talk to her about it about a week after Nora and Amalia left. Ivana and I had planned to take the girls to a movie, but Janey told me when I picked her up from school that she just wanted to go home.

"Are you sick? Do you not feel well?"

She just huffed at me. "Do I always have to tell you everything? Jeez. I just don't want to go, okay? Is that alright?"

Her attitude shocked me. She'd never spoken to me like this. "Jane," I started slowly. "I would just like to know what to tell your friend and her mom, that's all. You know you don't have to tell me everything, but I hope you know you can tell me anything."

Her scowl lessened. She gazed at me with her baby blues. "I'm sorry." She began bawling in earnest. I pulled over and took her hand in mine.

"I don't know what's wrong with me! I miss Daddy. I miss Nora. I feel like you're the only one who's there for me right now, and I'm sorry I yelled at you."

I leaned over and kissed her forehead. "I'm sorry, Jane. Your father can't help his schedule, but I know he wishes he could be here more. You know you can call him anytime, right?" She nodded pushing her red locks behind her ears. "What about Sasha? Can't you talk to her?"

She rolled her eyes. "All she wants to talk about is Gabriel. Ugh! I'm so sick of that name! I hope when I finally get a boyfriend, I'm not as stupid as she is. She makes me sick."

I snorted. "Wow. Okay. I can only imagine she talks about him a lot? Gets all mushy when she thinks about him?" I held back my laughter thinking Jane should be used to this since her father and I were like this all the time.

"It's just, really? He's a boy. He's a dumb boy, even. He sags his pants and acts like he's all gangster. Dude, bro, you live in Beverly Hills, not Compton!"

I spit out the water I was drinking all over the dashboard. She'd developed quite the sarcastic wit and regularly had me in stitches. She carried on and on about her poor best friend and her "bae."

"Oh, Janey. I really hope, for your sake, that Sasha has more patience when you experience your first crush, because, whoa."

She laughed with me. "You're right. I guess I'm just jealous. I don't think boys will ever ask me out."

I patted her hand. "Jane, you are so beautiful and smart that I'm sure they are all intimidated. Plus, there's your dad. What about the boy that was here at the Halloween party?"

She blushed and bit down on her lip. "We text a lot. His name is Carson. But I don't know if he likes me for sure. He has a band. He says he wants to play guitar together sometime." She told me all about young Carson Riley for the remainder of the drive. We seem to have crossed a bridge, one I knew we'd revisit from time to time. It was up to me to be there for her no matter what.

In all of this insanity, my health had remained better than ever. My pain was completely manageable and I had a lot more flexibility in my joints, especially in my hands and feet. I was dancing more and more with the kids at the studio and I felt great. Jane was still taking classes, but she'd decided to only do it through the summer. She was going to be joining a team at her barn to compete in equestrian events in the fall. She'd need to practice four days a week and there would be shows at least one or two weekends a month, with travel involved. I was beginning to worry that trying to handle Jane's busier schedule without Nora here would be too much for me and thought perhaps I needed to take a leave from teaching the next year. It was just a thought in its infant stage, but one I planned to discuss with Danny.

God, I missed him at times like this. He wasn't due home for another two weeks, and then only for a weekend before heading out for the month of May. He'd pop in maybe three days altogether for that month. Blackened was headlining the World's Loudest Month festivals all over the Midwest and southern states. The album was doing fantastic and the guys were flying high, excited to be at this peak in their career. I heard Blackened tunes everywhere I went. It was crazy. My students asked about it a few times, but I never discussed much more than to say yes, we were engaged and no, I didn't know when we were getting married.

Cosmo was finally getting around pretty good. He and Jinx were living together in a house out in Malibu. They'd decided the beach was more their speed and the ocean was "inspiring some deep grooves, baby." Legs and I visited them occasionally, but the chicks in bikinis hanging around were a bit much for me to tolerate. It seemed the party had followed them, even if they weren't drinking or using any drugs of any kind anymore. They both agreed to stay clean after their near-death experiences. Sam and Johnny were long gone. No one had heard from them. Danny assured them that he would help them shop around their demo when they were ready.

Patricia had taken a few months to get herself back together, and when she returned to Slade, she told them she wanted to focus solely on

Blackened. She needed to ease back into it and didn't want to be chasing the little boys all over the globe that kept getting thrown at her. She was just so good at what she did. They all wanted to work with her. She started to spend more time at our house, eating dinner with us and just hanging out like "a normal girl." She was fast becoming the best girlfriend I'd ever had. She had even smoothed things over with Max.

"How can I stay mad at the guy? If he wasn't getting off getting *me* off, then he needed to go find someone to get him off, right?" It had taken her a while, but her healthy outlook was impressive. I didn't think I could be that forgiving.

All of this chaos, or normal everyday life in the Blackenedverse, made time go by so quickly. Before I knew it, it was the end of May and school was almost finished. One morning I woke up and just realized that hey, I'd been a part of Danny's life for a year. A whole year of my life had gone by in the blink of an eye. And oh what a year it had been! So many surprises. So much love. So many changes. It was a Friday morning and I had nothing on the agenda today, except to maybe do some grading, but that didn't appeal to me right now.

I walked through the library and decided my desk needed some uncluttering, a task I often did when I was avoiding paperwork. I picked up a stack of books to return to the shelves and as I made my way across the room, the top two slid off. The one left on top was now Romeo and Juliet.

Memories assaulted me of reading the play to Danny and Alex over on the couches near the fire last summer. Danny and I were both struggling with our feelings for each other at the time so we'd needed Alex to chaperone. Ours was a forbidden love...Just like Shakespeare's characters experienced. Luckily the obstacles standing in our way were fairly easily overcome: Janey's approval, my job, Danny's Mr. Bossypants persona. We'd had a rocky road during our second act, during which we almost let our fears and other people's opinions tear us apart. Once we committed to each other, we gained the strength to fight. Our final act remained to be played out. Would we finally have our fairy tale wedding and live happily ever after? Or would we be doomed like Romeo and

Juliet? Morbid thinking had no place on this sunny morning. I picked up the books and slipped them back into their places on the shelves lovingly. I was not about to dwell in the dark when Danny and I had so much light.

Speaking of light, the day was much too nice to be hiding indoors with deep thoughts. I wandered out to the backyard to have some cuddle time with our enormous puppy. She joined me on a lounge chair, meaning I had barely any space for my legs, and we both sighed happily.

My cell phone rang and I picked it up with a smile. "Hey, baby." I always looked forward to calls from Danny. I hadn't seen him in a week and he and "the guys" weren't due back for another few days. I believed. I had a hard time keeping track of his schedule when he was on the road. Hearing his voice yanked on that tether between us, no matter how far away he might be.

"Honey, I need you to do something for me," he said hurriedly.

I sat up from the lounge chair, kicking Legs in the behind in the process. "Oh, sorry girl." She was so huge now. At a year old, she was one hundred and twenty pounds of scruffy looking love. I scratched behind her ears and kissed her nose. "What do you need?"

I walked into the house as I listened to his instructions. "Grab the copy of <u>Riders on the Storm</u> off the shelf in the library. I need you to take it to Roland at Universal. He's seeing Robbie Krieger this evening and he wants to have it autographed."

It seemed kind of silly that Roland would go to all of that trouble, but Danny had told me what a huge Doors fan Roland was. Since Robbie was the only surviving member of the band, I supposed it was a sentimental gesture.

"Now, you're going to have to take the studio tour to get there. Just let the driver know you need to get off at the spot where the offices are. Tell them you are going to meet Roland. It's too late for me to get you a pass to get you onto the lot through the regular means. Just hurry, okay? Roland was very insistent he needed it and I hate to keep him waiting."

Danny was acting so weird! He didn't even say "I love you" before hanging up on me. I shook my head. "Well, Legs, looks like I've got a mission. You hold down the fort."

We'd installed fencing around the pool and the back of the property so that Legs could have free range through the backyard. She even had her own entrance into the house. It made me feel so much safer with Danny gone. I'd refused his security guy at the house full time, but I knew his guy, Bob, patrolled out front. I'd seen him. One night I even brought him coffee, which he thanked me for, and we talked for a long time. He made me promise not to tell Danny he wasn't being inconspicuous. It was our little secret, as were the several other nights I took him food and drinks to keep him from being too bored on his long shifts.

I grumbled about having to change out of Danny's boxers and t-shirt and slipped into one of my new dresses Patricia had pushed me to buy the last time she took me shopping. The hem of the ivory dress was just short of knee length with embroidery on the bodice. I threw my hair up into a bun and added a dab of eye makeup just so I didn't look tired. My skin was very tan from all the time I spent in the backyard with Janey and Legs. I used sunscreen, but this was the darkest I'd ever been. The Vitamin D was good for me.

I drove quickly but safely to Universal Studios, trying not to get too irritated with the traffic at this late morning hour. I arrived at ten thirty and used my season pass to get into the park. I walked through to the back where the several-story-high escalator took me down to the bottom level where the studio tour was. The park was not very crowded today since most of the kids were still in school. I was able to walk right up to the front of the line.

"Excuse me," I said to the attendant at the front of the line. "My name is Jesse Martin and I'm supposed to meet with Roland Curtis. My fiancé, Danny Black, told me to take this tram to the offices"

"We don't stop the tour for visitors to get off. You'll have to call and make an appointment."

I frowned. I clutched my bag with Roland's book a little tighter. "I promised I would get this to Mr. Curtis, is there any way you can—"

"Ma'am? If you want to ride the tour, you'll ride the whole tour. Do you understand?"

Wow. This woman was good. But my teacher voice was tougher. "I understand. Thank you for your assistance," I said tersely.

The gates opened and I walked up to the tram, thinking I might be able to speak to the driver. Unfortunately, I was elbowed out of the way by a group of tourists from Germany or the vicinity. There were about ten of them and they were all talking loudly and laughing as they cut in front of me and took up the two rows between the driver and me.

I growled in frustration and tried to figure out what to do. The screens at the front of the tram came to life and there was Jimmy Fallon doing a very goofy introduction. A very friendly-sounding young woman took over the tour guide duties, but I couldn't see her well from where I was sitting.

"We will be passing through the set of a pilot being filmed today, so be sure you watch for my cue when it's time to be quiet." She chatted amiably about the history of the tour and all of the most recent films being shot there on the lot.

Our tram wound its way through warehouses and then we passed the cute bungalows where I was supposed to get off. I even saw a sign marking Roland's parking place. I contemplated jumping off, but didn't want another run in with security or police. Vegas had been enough for me, thank you very much. My life of crime was over.

The guide's cheerful voice was starting to really grate on my nerves. If she pretended to be surprised by one more thing, I was going to snatch the mic out of her hand and beat her with it. I leaned back against the seat and groaned as we made our way onto the water where Jaws was about to come up and snap at the German tourists' unsuspecting feet. They all whooped and hollered when the shark came up and cheered wildly.

The next stop was the set from the Grinch film, the brightly colorful buildings now dirty and gritty like a ghost town. It was a little creepy in the daylight. Around the next bend was the Bates Motel set, but the tram stuttered to a halt before we rounded the corner of the building.

"I'm sorry, folks. It seems like we have a special guest on this tram. Is there a Jesse Martin on board?"

Startled, I looked around before raising my hand timidly. The guide smiled brightly and said, "Wonderful. Everyone say hello to Jesse." I was greeted in German, Spanish, and even Japanese by a group in the back row. I waved to them all and then looked back at the guide with a puzzled expression.

"Miss, would you please come with me?" Another guide was now standing at the side of the tram. His hat covered his face, but his build seemed familiar.

I took the hand and stepped down off the tram. I looked up into Cosmo's face. "What are you doing here?" I asked in a whisper. The giggling on the tram and the curious voices had me feeling really uncomfortable.

Cosmo took my hand and wrapped it around his arm. "Right this way," he said with a wink.

His hair had grown into a mop of curls that framed his face, but right now it was tucked under a silly looking Safari hat. He walked me down the dusty trail a bit to the edge of the building where my father stood, dressed in the same silly uniform, smiling brightly with a bouquet of roses in his hand. He pulled me into a hug, not holding back his strength. I felt something pop in my back.

"Dad! What the heck is going on here?" He handed me the flowers, I looked to Cosmo for explanation, but he just grinned.

"Come on, Jess. Danny's waiting."

All the breath whooshed out of my lungs. The flowers. Danny's weird call. Roland here at Universal.

"That little shit is throwing a surprise wedding?"

My father laughed and tugged on my arm. "Come on, now. Let's not keep your groom waiting at the altar. He's been in a panic all morning."

Cosmo stepped around the building and the next thing I heard was the wedding march being played on two guitars. My feet were stuck in cement. I felt my palms sweating and my heart racing.

"Daddy," I squeaked out nervously.

Dad leaned down and kissed my cheek. "You look beautiful, sweetie. I'm so happy for you." He had tears in his eyes as he tugged once more to get my feet moving. We rounded the corner of the building and there, in front of the dilapidated Bates Motel set, was my family. Mom, Jane, Nora, Amalia, Patricia, Jinx, Rebecca, "the guys," and my devilishly handsome fiancé dressed in black slacks and a white dress shirt. An arbor had been set up with flowers intertwined in the latticework and Roland stood in the middle on a raised step. My dad led me down a path marked by a roll of artificial turf.

My face hurt from smiling so wide. This was it. We were finally going to do this. I was going to marry Danny. As we approached him, my father started to shake. I looked up into his strong face and was shocked to see him falling apart.

"Daddy?"

"I can't help it. You're just so beautiful and grown up." He wiped at the tears with a laugh and hugged me tight again. I had to tap out in order to get some oxygen. He apologized and reached over to shake hands with Danny. "I don't even have to say it, do I," he warned.

Danny shook his head. "No, sir." Then those warm, brown, heavenly eyes descended on me and there they stayed throughout the entire whirlwind that was our ceremony.

I vaguely remember Roland talking about the Universal Life Church and how honored he was to be officiating our wedding. I think he talked about meeting Danny, but I was completely dumbstruck staring at my soon-to-be-husband. He'd gone to all of this trouble and had put together the most perfect wedding we could ever have had. Forget breathtaking Spain, or wacky Vegas... Our perfect wedding was in front of a historic movie set where horrors and camp were so well known. It was us. We'd been through horrors, we had plenty of camp, and I hoped our love and marriage had the staying power of the Alfred Hitchcock classic. I just prayed Danny didn't develop a taste for women's clothes.

"I do," I said suddenly.

Danny's eyes bugged out and he laughed, looking to Roland for help. "Darling, we haven't gotten to that part yet," Roland said softly.

"I don't care," I said, squeezing Danny's hands tight. "I just want to say it and let it be real. I don't want anything to stop us this time."

Danny's eyes watered. He stepped closer to me and put his hand on my waist. He leaned in and whispered in my ear, "Nothing will stop us, but I have some things I want to say and I've got this ring and everything, so can I just—"

"I'm sorry," I said, feeling my cheeks flush. "Go ahead."

He proceeded to recite the poem he'd written for me almost a year ago, but this time it had a different ending.

CAGES

We all live in cages
some are solid, some imagined
Some keep us in and hidden
some keep us from what we've been given
To break free one must hold the key
but if we don't know what it is
then how can we see?

My cage is right here
mine is patient, mine is loving
finally with all I could desire
a family was all I desired
To break free I had to find my key
I found it in you
And now I am free

For this cage protects
It is safety, it is home
This cage surrounds us
It will always be a part of us
And together we are free

I gasped at his words. If I'd had any doubts that this man loved me completely, they were gone now.

Roland looked at me and spoke. "Jesse, do you have anything to say?"

I smiled nervously, remembering the vows I'd written for our last attempt at this before tossing them out of my head. "I do. Danny, you've had my heart and soul for some time now. Today, I give you my life, for better or for worse. I give you all the breaths I have left in me, all of the remaining beats of my heart. I give you my all, as you've given me, from now until the end of time. I love you, and I'm so grateful we made it to this moment together."

Danny closed his eyes, perhaps to pull his emotions together. He squeezed my hands and spoke as he opened his eyes. "Thank you, honey."

All that was left to do was exchange the rings and then Danny was on me before Roland could say, "You may now kiss the bride." It was a whole body kiss that I felt all the way down to my toes. He held my body against his as he claimed my lips along with all of the rest of me that I'd offered up to him. The cheers and roars were much louder than just from our little crowd. Cringing, I pulled my lips away and looked to find six tour trams lined up along the road, all witnessing my marriage to Danny Black. The applause was almost as loud as one of Blackened's concerts.

"Oh my God, Danny," I whispered, mortified.

He pulled me tighter, took my lip between his teeth and grunted. "I can't wait to get you out of here." Snickers and whispers surrounded us.

"Ladies and gentlemen, I now introduce you to Mr. and Mrs. Daniel Adam Black."

The cheers grew louder as another tour bus rounded the corner. Out of the corner of my eye, I watched in horror as a man stepped from the office of the hotel carrying a wrapped object shaped like a...

"Yes! Do it, man!" Danny raised his fist and gave the horns to the Norman Bates look-a-like as he loaded the body in the trunk of the car and drove off in a cloud of dust. Everyone clapped and cheered when they saw Danny's Challenger parked on the other side of Norman's classic car. The Challenger had writing all over it and trails of tin cans strung from the bumper. Danny swooped me up into his arms and started running for the car.

"Aren't we going to say goodbye?" I joked.

Danny cursed. "No fucking way am I putting you down. Nothing is getting between me and my happy place, God dammit!"

I laughed as he tossed me unceremoniously in the car. I caught Janey's eye and mouthed, "I love you. Thank you," to her.

She mouthed it back, gave a thumbs up, and then turned into Nora's waiting embrace. The last thing I saw before Danny pulled away with a roar of his engine, was my parents in an embrace and my father kissing my mother sweetly.

Epilogue

Cosmo

I watched the only woman I'd ever loved drive away with her new husband. I remembered what she'd said about everything happening for a reason. Didn't mean I wasn't going to drown my sorrows in about a dozen beers tonight on my deck overlooking the Pacific Ocean. Jinx and I agreed tonight we could put our sobriety on the shelf and toast the newlyweds, but in a mourning fashion. I'd finally made Jinx stop telling me what was going on over at the house while he stayed with them. Recovering from a broken leg while mending a broken heart was hard enough without his constant updates shoving more hot pokers in my chest.

I'd done the valiant thing. I'd let her go, even though every bone in my body was screaming for me to drive over there, sweep her up in my arms, and carry her away from all the bullshit in Danny fucking Black's life. She'd hate me, but whatever. It would be easier than worrying about her all the time. But once they got serious with this wedding talk and I saw how miserable she was after two failed ceremonies, I had to let her go. She was seriously in love with the dude, and all I wanted was for my Jesse Baby to be happy.

The rest of the crowd climbed on to the trams to finish the tour and head over to the Dresden, where the newlyweds were supposed to make an appearance, but I was over it. I was just about to climb onto the rear of the tram so I could sulk in peace when I noticed Patricia standing off by herself, her arms wrapped around her middle.

The redhead was all class. She'd been phenomenal in arranging shit for me and Jinx, despite everything falling apart with the Tragedy. She'd even helped me find my house out in Malibu, which I really wanted to get back to after stopping to pick up a case of whatever beer caught my fancy. But something was off with the lady, and I felt an urge to soothe someone else all of a sudden, although I had no fucking clue why. I walked over to her and just stood, waiting for her to speak. When she did, she continued to stare off in the distance.

"He'll take care of her, you know," she murmured.

I grunted. It was as if she was reading my fucking mind. I looked down and saw her eyes were watery, but her perfect makeup hadn't run. Maybe she was trying to hold it in with that death grip she had going on.

"You want to go get drunk?" Her question caught me by surprise. I looked around to make sure it was directed at me. "Yes, I mean you, Cosmo. You look like you need a beer, and you're probably the only other person here besides me who can't be totally excited for the lovebirds."

Ah. Her dumbass husband. Patricia had had a rough time of it. I can't even imagine how I would have felt if I walked in on what she did. He'd done her dirty, that's for fucking sure.

I wrapped an arm around her and squeezed. "That sounds like a perfect end to this day."

She nodded and took a deep breath. I started to say I needed to tell Jinx, but he'd already found a skirt to get under, some chick on the tram who already had her fingers in his hair. I smirked and then looked down at Patricia. I was immediately lost in her blue eyes. There was so much pain and longing there, feelings I recognized in my own heart. I couldn't help myself. I brushed a thumb along her cheekbone and took a deep breath.

"Let's get out of here," she said in a husky voice that grabbed me by the balls. Things were about to get interesting, and I for one was going to let the lady drive...In her little red Corvette...To wherever the night carried us.

The End... Of this trilogy. Stay Tuned for More Rock n' Romance!

Acknowledgements

My family members are my biggest supporters and have made it possible for me to share my brand of crazy with all of you. Thanks to my husband, children, Mom, Dad, and sister for always being there when I needed a kick in the ass or a big hug.

I'd like to say a huge thank you to Bob Houston, the most patient, kick-ass formatter on the planet, for all of his patience. He and Yosbe, the designer for the print editions of my books, were so wonderful while I clumsily made my way through this new journey.

My amazing writing partners, Ellay Branton and Kimberlie L. Faye, were instrumental in keeping me sane while I worked to get this book out. Their encouragement, knowledge and patience are invaluable in my writing process. I don't know which of the Fates decided to put them in my path, but I'll be eternally grateful.

Thank you to my friends in the Indie Author community for your continued support. I consider myself blessed to have you all in my life.

To my beta readers, those who have been with me from the beginning, and the new ones I've recently come to call friends, thank you for the use of your eyes and for allowing me to corrupt, I mean, entertain you with my tales of Rock 'n' Romance! Thank you for always being available to check over some crazy idea no matter the time frame or task. Without you I'd be nowhere.

To the Sexy Rock Goddesses of our Street Team…You ladies are always there to support us, be it with pictures of yummy food, pictures of yummy men, or a great song to get me through the day, thank you for sticking with Ellay, Kimberlie and I and helping us live the dream! Big hugs to you all.

Connect With R.L. Merrill

I would love to connect with you! Here's where you can find me lurking:
Facebook at: www.facebook.com/rowritesrocknromance
Email at rlmerrillauthor@gmail.com
Twitter @rlmerrillauthor
And my groovy website: www.rlmerrillauthor.com where you can find my newsletter-y thingie and stay up-to-date with the latest from my world of Rock 'n' Romance! You can even pick up passwords to unlock short stories set in the Teacher, Haunted and The Rock Season worlds.

Reviews

Reviews are incredibly important to authors. If you enjoyed Teacher: The Final Act, please leave your review for others at Amazon, GoodReads, or whichever rooftop you'd like to shout it from!

Coming Soon!

Road Trip: A Rock Season Novel

Read on for a sneak peek at the story of Abra and Kelly.

Road Trip: - A Rock Season Novel

July 2014
Abra

Ahhhh… Summer vacation! Work hard all year, two and a half months off every summer. Greatest gig in the world, right? Actually, I really did have it good. As a counselor at a continuation high school, I worked my ass off nine months of the year with the most desperate kids, so I allowed myself to play hard every summer. Playing hard for me meant going to as many concerts and festivals as I could squeeze in. Sweaty, hot, and loud…That's what I needed, and I was about to have a fantastic fix this weekend, even if I was flying solo for the first time in a long time.

Interstate 5 ran the length of California and driving it was always an adventure. Running only two lanes in each direction, it was a constant game of Frogger trying to avoid the big rigs, tumbleweeds, assholes speeding in their Smart Cars—

Oh, hell no! I was not about to be passed by a damn Smart Car in my 2010 Mustang GT. There were some things that could not stand. The speed limit was seventy, I was going eighty, and this old guy was passing me at eighty-five… *Uh uh!* I stepped on the gas and flew right by him, my Metal road trip soundtrack urging me to step on it.

Heavy Metal was honestly the soundtrack of my life. It allowed me to sing and scream along and get out all the aggression, anger, frustration, sadness, and yes, depression that my job brought along with it. Healer heal thyself? Yes, please! Some Korn will do just fine, thank you!

In fact, I was headed to see Korn this very weekend! I was going to headbang, crowd surf, people watch, and just fucking LIVE! Yes! If only I didn't have a seven hour drive ahead of me. Oh well. It would be worth it.

I drove the 580 to get out of the Bay Area and the traffic on this Friday night was killing me. I'd waited to leave until ten o'clock, figuring I'd miss the traffic that way. No such luck. It seemed many of the East Bay's inhabitants had the same idea: Beat the dog days of summer by getting out of town. On the road there were tour buses, fifth wheels, RV's towing cars and big trucks towing boats…It was insanity!

My first pit stop of the night was an hour into the trip. Why did I do this to myself? Some day I would learn to not start my trip with a 44 oz. Diet Coke! There were a few families with screaming kids hanging around and others walking their dogs. I stood in line for the restroom and got back in my car as soon as I could to avoid any unwanted attention. Dressing the way I did usually kept people away from me, but there was always some jackass who saw a woman alone at night and figured she might 'need some good lovin'. *Barf.*

I managed to make it another three hours without having to stop. Barely. By the time the next rest stop came into view I was nearly in tears from the pain in my bladder. I'd been contemplating which would be worse, cleaning up an accident in the car, or copping a squat in the wide open space next to the road. Luckily I didn't have to resort to either of those.

I pulled off the interstate and breathed a sigh of relief that not much was happening at this rest stop. I'd been pushing ninety miles an hour for some time now and I'd left most of the other traffic behind. There were only a couple of big rigs parked on the side closest to the highway, and one other car near the restrooms. It was nearing three in the morning and I wasn't the least bit tired, so when my headlights illuminated the horrific scene in front of me, I knew I hadn't fallen asleep at the wheel and succumbed to a nightmare.

Two guys were beating an unmoving body on the ground and another was pouring liquid out of a red can onto the body. Before I could think, I laid on the horn and revved my engine. The rough-looking guys looked up and scattered, piling into a van I hadn't seen parked out of the light. The van and the lone car peeled out and sped off down the on ramp.

I scanned the area and didn't see anyone else. We were miles from civilization. I prayed quickly that the body on the ground wasn't dead as I climbed out of my Mustang and hurried around to the trunk where I grabbed a Mag-lite that was as big around as my arm and my softball bat.

I remained aware of my surroundings as I cautiously crept over to the man lying on the ground. I could make out black work boots, black utility pants, a vest covering a plain white t-shirt... *Holy shit!* This was a cop on the ground! And there was no police car anywhere. And I'd left my phone in the car. And the smell of gasoline was burning the shit out of my nostrils.

I stepped up next to him and could see he was breathing heavy. I heard soft moans as I knelt next to him and touched his shoulder.

Kelly

"Don't touch me," I snarled. I thought they'd all left after stealing my car and pulling off my uniform shirt. I sat up quickly and tried to get to my feet, but all I succeeded in doing was staggering around before falling against something, or someone soft.

"OOof! Relax! Dude, you weigh a ton. Stop moving and I'll help you." Her high-pitched voice shocked me into a little bit more of a coherent state. I couldn't see anything other than the halo of the flashlight she'd dropped. I lunged for it, nearly falling on my ass, and spun around.

"Fuck! That's really bright, dude. I'm not going to hurt you, okay? I'm trying to help you. Just relax!"

This tiny creature in front of me looked more like a ragdoll than a potential threat. Torn up stockings stuck up out of black combat boots, a short black dress draped over her small frame, and she was looking at me like I was the crazy person in this scenario.

"Who are you?" I demanded, then felt something crunch in my mouth. Was that a tooth? I spit onto the ground and shone the flashlight on the blood and-yes! That was a tooth. "Son of a beehive," I spit out. The girl in front of me laughed.

"I'd be using a helluva lot stronger words if I'd just had the shit kicked out of me." I put the light back on her and she cringed, covering her face a bit.

"Would you get that thing out of my eyes and let me help you?"

"Why do you have a bat?" I shouted, noticing what she was brandishing. I felt for my weapon, knowing at the same time I wouldn't find it.

"Because I'm a chick traveling at night. Duh. Now put that down. I'm not going to hurt you, you big lug!" She dropped her bat and walked toward me. I stepped back.

"DUDE! I am not going to fucking hurt you! The guys who did this just took off, all right? I'm just going to look at your head, okay? You're bleeding."

She stepped cautiously towards me. I kept the flashlight on her, still not trusting her. Her tiny hand touched my shoulder as she stepped behind me. She was so small, I might have mistaken her for a young teenager, but on closer examination, I could see faint lines around her mouth. She had huge brown eyes with dark brows that were furrowed with concern. Her touch wasn't light. She'd obviously been in situations like this before. I could feel her touching the back of my head and I cried out.

"They hit me with something. I went to get out of my car and they rushed me. I got hit in the head, and then I don't know... Whoa, what is that smell?"

"You almost became your own private Burning Man festival."

"I, what?" She finished walking around me and tried to take the flashlight from me. I yanked my arm away and she calmly stepped back.

"It's gasoline. They were going to—"

"Whoa," was all I could say. I pulled the Velcro off my vest, grateful they hadn't gotten it off of me as it protected me somewhat from their blows, although my thigh and butt were stinging like the knife one of them had connected. My whole body screamed as I pulled my shirt off over my head.

"I've got first aid stuff and a phone in my car. You need help, dude. You're bleeding back here," she said as she gently pressed the back of my head, "and your pants are ripped—"

"They got in a couple of cuts." I looked around the area to see if they'd left anything but it was all gone. "Crumb! They got everything. My belt, my keys, my badge." Gasoline. Holy Mother, they were going to burn me alive…

"Come on, Officer. Let me get you to my car." She'd somehow managed to catch my weight and was guiding me over to the passenger side of her car. I started to panic, but then she was talking and her voice instantly calmed me.

"My name is Abra Moore. I'm not going to hurt you. Let's just sit you down and then you can tell me who to call, okay?" Her voice was so sweet. It allowed me to let some of the tension go, but then I got the shakes so bad she had to support me almost completely. Somehow she got me to her car, although she barely came up to my shoulder. She got the door open and helped me maneuver into the low seat, using her other hand to guide my head in so I wouldn't smack it. Then she leaned across me and grabbed her phone off the console.

"Who should I call, Officer—"

"Graham. Kelly Graham. I guess just call nine-one-one. The CHP will hopefully respond. Do you know where we are?" She dialed the phone and shook her head, her dark hair grazing her pale shoulders.

"Yes, my name is Abra Moore and I am here with an officer who has been injured… We're at a rest stop on Highway 5… I don't think we are in danger. I think they left… Yes, I will stay with him… He's bleeding from the back of his head. He said they hit him… Yes, he is able to move and walk… Breathing is labored but normal… Ok… Thank you…" She hung up the phone and stepped closer. It was so dark I could only make out her silhouette from the distant bathroom lights.

"Thank God you pulled in," I said quietly. "I can't—"

"Yeah. No, I'm glad, too. Were you on duty?"

"No. I left work at ten and hit the road. I can't believe—"

"Where are you from?" she asked, squatting down in front of me. She wrapped her arms around her knees and looked up at me, worry creasing her forehead. The light was hitting her just right so I could get a good look at her face. She was absolutely gorgeous. Not my usual type, I guess. I don't know that I had one, but she was definitely not a woman that would have caught my eye normally. Heavily tattooed, small-boned… Her face was angelic, but like a dark angel. I blinked hard a couple of times, starting to wonder if I was…

Want more? How about more Maggie's Bones!

Fated: – A Haunted Novel

September 2012
Sammara Gunderson
Hollywood, Los Angeles

When news first came out that Maggie's Bones were working on a follow up album to their smash from last year, I begged my editor to let me do a feature on them. As a reporter for Feedback Magazine, the premier Rock magazine in the U.S., I followed their career since the beginning and loved their music. Then, when tragedy struck and they lost their manager in a freak accident, I became even more intrigued. The guys had put on a brave front for a bit, then their lead guitarist, D, disappeared. The next thing everyone knew, they were all back in New Orleans writing their follow up album, tentatively titled Haunted. The Rock world was dying for news on what was happening to them. I was in contact with their manager, Sherry Jordan, and she assured me she would ask the guys to do the interview. I could barely contain my excitement. There was something about their music that called to me, and though I knew I needed to remain objective, I couldn't wait to meet them and experience their magic in person.

That was four months ago. The next thing I heard was that they were back in L.A. with Scott Cross, an amazing producer who had given several bands their masterpieces. I figured I'd never get access while they were recording, but I was hoping for a break. Luckily I ran into Sherry at the Formosa Cafe on a random September afternoon.

"Sammara! How are you, girl?" We hugged and Sherry invited me to sit with her and the two women she was dining with. "Sammara, this is Mackenzie McGowan and Jaylene Charles. Ladies, this is Sammara Gunderson, reporter extraordinaire from Feedback magazine."

I scoffed at her introduction. "Extraordinaire? Please! How do you do?" I asked as I slid into the booth next to her. The restaurant had a cool spot in the back that looked like an old railroad dining car. I loved the mix of food here and the service was tepid as all of the servers were bored locals. I'd had several meetings here in the past and loved the atmosphere of feigned disinterest.

"Jaylene and Mackenzie snuck out here to visit the guys while mixing is going on and I promised I would show them the town. What brings you to Hollywood?"

I tucked some hair behind my ear. "I had a meeting with Patricia Gordon about interviewing Blackened. They are about to head into the studio as well and I was hoping to catch them before that." Sherry and her friend all sighed at the prospect.

"Have you met them before?" Mackenzie asked. When I nodded, she exclaimed, "Oh my hell, Danny Black is so friggin' hot!" Sherry laughed at Mackenzie and Jaylene rolled her eyes and sipped her soda.

"I have interviewed them before. If you can get past his gruff exterior, he's pretty damn funny. He's just kind of a dick when you first meet him," I said with a laugh. My first piece on Blackened cemented my position as a features writer with the magazine and since then Danny only wanted to deal with me. I was grateful for that.

"I was going to call you and see when we could have you meet with the Bones. They're ready to talk... About everything... I told them you would be the best person to tell their story." I dropped my suddenly slimy hands into my lap.

"Really? That would be...Thank you, Sherry. I would love to work with them! When were you thinking?"

Sherry opened up her calendar on her phone and chuckled. "They have tonight free, or Saturday. I think it would be perfect if you came out to the house they're staying in. It's totally them."

I checked my own calendar and frowned. I was supposed to attend a work function tonight and Saturday I was supposed to see a show at the Whisky. "I can do either. You tell me and I'll make it work." My managing editor would let me out of my commitment tonight for this and I could catch the other band at another venue. I wasn't going to miss my chance to interview Maggie's Bones! For some reason I couldn't put my finger on, I knew in my heart I had to do this, that the repercussions of this interview would be massive in my life. I needed massive repercussions to combat the stagnation I had felt for so long.

"Why don't you come by tonight then? You're always bound to get them at their goofiest at night. They're so serious during the day."

I opened the GPS app on my phone. "Where should I meet them?"

Sherry and the other women laughed. "Uh, they're staying at the Los Feliz Murder Mansion."

My phone clattered onto the table. "Say what? I thought the owners wouldn't let anyone in that place?" The mansion had one of the creepiest histories in Hollywood history. I was definitely intrigued.

Sherry laughed. "It just so happens that one of their kids is a huge fan of Maggie's Bones and she talked her parents into letting the band use the place after they initially refused. They cleaned it all up, only leaving a couple of the rooms untouched. The owners hadn't changed anything since the night in 1959 when the dude killed his wife. Mage was all excited about it. He thought it would be an inspirational place for them to stay while they were in the studio."

Sherry shuddered and Mackenzie barked out a laugh. "That guy is obsessed, I'm tellin' ya! You should have seen the creepy ass house he wanted to buy in New Orleans. He's even convinced the guys to go ahead and purchase the St. Germaine in the French Quarter and turn it into a club! Club Haunt, he wants to call it."

Jaylene swirled her straw around in her glass and smiled fondly at the mention of Mage's name. "Poor guy. He swears the building was haunted, but nothing happened while I was there."

Sherry laughed and turned to me. "Jaylene stayed with the boys while they were writing for the album. She's a tattoo artist."

Jaylene raised an eyebrow in surprise. "It's fine, Jay," Sherry laughed. "The guys are going to give her complete access so she'll find out anyway. Don't worry." Jaylene relaxed noticeably. Her eyes darted between her two friends, then her phone started buzzing. She picked it up and her cheeks turned rosy.

"Is that loverboy," Mackenzie said, peeking over her shoulder. Both of their eyes went wide. "O-kay! I didn't need to see that... Or maybe I did. Bring that back up!" Jaylene was trying to respond, her bottom lip between her teeth, while trying to block Mackenzie's view. "Damn he's got a fine—"

"Kenz! He'll be so embarrassed if he knows you saw that, now stop!"

Mackenzie winked at Sherry, then frowned. "How come mine doesn't send me hot pics like—WHOA!"

It was Mackenzie's turn to blush at whatever had just buzzed her phone.

Jaylene peeked over her shoulder and gasped. "He wants you to do THAT?" Mackenzie got a dreamy look.

"Ahhhh, I always dreamed I'd find a man brave enough. Sherry? When does their tour start?"

Sherry laughed nervously. "Why? You aren't thinking of... Let me see that picture!"

Mackenzie held the phone to her ample bust. "I promise he will be okay to play! Scouts honor!"

Jaylene snorted. "Yeah, you're just lucky he hasn't yanked out his nipple rings while playing yet!"

"That was so much fun," Mackenzie sighed. I thought I was picking up the gist of what this conversation was about. Mackenzie showed Sherry the phone across the table and as much as the reporter in me wanted to be nosy, I really didn't want to be tempted to print something this salacious.

Sherry looked horrified and intrigued at the same time. "How do you even do that? Can't that cause permanent damage?"

Mackenzie shook her head. "Not if you do it right, and I've done plenty. Yes, ma'am, there are plenty of dudes walking around New Orleans with these babies!"

Okay, that was too much temptation for me. "So you do body modification?"

Mackenzie smiled wickedly. She swirled a lock of her teal hair around a manicured finger with polish in a matching shade of teal. "Give me a needle and I can pierce anything," she said with a wink.

I shivered. I had my ears pierced three times on each side and had considered piercing my navel for about five minutes, but anything lower… "Gotcha. Why do people want to pierce their, um, their—"

"Dicks? Adds sexual pleasure. I have yet to actually get to experience it, though. Sadly. I've provided pleasure for hundreds of other women." She sighed and her face relaxed into a dreamy expression. She clasped her fingers together and rested her chin on her hands. "But now… I just might—"

"Kenz," Jaylene interrupted by throwing an elbow into Mackenzie's boob. "You do know she's a reporter? You really want Star's business about his business out there?" Jaylene's eyes bugged out. "Oh God. You won't report that, will you?"

I laughed and shook my head. "I'm off the clock right now, don't worry. I can't say I'm not intrigued, though. So you tattoo them and Mackenzie—"

"Only Star has been brave enough to let me go to work on him. Jaylene's tattooed them, but for some reason they're afraid of little ole me!" Mackenzie tried to do her best to look demure, but she didn't fool me. "If you're ever in New Orleans, you could come see my portfolio," Mackenzie purred, wiggling her eyebrows. "Maybe you might want a little something yourself."

I gulped. As a reporter for Feedback, I'd worked really hard to overcome my naiveté about the more worldly world of rock n' roll, but there was still a lot out there that shocked me. I'd had quite an education since moving to Hollywood from a bedroom community in the East Bay after attending UCLA's school of journalism. Luckily, I had a good poker face when faced with something a little 'out there.'

"Then it's settled," Sherry said while working her phone frantically. "Sammara, you'll meet the band out at the house tonight. I've texted you the address. Let me know if you need anything further."

Jaylene frowned as Sherry packed up her things to go. "But aren't you coming, Sherry?"

The usually poised and self-assured manager for the band looked flustered. "I'm going to pass I think. I'm not in the mood for a certain person. He's been texting me all week and I just don't want to hear it."

I wondered who she was talking about but didn't want to butt in if Sherry didn't want to share. We'd been friends since college and had confided in each other many times. It was obvious this was a detail she'd decided to keep from me. I wasn't upset. She didn't always tell me who she was seeing. Unfortunately, the ones she kept from me in the past were ones who hurt her really bad. I hoped that wasn't the case this time.

"But he really wants to fix things with you," Jaylene pleaded gently. "He's been such a good boy since New Orleans, I swear. I'm not asking you to do anything other than talk to him." Jaylene seemed like such a caretaker. She was guarded, or maybe just quiet. I couldn't tell for sure yet, but I could tell she didn't know how much she could trust me no matter what Sherry said by the way her eyes darted to me with every topic of conversation.

Sherry exhaled loudly. "I'll think about it. Let's get you two back to the house before Devon starts blowing up my phone looking for you. I swear, it's like you're his security blanket or something!" Jaylene blushed, Mackenzie laughed and Sherry winked.

I was already thinking of questions I wanted to ask tonight. "I'm really glad I ran into you, Sherry. I'll see you all tonight. About what time?"

Sherry checked her watch. "Come over around eight. They should be back from the studio, fed, and will have had time to snuggle up with their ladies for a bit." Jaylene and Mackenzie groaned and laughed.

"No problem," I said. I wanted the women to feel comfortable around me. "And don't worry. I know they've had a rough year. I won't push."

Sherry's smile dropped. "Thanks, Sammara. I reassured them that you would take good care of them." I was grateful for Sherry's confidence. It was hard to earn respect in this crazy business.

Sherry stood from the table and said, "Now, I need to get my lovely guests to the spa-"

"Oh Sherry! Can we skip the spa and go to that Hollywood History Museum? Devon said they are finished for the day and wants to meet up there. He says there's a replica of Hannibal Lecter's cell in the basement!"

Sherry's expression was priceless. "You and your horror movie fascination. You guys are creeps!" She shuddered and shook her hands out like she'd just seen a big hairy spider in her bathroom. Jaylene just smiled innocently and bounced on her toes.

Sherry rolled her eyes. "Fine, sure. No problem. Sammara we'll see you tonight, ok?" I waved good-bye and gathered my sweater and purse. I had a night with Maggie's Bones to look forward to. Whoa.

Stay Tuned for more Rock 'n' Romance!